"Look, I'll keep sea[rching] but the very least yo[u can do is tell me] what the hell it is I'm looking for."

For a few moments Libby glared at him. Carson could see that tears were about to spill over and her chin was trembling as she fought for control. Why was it such a big secret?

"You're looking for bones," she blurted out abruptly.

"What?"

"*BONES!*" she shouted at the top of her lungs, the tears finally brimming over. "*My father's bones!*"

As soon as she'd said the word *father*, all the pieces of the puzzle clicked together.

"If we can find just one bone in that wreckage, the DNA will prove my paternity and Frey will never be able to stop us from recovering the plane." Her eyes were wide, fixed on him, riveting him in his seat. "Well?"

"Well, what?"

"I suppose now you're going to want to charge me more money."

Carson stared at her, then shook his head. "You have a really high opinion of me, don't you?" He started the motor. "I'm going to take a quick break. I'll be back out in an hour."

"Pick me up at the dock at seven," she said. "And don't tell me no. I have way too much at stake for you not to let me help."

Before he could respond, she started her own outboard and veered around his boat, heading at top speed for the lodge. He muttered, "Yeah, I guess maybe you do at that. Several billion dollars is a pretty big stake."

Dear Reader,

Deep beneath the icy waters of Alaska's Evening Lake lies the wreckage of not only a plane, but also three lives: the pilot of the ill-fated craft, the bride he was flying off to meet on their wedding day and their unborn child. Twenty-eight years later, that child, Libby Wilson, is determined to prove her paternity by salvaging the wreckage and recovering her father's remains. Her journey into the past reveals the secrets of the lake and unlocks long-dormant family mysteries...mysteries that change her life in ways she never imagined.

Every so often, a person's future is dictated by events long past. The desire to know where we came from and who we are within the context of our family's past can be a powerful driving force. Deciphering the clues can take us on new, wholly unexpected adventures with amazing outcomes in the here and now. Whether it's simple genealogical research or more complicated scientific genetic testing, we never know where the search might lead. Perhaps this book will light a spark in you to delve into your own family history. Who knows what secrets (and skeletons) you might discover when you peek into the far corners of the family closet?

Nadia Nichols

P.S. I'd love to hear from you. My e-mail address is nadianichols@aol.com.

EVERYTHING TO PROVE
Nadia Nichols

TORONTO • NEW YORK • LONDON
AMSTERDAM • PARIS • SYDNEY • HAMBURG
STOCKHOLM • ATHENS • TOKYO • MILAN • MADRID
PRAGUE • WARSAW • BUDAPEST • AUCKLAND

ISBN 0-373-71341-X

EVERYTHING TO PROVE

This edition published by arrangement with Harlequin Books S.A.

® and TM are trademarks of the publisher. Trademarks indicated with
® are registered in the United States Patent and Trademark Office, the
Canadian Trade Marks Office and in other countries.

www.eHarlequin.com

Printed in U.S.A.

Books by Nadia Nichols

HARLEQUIN SUPERROMANCE

Don't miss any of our special offers. Write to us at the following address for information on our newest releases.

Harlequin Reader Service
U.S.: 3010 Walden Ave., P.O. Box 1325, Buffalo, NY 14269
Canadian: P.O. Box 609, Fort Erie, Ont. L2A 5X3

To John, for pointing out that the exception proves the rule.

PROLOGUE

For the sixth time in less than twenty minutes, Connor Libby knotted his tie then studied his handiwork in the small mirror that hung above the bathroom sink, and for the sixth time it failed to pass muster. If he didn't hurry up, he was going to be late. He tore it out again and started over. His hands were shaking, which didn't help matters much. He'd had to borrow the tie from Dan, a green strip of silk with little brightly spotted rainbow trout jumping all over it. It went well enough with his white shirt and dark slacks. Dan was lending him the jacket, too, a fine wool tweed with leather elbow patches. If not for Dan's help, Connor would be decked out in faded jeans and his favorite red flannel shirt, and would no doubt be a whole lot more comfortable than he was in these fancy duds. But suffering a gentleman's fate for a few hours was worth it, for Marie.

Marie. Just the thought of her kick-started his heart and made his hands shake even worse. She was as beautiful as an early spring sunrise over the Brooks Range, and in less than three hours she was going to become his wife. He'd met Marie nearly a year ago, when she came to work for him and Dan. The war was over and he'd arrived back at the Alaskan lodge, still trying to make sense out of four years in the air force, the last two spent in Vietnam.

She was a slender, quiet girl and an excellent cook, minding her own business and keeping apart from the others. In her spare time she would read books outside the cabin where the hired help stayed, and Connor's dog, a three-legged mongrel named HoChi that he'd brought back from Vietnam, liked to hang out with her. He took that as a good sign, since HoChi was by nature and experience a very wary and distrustful dog.

One day he braved it all and dropped onto the wall bench beside her. "What're you reading?"

She glanced up with those shy, dark eyes, as startled by his boldness as he was. "*War and Peace*. One of your guests left it behind."

"Have you figured out which is better?"

She closed the book, a piece of birch bark marking the page. "I do not like war."

"Me, either. You like to fish?"

"My family is at fish camp right now. If I were there, I would be gutting and splitting and drying dog salmon."

"And you'd rather clean rooms at the lodge?"

"The money I make here helps my family. My father's health is not so good. He can no longer do all the things he needs to do. We need a lot of supplies to get through the winter."

Through quiet conversations, Connor learned that Marie Wilson was an Athapaskan whose family lived on the Koyukyuk River, and in the weeks that followed, the friendship that developed between them became the highlight of his summer. Walks along the river or paddles in the canoe were moments to be savored. Connor was smitten, though he was unsure if Marie felt as strongly about him as he did about her. As the end of the season drew near, he asked Dan for some advice. Dan, whom Connor regarded as more of an uncle than a godfather, was a confirmed bachelor. He didn't have a high regard for women in general, and disliked native women in particular, hiring them only because help was so hard to get out in the bush. To Dan, the indigenous people were to be tolerated with barely concealed contempt. He believed them to be lazy, incompetent and untrustworthy—a racist attitude that Connor never understood. He smoked his cigar and listened to Connor relate his feelings about Marie, and when Connor asked him what he should do, Dan took his cigar out of his mouth and spat.

"Soon enough, she'll go back to her village and take up with some young buck," he said. "She's a squaw, for God's sake. Forget about her."

When the summer was over, Marie returned to her people. The geese flew south, the lake froze up and deep snows filled the long cold darkness. Conner ran a trapline out of the guides' camp and suffered endless torments thinking about Marie falling in love with some young man from her village. He went to the lodge from time to time when his need for companionship outweighed his desire for solitude and shared a whiskey or two with Dan. He told Dan he planned to marry Marie and bring her back to the lodge to live. Dan never said anything in response, just shook his head and threw back another slug of hooch.

Spring came and filled Connor with a restless yearning as the days lengthened and the sun rose higher in the sky. The ice went out on the lake. The great flocks of geese returned, their long ragged Vs darkening the pale sky. Connor wondered if Marie had missed him during the cold dark winter, and if she would return as promised.

In early June the accountant from New York City had made his annual trip to the lodge before it opened for the season to report that Dan and Connor had done well in all their business ventures, though Connor knew that was all his father's doing. Ben Libby's death had made both Connor and Dan Frey very wealthy men, though Connor had little use for money. As long as he had a sound canvas canoe, a couple of fly rods and plenty of food to eat, he was content. But Dan, although he professed no interest in a fancy lifestyle, liked expensive toys. After the accountant had departed, Dan went to Anchorage and bought a de Havilland Beaver, a bright shiny yellow six-passenger plane on pontoons. It was delivered the next day.

"You might as well use those Air Force skills of yours," he'd told Connor, gesturing to the plane with his cigar. "You can fly our clients to surrounding lakes and charge extra money for doing it." Dan, who didn't need to make any money at all and had a flying service at his beck and call, nonetheless liked to emphasize that the plane was not a frivolous extravagance but a sensible business expenditure. Besides, float planes in Alaska were as common as pickup trucks in Montana. Everyone who lived in the bush either owned one or knew someone who did.

The first place Connor had flown was to the tiny village on the Koyukyuk to see Marie, and she was as glad to see him as he was to see her. Her father had died that winter and she'd been running his trapline. Times had been hard and their winter had been lean, but she was glad to see him, and Connor felt hopeful. He spent several days at their cabin, eating stews her mother cooked from the beaver Marie had trapped, helping her tend the sled dogs and mend a broken sled. When he told her he wanted to marry her and bring her to live at the lodge, Marie looked troubled and shook her head.

"My mother would be all alone then."

"She could live with us," Connor offered, and Marie had consented.

And so it was arranged, as quickly and as simply as that. After supper that night Connor and Marie walked a long way down the river. He held her hand and kissed her for the first time. He gave her a gold necklace with a pear-cut blue diamond that had belonged to his mother. She gave him her body there beside the river, while the wild geese clamored across the arctic sky.

He remembered her gift as he stood before the mirror, thinking how much more precious it was than a blue diamond on a gold chain, and his seventh knot was as bad as the first. He picked up the jacket and stumbled out of the lodge into a brightness that startled. He left HoChi behind him in the lodge. "You weren't invited," he said through the door in response to the dog's plaintive whine.

Dan was standing down on the dock, smoking a cigar.

"I can't knot the tie," Connor said. "My hands are shaking."

Clenching the cigar in the corner of his mouth, Dan did it for him.

"I guess I can't get you to change your mind and come," Connor said.

Dan uttered a grunt of disgust and shook his head. "Hate weddings with a passion," he said around his cigar. He finished the task and took the cigar out of his mouth. "I'm going to head up to the mouth of the Kandik, camp up there for a week or so. That'll give you and your bride the run of the place for a few days. It'll be the last privacy you get all summer. Make the most of it, boy. And good luck."

Connor shrugged into the jacket and stuck out his hand.

Dan clasped it in a firm handshake and slapped his shoulder before heading back up to the lodge. Connor walked out to the end of the dock where the plane was tethered, threw off the lines and climbed aboard. A man only got married once. He guessed he had a right to be nervous. He started the plane's engine and was about to leave the dock when he spotted HoChi running nimbly down the gangway. Dan must have let him out of the lodge. He opened the plane's door and HoChi jumped in, immediately hopping into the right-hand seat.

"Okay then, you'll be the ring bearer," Conner said, taking the leather thong from around his neck and draping it over HoChi's head. The simple gold band with their names and wedding date inscribed on it glittered against the dog's neck. "But remember, best behavior. This is an important day."

He did a quick preflight while he taxied the Beaver out onto the lake. The weather was good, the lake was calm, and the Brooks Range reared its glorious snow-cloaked majesty against the northern sky. The flight to Marie's village should take less than forty-five minutes. The wedding would be held there, an Athapaskan celebration officiated over by a missionary priest and followed by a traditional potlatch. Afterward, they'd fly back to the lodge and enjoy a whole week of uninterrupted bliss. Life was good. Connor pushed the throttle up and the plane accelerated through the light chop.

It wouldn't do to keep his beautiful bride waiting.

SOLLY JOHNSON HAD LIVED out on the land most of his life, like his father and his father's father, way back to the time when Raven first created the world. He had a wife who lived in the village, a woman who talked too much and made him crazy. He'd given her three sons, the last one two years ago, and left her with her family down on the Yukon while he ran his trapline up in the mountains. He liked it that way. He liked being alone. She raised the boys; he brought home the furs that gave her the things she wanted. He listened to her talk for a few weeks, a month maybe, nonstop, while she mended his clothes and made him a new pair of mukluks, and then he left her again and was glad to do so.

He didn't like noise, and people were noisy. When he first came here to live in the mountains as a young man, there was no noise. There was just his canoe and his dog team, and the animals in the wilderness. It was quiet then. The only loud noise he heard was the sound of the river breaking up in spring, the thunderstorms in summer and the wild keening roar of the wind through the high mountain passes. And then the whites came. At first they came looking for furs and gold, but they went away when they couldn't find any gold and all the furs got trapped out. But then a few years later they came back in those noisy flying canoes. They came for the fish they could catch in the rivers and lakes, and the animals they could shoot on the land, and some of them stayed and didn't go away.

This was the beginning of the bad times.

The place he loved was where he built his cabin, near the mouth of the Yaktektuk, a small river that fed into the lake the whites named Evening but his people had always called Dayhehas. He had lived in this place for most of thirty years now. He was still a strong man, and he still had good strong dogs, but the winters seemed longer now, and the darkness was colder. The quiet places were quiet no more. The skies were full of the flying canoes that brought men to the big log house over on the warm shore.

The white man who lived there was called Dan Frey, and he didn't like Indians. This much was true. He had been there long enough so Solly knew to keep away. Frey thought Indians stole things. He thought Indians were drunks. He hired them to work at his fancy log house on the lake, but he didn't like them. Solly heard these things when he went to his wife's village on the Yukon. He heard how the white man treated his Indian help. When Solly went back to his cabin on the Yaktektuk, he stayed away from the white man's lodge. But he still came down to the shores of Dayhehas. He still liked to see both faces of the great mountain at the same time, and the way the sunlight sparkled over the big waters when the ice went out and the days got long. He liked to watch the loons when they returned to raise their young, and he liked to watch the moose eat lily roots in the coves. He was at the lake, crouched on his heels at the water's edge cleaning a pretty good fish, when he heard the flying canoe taking off from the white man's lodge.

He watched it race along the water, roaring like a hundred of the white man's snow machines, those noisy stinky things that were taking the place of sled dogs. He watched it lift off the water and skim along just above the surface for a long time, as if trying to decide if it wanted to keep flying or return to the water. Then he watched it climb abruptly toward the sky the way this yellow one always did, and he saw it do something he'd never seen it do before. It climbed straight up, so steep it nearly went over backward before it stopped climbing and hung in place above the sparkling waters. The loud noise stopped and there was sudden quiet, just the lap of the waves against the shore and the brush of wind through the trees.

Then the flying yellow canoe fell out of the sky, tumbling forward and dropping nose first into the lake. Solly saw and heard the great crash of waves as it hit the water. He saw the canoe's two legs break off and float away. He watched as it settled onto its belly and then sank so quickly that before he could rise to his feet to properly mark the spot the big canoe had vanished. He was still standing there when he saw something bob up from the water between the floating legs and begin swimming to shore. He thought maybe it was the white man, the mean one from the lodge. But as it came closer he saw that the head wasn't human. It was a short-haired dog like none he'd ever driven before his sledge. The dog came out onto the gravel strand a quarter mile from where Solly stood and he saw that it had only three legs.

Not long after the dog reached shore, Solly heard a boat coming from the lodge. The boat was coming fast. He thought it must be coming to rescue the white man trapped inside the sunken canoe, but he was wrong. The boat circled the two legs that were still floating and Solly saw the driver tie them together. Then the boat sped down the lake toward the outlet, screaming like an angry woman and towing the two big yellow legs behind. The man in the boat had been the mean one, the one called Dan Frey. Dan Frey hadn't seen the three-legged dog on the gravel strand. He hadn't seen Solly standing on the shore not a quarter of a mile away from where the flying canoe sank. But this was no surprise. Dan Frey was a white man, and it was well-known among the Athapaskan that white men didn't see too good.

CHAPTER ONE

Twenty-Eight Years Later

IT WAS THE ARTICLE in *Forbes* magazine that gave Libby Wilson the sudden impetus to throw all caution to the wind and do what she'd been waiting to do for the past twelve years. She read that article and realized that she had to go back home and make things right. Not five years from now as originally planned, when her bank account would be healthy enough to finance what was certain to be an expensive undertaking. She had to go *now*. The truth had remained buried for far too long. She knew her mother would object, but her mother could no longer tell her that the past didn't matter, because it did.

Libby knew exactly how much it mattered. She'd grown up in the same village that her mother had. She'd lived in the same little government-issue house, been shipped out to the same boarding school in Anchorage to attend high school; she'd worn the same clothes, eaten the same foods and felt the same bleak desolation when one of the village kids sniffed too much gasoline and was buried beneath the permafrost. The only difference between the poverty her mother suffered and her own fate had been the color of Libby's eyes.

The teacher in Anchorage had commented about her eyes. Ms. DeFranco had been young and earnest and from a well-to-do family in New England that believed in helping less fortunate cultures. She had made Libby's future her personal crusade, which was the only reason Libby ended up going to college back East, being accepted to Tufts medical school and graduating top of her class. Proof positive that sometimes a little bit of racism could work to a minority's benefit. Her internship was in forensic pathology and her ticket to success had been a reasonably sharp intellect and a pair of the prettiest blue eyes that ever came out of an Athapaskan villager…compliments of a Russian fur trader two generations removed on her mother's side, and a father she'd never known.

Libby's internship at Massachusetts General had just recently ended and two months ago she'd been offered a residency, an impressive nod to her potential from such a fine hospital. She might have accepted it and spent the next five years bolstering her bank account and carefully plotting her return to Evening Lake, but that very week *Forbes* magazine hit the newsstands and a copy ended up on the table in the doctors' lounge. Idly thumbing through the pages in one of those rare quiet moments that sometimes occur in the middle of an endless shift, Libby had stumbled over that fateful article with all those glossy color pictures and a lengthy feature profiling one of Alaska's wealthiest and most eccentric residents: the silver-haired and distinguished-looking Daniel Frey.

Libby had taken the magazine back to her apartment and read the article again, and yet again after that, studying the pictures of the massive log lodge, the lake and the man; all the while her blood pressure nudged toward the boiling point. Daniel Frey. Even the man's name sickened her. She should write a letter to the editors of fancy *Forbes* magazine about the eccentric billionaire Daniel Frey and tell them the stories her mother had told her. She'd tell them what it had been like to work for the rich white man who hated Indians. What it had been like to be treated with contempt, to be unfairly compensated for long hours worked, to be housed in crowded conditions and poorly fed. What it had been like for her mother to fall in love with Connor Libby, Frey's godson, only to lose her beloved on her wedding day in a suspicious plane crash. A crash her mother believed Frey had rigged both to keep Connor from bringing an Athapaskan bride back to the lodge and to claim the entire Libby fortune as his own.

She'd tell them what it had been like for her mother to go to Frey after learning she was pregnant with Connor's child, only to be driven from the property.

"I know how you squaws sleep around," Frey had said. "That baby could be anyone's."

Connor Libby had been mentioned only briefly in the article. Two sentences made reference to the fact that Ben Libby's only son had been killed in a plane crash shortly after returning from Vietnam…and that Connor's will had specified that if he died without heirs, Frey would inherit his share of the Libby fortune.

What Libby had to prove was that Connor in fact had had an heir, and she was determined to do just that. She remembered vividly that fateful day in high school biology class when she'd first learned about DNA, and how it could be used to prove a person's paternity. That knowledge had changed her entire life's focus, and had even steered her medical studies toward specializing in forensic pathology.

Libby had long been planning to return to Evening Lake,

where her father's plane had crashed, and salvage the wreckage. The only thing that had stopped her from doing it years ago was the large amount of money it would take to find and recover the plane. She'd made inquiries to salvage operators while she was in college, but none of them could be specific as to the costs because each salvage operation was unique. All they could tell her was that it would be expensive.

As a medical student, Libby had worked part-time during the school year and full-time in the summers to help cover the cost of her books and tuition. Scholarships and student loans had covered the rest, but saving any amount of money had been impossible. As an intern, she'd struggled to make ends meet and pay off her school debts. Logically, she should have accepted the residency that had been offered to her and worked until her finances improved, but none of that would matter if she could find just one of Connor Libby's bones and prove she was his daughter.

The magazine article had become the catalyst, and after Libby had finished reading it for the third time, she'd made her decision. Her mother had told her over and over again, throughout years of listening to Libby rail against the injustices of poverty, that there was no way to prove anything, and it no longer mattered. But it did. It mattered twenty-eight years ago, and it mattered just as much today. And her mother was wrong. There *was* a way to prove not only her paternity, but what kind of racist Frey really was.

Which was why she turned down the offer of a residency at one of the best hospitals on the Eastern seaboard and was now flying to Alaska. The flight was a long one and gave her time to think about her strategy. What she actually thought about was the fact that she didn't have a strategy, and had no idea how to start the search for her father's plane other than by confronting Daniel Frey in person, something she'd always wanted to do but never dared. This strategy was a poor one, given his attitude toward the native people. He'd certainly never admit to any wrongdoings, never admit that it was strange he hadn't wanted to attend his own godson's wedding, and equally strange he hadn't been anywhere in the vicinity of the lodge when the plane crashed.

Her mother had mentioned a warden, Charlie Stuck, who had been kind to her after Connor's death. He'd taken her in his plane while he searched for her missing fiancé. They'd searched for over a week before declaring him lost and presumed dead. No plane wreckage was ever found, just the two pontoons hung up in the rapids about a half mile down the Evening River, which led searchers to believe that the plane had gone down in the deep waters somewhere near the lake's outlet. Charlie Stuck had been in his late fifties then, but with any luck he might still be alive. He might remember something helpful, and it was a starting place.

When her flight touched down in Anchorage it was 10:00 p.m. and still broad daylight. Libby rented a car and threw her bags in the backseat. She drove down Highway One to a right-hand fork that took her along Six Mile Creek to a place called Hope. An empty state campground, open for the season but devoid of tourists, offered her the choice of sites overlooking Turnagain Arm. She pitched her tiny tent, ate a can of cold beans sitting on the edge of the bluff then walked a short way in the violet dusk down Gull Rock Trail. She walked until the twilight thickened and jelled, then carefully retraced her way back to her tent site and climbed into her sleeping bag.

An hour later she heard a mysterious noise and crawled out of her tent to watch the ghostly movements of a pod of Beluga whales through the dark waters of Chickaloon Bay. Sitting with her arms wrapped around her knees, she listened to them breathe as they surfaced and swam past, and she wondered why it had taken her so long to come back home.

Two hours later she was making coffee on her tiny camp stove, drinking it in the dawn while a cow moose browsed along the water's edge. She cleaned up the site, packed her gear back into the rental car and returned to Anchorage. Once there, she headed for the regional office of the Department of Fish and Game and had to wait outside for an hour before the first employee showed up, still blinking sleep from his eyes. He introduced himself as Elmer Brown, and appeared surprised to find her waiting on the doorstep. He ushered her into the office and listened to her story while he made a pot of coffee. Libby told him about the plane crash, omitting any mention of her relationship to the pilot or any implications of foul play. She expressed her interest in locating the plane and speaking to the warden who had been involved in the search.

"So, you're looking for this Charlie Stuck," Brown concluded.

Libby nodded. "I'm hoping he's still alive. He was in his fifties then, based out of Fairbanks."

Brown reached for the phone book and placed a call to the Fairbanks office, briefly describing the circumstances and asking if they could look into their records, then hung up. "They said they'd call back. Coffee?"

"Love a cup, thanks," Libby said, taking the offered mug. "Assuming the plane is still in the lake, how would one go about finding it?"

"Well, it'd be easier now than it would have been back then, but still, that's a mighty big lake. Deep, too," Brown said. "There's a good salvage outfit not too far from here. They're expensive, all those outfits are, but Alaska Salvage just about always get what they go after. They've hauled a lot of planes and boats out of a lot of deep water. The company is owned by a guy named Dodge. He spent eight years as a Navy special forces combat and demolition diver before starting Alaska Salvage maybe six, eight years ago. Loads of experience, but he nearly bought the farm in a freak diving accident while salvaging that commuter plane that went down in the inlet five weeks back. You probably saw that in the news."

Libby shook her head. "No. I didn't."

Elmer seemed pleased to be able to enlighten her. "He had a new employee on board the salvage vessel, and the kid accidentally started the winch while Dodge was attaching the cable to a piece of wreckage a hundred feet below. He got tangled up in a big jagged piece of plane wreckage. His divers managed to free him and get him to the surface but he was more dead than alive when they brought him up. Spent over a month in the hospital getting put back together. Just got out. He'll probably never dive again but he still ramrods the outfit and he'd be the one you'd want to talk to. His office isn't far from here."

"If he just got out of the hospital, I doubt he'll be at work."

"He'll be at Alaska Salvage. He lives and breathes that place." Brown wrote the name and phone number on a card, handing it to her just as the phone rang. He picked it up. "Oh?" he said after a long pause. "I see. Okay, I'll pass that information along. Thanks, Dick." He hung up and gave her an apologetic shrug. "Well, I'm afraid you're out of luck when it comes to Charlie Stuck. He died last winter in the old folks' home, but he had a son, Bob, who still lives in the Fairbanks area. Runs a garage out toward Moose Creek. Might be worth talking to him."

He scrawled another name on another card, then went through the phone book and wrote the phone number down. "You might also check with the warden service based out of Fairbanks. They keep pretty good files on that stuff. They probably still have Charlie Stuck's report on that particular search. Good luck."

THE SUN WAS WELL UP when Libby pulled into the Alaska Salvage parking lot in Spenard. The building was a huge blue Quonset hut with a neatly lettered sign spanning the wide doors and three late-model pickup trucks blocking the entryway. The metallic sound of banging and clanging came from inside. She stepped between the trucks and into the dimness, startled to see several massive pieces of what appeared to have been a large commuter plane scattered all over the floor. Hoses snaked across the concrete, and in a separate alcove she caught the bright flash of welding light.

A side door opened into a small office, and when the man bent over a large nautical chart spread open on the desk glanced up and spied Libby he straightened, lifting his hands from both sides of the map, which immediately snapped back into a tight scroll. He was tall, broad-shouldered and clad in a pair of well-worn coveralls that could have used a good washing. His eyes were blue, his dark hair cropped short, his jaw shadowed with stubble. He looked to be in his mid to late thirties, long on experience but short on sleep. A jagged, raised welt slanted across his forehead and disappeared into his hairline, tracked with the marks of stitches that had been recently removed. Another shorter scar crossed the bridge of his nose, his left cheekbone was seriously abraded, and one hand was wrapped in a wad of bandages that allowed only the fingertips to show. Libby could only imagine what the rest of him looked like if his face had taken that much abuse.

"What can I do for you?" he said in a voice as rough as his appearance.

Libby indicated the wreckage on the concrete floor behind her. "Did you salvage this plane?"

"Most of it," he said, his eyes narrowing. "Look, lady, if you're with the press, I have nothing to add to what's been said, and if you're a relative of someone who was on the plane, you'll have to talk to the state police."

"I'm neither," Libby said. "You were recommended by Elmer Brown of the Fish and Game Department. He told me Alaska Salvage always got what it went after."

"Almost always," he corrected. "That plane behind you crashed in Cook Inlet just after takeoff with six souls aboard. The riptide took some of the wreckage out before we could get to it. My crew's still looking for the missing pieces."

"Was anyone killed?"

"There were no survivors."

Libby glanced back at the pieces of wreckage and wondered who the people had been, and what their last moments had been like. She felt a sudden chill. "Did you...?"

"We don't recover bodies. The state police dive team was in charge of that. We assist as necessary, of course. Their dive team isn't nearly as good as mine."

"What do you do with the wreckage?"

"The FAA likes to look it over, so we lay everything we find out for 'em in here. It's a convenience for them and they pay us for the privilege. When they're done with their investigation we'll sell what we can and scrap the rest. Why? You looking for a grisly souvenir? Something with a little blood on it, maybe? If so, you're out of luck. I already sold all that stuff off to help pay my medical bills."

Libby's chin lifted in response to the hostile sarcasm in his voice. "I'm looking to hire a salvage outfit to find a plane that went down twenty-eight years ago in Evening Lake, just south of the Brooks Range."

Now that she'd announced her business for being there, he eyed her up and down as if trying to decide if she was worth talking to. "Evening Lake?"

"Yes."

"Any idea where it crashed?"

"Not exactly. I'm hoping to find out more after I speak with some people."

"Evening Lake is big. I've fished it. Spent a couple weeks camped up there a few years ago. Must be a good three, four hundred feet deep in some places."

"So I've been told," Libby said, wishing he wouldn't stare at her quite so brazenly. She decided that he was both crude and rude and any sympathy she'd initially felt for his battered condition evaporated as the heat came up in her cheeks.

"When you're talking remote salvage operations, you're talking big bucks."

"How big?" Libby asked.

"For a salvage operation on Evening Lake…that'd take a crew of at least three people, flying in all that gear and some pretty sophisticated equipment. Just finding the plane could take some time. Once it's found, purchasing the salvage rights and getting the wreckage to the surface could run you maybe seventy-five, eighty grand. Possibly a lot more."

"I see." Libby was staggered by the sum. "What if the plane crashed in shallow water?"

"If it were in shallow water, the initial search party would have spotted it." He rubbed the stubble on his jaw. "I'm assuming there was a search?"

Libby nodded. "But they may have been looking in the wrong location, and if there was a lot of chop on the surface, wouldn't that have made it difficult to spot anything?"

"Maybe. But over the years a helluva lot of planes have flown in and out of there. If nobody's reported seeing anything in all that time, I'd have to assume it's way down there, and if you're not sure the plane really crashed in the lake, you could be wasting a lot of time and money. Were there any eyewitnesses?"

Libby shook her head. "Not to my knowledge. But the plane was taking off from a lodge, the only one on the lake at that time. They think it went down just after takeoff. The pontoons were found half a mile down the outlet of the lake."

"Must've crashed real close to the mouth of the river, then. The wind blows pretty strong through the pass there and would've pushed the pontoons clear to the opposite shore otherwise."

"That's what the searchers figured. How do you base your salvage fees?"

"Depends on the size of the plane."

"It was a de Havilland Beaver. Six-seater."

"We require a deposit of ten grand up front. You'd pay a straight hourly fee contingent upon the size of the crew and the equipment being used. When we find the wreckage, we're willing to negotiate fair salvage trades toward payment if the plane is deemed restorable."

"What shape do you think the plane would be in after all that time?"

"Pretty good, if it was down deep and wasn't demolished when it hit the water. It's the ice and salt water that plays hell with wrecks. The plane would probably be in close to the same shape as it was when it crashed."

"If you found the wreckage in just two hours and raised it the same day, would that be less than ten thousand?"

"The minimum charge for any remote salvage operation is twenty-five grand. The retrieval cost of the last plane we dredged up out of a lake ran three times that amount. If you don't mind my asking, why is salvaging this plane so important after twenty-eight years?"

"It's not the plane so much as what it was carrying," Libby said. "Thank you for your information. It's been helpful."

He gave her a keen look and rubbed the stubble on his jaw again. "My name's Dodge. I own this business. Let me know if you want us to take a look."

"Thank you," Libby said, accepting the business card he pulled out of the chest pocket of his coveralls and glancing down at it briefly. Carson Colman Dodge. Fancy name.

She left the Quonset hut in a discouraged mood. Twenty-five thousand dollars was an impossible amount for her to come up with, never mind seventy-five. She had the sinking feeling that she'd made a terrible mistake in giving up the residency at Mass General. But she was here, so she might as well persevere for as long as she could. By 10:00 a.m. Libby was on a flight to Fairbanks, hoping to speak to Charlie Stuck's son, Bob, about what Charlie might have told him about the incident.

CHAPTER TWO

"MY FATHER NEVER said nothin' to me about anything," an overweight and balding Bob Stuck said seven hours later, standing outside the door of his one-bay garage in Moose Creek in the watery spring sunshine. Six rusted trucks cluttered the small yard and another took up the garage. He sported a gold hoop in his left ear, a diamond stud in his right and his hands were black with grease. "He was never home. Always off chasing poachers and fish hogs and women. That was more important to him than raising a son." He spat as if talking about his father put a bad taste in his mouth.

"Did he have any close friends that you know of? Anyone he might have talked to about that plane crash?" Libby asked.

"Most of 'em are dead now. But Lana's still alive. She lives over on the Chena. She and Charlie shacked up together about ten years back. She took care of him better than he deserved, cooked for him, cleaned his cabin, washed his clothes and waited up nights till he came home from the bars. Then he had that stroke and the hospital put him in the old folks' home. She wanted the doctors to let him come back home. She ranted and raved in the hospital, made a big scene, said she could take care of him better than any nursing home." Bob shook his head. "Yeah, she might remember something. She don't talk to me, but she might talk to you." He gave her a baleful stare from red-veined eyes. "You're Indian, ain't you?"

LANA PAUL LIVED IN an old cabin sitting on sill logs that had rotted into the riverbank over the years, giving the building a decided tilt toward the water. When Libby parked her rental car next to the dilapidated wreck of an old Ford truck, the cabin door opened and a stout older woman with a bright blue kerchief tied over her head peered out.

"Lana?" Libby said, climbing out of the car. "I'm Libby Wilson. I'd like to talk to you about Charlie Stuck."

The black eyes glittered with suspicion. "Charlie's dead. They locked him away in a place full of old people and bad smells and he died."

"I know that, and I'm sorry. But I want to talk to you about what he did, about his job as a warden. I think he might have known something about my father's death. My father was Connor Libby. He lived in a lodge on Evening Lake."

"Charlie might have known something, maybe, but I don't," she said, and the door of the old cabin banged shut. Libby stood for a few moments in the drab detritus of mud season, listening to the Chena rush past and wondering why the cabin hadn't been swept away by floodwaters years ago. She was turning to leave when the door opened and the woman leaned out, giving her a sharp look.

"You got any tobacco?" she said. "I got papers but no tobacco."

"I can bring you some," Libby replied.

The woman nodded and the door closed again. Libby drove into Fairbanks and at the big grocery store she bought rolling papers and tobacco. She also bought a cooked rotisserie chicken and a tub of coleslaw from the deli, half a dozen freshly baked biscuits and cookies and two bottles of wine, one red, one white. When she returned to the cabin the door opened immediately and Lana Paul ushered her inside. The interior was surprisingly neat and clean, in stark contrast to the muddy, cluttered yard. Libby set the bag of groceries on the Formica table and took out the contents. "I picked up some food, too, in case you hadn't eaten supper yet," she said, handing the foil-wrapped package of tobacco to the woman.

Lana took it from her with gnarled, eager hands. "I remembered something while you were gone," she said, unwrapping the package. She sat down in an old wooden rocker near the woodstove, which threw a welcome warmth to the room. "I remembered how Charlie talked when he came home from the bars. Sometimes, he would talk about his past." She was filling a paper with tobacco as she spoke, and rolled it with swift, practiced dexterity. "I remember a story he told me about a boy with eyes like yours and a three-legged dog. They lived on Evening Lake."

Libby froze in the act of setting the chicken on the table. "That was my father."

"Charlie told me this story." Lana reached for a wooden match in an old canning jar on the table and scratched it to life on the top of the woodstove. She lit the thin cigarette and inhaled with an expression of reverent content, smoke wreathing her deeply wrinkled face and sharp eyes. "The boy came home from a place faraway and brought a three-legged dog with him."

"He came back from the war in Vietnam with a dog he called HoChi," Libby said, sinking into a chair and staring transfixed at the old woman. "The dog's hind leg had been blown off by a land mine that killed three soldiers."

"This boy fell in love with a young girl from a village on the Koyukyuk," Lana continued.

"My mother," Libby said, her heart hammering with hope that Lana would say something that would help her find her father.

Lana pushed her feet against the floor and made the old rocker move back and forth as she smoked her cigarette. A floorboard creaked in time to the movement. "They were going to be married, but the boy was killed on his wedding day."

Libby waited for several long minutes while a big water pot hissed atop the woodstove and the old woman rocked and the warm, delectable aroma of spit-roasted chicken filled the little cabin. "Is that all he said?" she finally asked.

"Charlie was drunk," Lana mused, rocking. "He was sad. He walked back and forth and said he wished he found the boy's plane. He said he always wondered about the plane."

Libby leaned forward in her chair. "What do you think he meant by that?"

Lana shrugged. "I think he wondered why the plane crashed." She looked toward the food Libby had placed on the table. "Boy, that chicken smells good."

Libby got up, found two plates in a drain rack on the sideboard and a sharp knife in a kitchen drawer. She carved up the chicken and heaped generous portions onto both plates. She hadn't eaten anything since the can of cold beans the night before, and she was hungry. She put two biscuits on each plate, divided the coleslaw into two green mounds, then found eating utensils in another drawer and placed them on the table. Lana threw the stub of her cigarette into the woodstove while Libby opened the bottle of red wine and poured two glasses. They sat at the table together and ate in silence. The food was good and the warmth of the woodstove a welcome

radiance in the cooling evening. Sagging into the earth and
leaning toward the river, the weathered old cabin gave Libby
a sense of peace.

The old woman cleaned her plate. She ate deliberately, as
if trying to memorize each mouthful of food. She drank her
wine and Libby refilled her glass. Lana kept her attention on
the meal until it was finished, and then returned to her rocker
and rolled another cigarette and lit it as she had the first.

"Charlie said the young girl was very beautiful, and he
didn't know why the old man didn't like her."

"The old man? You mean Daniel Frey?"

Lana nodded. "The rich man who lived on the lake and
didn't like Indians."

Libby gathered up the plates and silverware and carried
them to the sink. She poured hot water from the pot on the
stove into the dishpan and added a squirt of detergent from
the plastic bottle on the sideboard. There was a small window
set into the wall above the sink and Libby could look out at
the river rushing past as she washed. It made her a little dizzy.
When the dishes were done she wiped off the table and draped
the dishcloth over the faucet. "Did Charlie ever mention that
the young village girl had a child?"

The old woman shook her head, but as Libby was leaving,
Lana pushed out of her chair. "Take this with you," she said,
reaching onto a shelf and lifting down an old tattered leather-
bound journal. "It belonged to Charlie. He scribbled in it ever
since I knew him. It was important to him, but his son don't
want it and it don't do me no good. I can't read."

THERE WERE SEVERAL STORES in Fairbanks that Libby visited
after stopping at the warden service's office to get a copy of

Charlie Stuck's report and before flying to the village the following morning. She bought a pretty dress for her mother, bright with the colors of spring, and outfitted herself for a few weeks in the bush. She had no idea how long it would take for her to accomplish her mission, so she erred on the side of caution with the clothing. Warm long underwear, thick wool socks, serious field boots, a parka that would turn the worst weather, iron-cloth pants, several pairs of warm gloves and a good fleece hat. She packed all of it into a duffel bag in her hotel room near the airport and lastly, before checking out, took one last and very long hot shower, knowing that the amenities in the Alaskan bush wouldn't be nearly as luxurious as these.

The flight from Fairbanks to Umiak took two hours, giving her time to reread the photocopy of Charlie Stuck's official statement regarding the search for Connor Libby's plane. The report was disappointing. It mentioned the daily weather, the specific grid patterns flown, the pontoons found in the Evening River, and concluded with the assumption that the plane had crashed near the outlet in very deep water. No hidden clues and nothing that Libby didn't already know.

Next, she started on Charlie's journal. She'd already scanned the dates. The entries began four years after the plane crash, but Libby read every single one, hoping he'd make some reference to the crash and the subsequent search, perhaps reflect some of his own theories on what might have happened in a retrospective entry. It was slow reading because Charlie Stuck had terrible handwriting which deteriorated steadily over time. The entire journal spanned almost twenty years, the entries being very brief. A sentence, maybe two. Sometimes months would pass without an entry. The journal read like a warden's trophy log.

Caught R. Drew red-handed with twelve over the limit, gave him maximum fine, bastard deserved it.

There were also entries on the state of wildlife.

Moose population down fourth year in a row. Hunters are crying wolf. I'm sure it's poaching. Wolves and moose have always coexisted. Increasing human population and hunting pressure are new on the scene, and where there are humans, there is poaching. No stopping it.

Libby decided she liked the way Charlie Stuck thought. She pored laboriously over his entries until, finally, she read one that was totally out of context, and the words jumped out at her, causing her to sit up in her seat and bend over the journal.

Two weeks late to Lana's due to crash landing the plane in a white-out, bending the prop and being stranded until villagers found me south of the Dome, but she asked no questions. She waits the way that girl Marie waited. Still wonder what became of C. Libby but think my instincts are right about D. Frey. Why didn't he go to the wedding? (This was underlined twice.) I know Frey had something to do with that crash. Wish I could have found that plane. Wish others would have listened to my theory, but money talks loudest and always has.

Libby read the passage several times, her heartbeat racing, dizzied by the words. Charlie Stuck had believed that Frey had something to do with her father's death! The rest of the journal revealed nothing relevant to Connor Libby, but that one passage gave her hope that maybe, once the plane was found, others *would* listen…especially if it could be proved that the crash hadn't been an accident. Was it possible? Could Frey have deliberately killed her father? Somehow she had to come up with the money to salvage the wreckage!

The commuter flight stopped in Tanana, Ruby and Galena before landing in the Koyukyuk River, dodging several large ice floes and a flock of Canada geese while taxiing to the village dock. Her gear was put out of the plane and for the first time in six years Libby stood in the village of her childhood. Umiak hadn't changed much. There were a few more houses, a few more junked vehicles, a few more boats drawn up on the gravel bank next to the fish wheels. The place looked bleak and dreary to her, and she felt guilty for feeling that way. This was, after all, where she'd been born. She waited for a few moments, searching for her mother among the faces, some familiar and some not, who had come to see if the plane had brought mail or supplies, but if Umiak hadn't changed much in her absence, nothing prepared her for her mother's appearance.

Libby felt a jolt clear to the bottoms of her feet when she saw how Marie had aged. Fear clenched her up inside and her heart raced.

Marie came to a stop at the end of the dock. Her hair had gone almost completely white. She had shrunk. This couldn't be real. Her mother had always been so strong and vital, the anchoring cornerstone of Libby's existence, always there for her. Weekly phone conversations had perpetuated the myth that her mother was the same as always, that nothing had changed, yet obviously it had. Libby felt the hot prickle of tears beneath her eyelids.

"Mom?"

Marie spotted her and her eyes lit up. "Libby?" She came toward her and raised her arms to clasp her in a trembling embrace. "Libby. It's good to see you. I'm so glad you came. How long can you stay?"

Libby hugged her mother gently, kissed the velvet of her cheek, slipped her arm around her mother's frail shoulders and picked up her duffel. "As long as you want me to. I don't have to go back to Boston."

Confused, Marie looked up at her. "But you work there."

"Not anymore. Come on. Let's go home. I have a pretty dress to give you, and lots of stories to tell."

Her mother's dreary little house was exactly the same. Libby could see that Marie had done nothing with the money Libby had sent her every month. No doubt she had put it all in the bank, saving it just in case times got hard because she didn't realize that her times were always hard. The furniture was shabby, the linoleum worn almost to the plywood underlayment, the cupboards nearly bare. Libby wanted to rage at her mother one moment, then weep the tears of a heartbroken child the next. While her mother made coffee, she paced the confines of the shoe-box house and looked out the windows as if she were a prisoner. She'd been back less than twenty minutes and already couldn't wait to escape.

Marie was happy with the brightly colored dress. She went immediately into her room and put it on. She'd lost so much weight the dress hung from her frame and filled Libby with a terrible premonition. "You look beautiful," Libby said.

They drank cups of instant coffee with lots of sugar and powdered creamer. Libby told her mother about her internship at Mass General and the prestigious residency she'd been offered, and that she'd turned it down.

"Was this residency you were offered like what you were doing before, with the dead bodies?" she asked.

"Yes."

"Then I'm glad you didn't take it. That isn't what a doctor should be doing. You should be delivering babies and healing people."

"Forensic pathology is just as important, Mom. I can help solve the mysteries of a person's death. I can help solve murders. But if it makes you feel better, I know how to deliver babies and heal people, too. And as long as we're speaking of doctors, who's at the clinic now?"

"Nobody. We have a doctor who comes in once a month. If there is an emergency we go down to Galena, or to Fairbanks if it's really bad."

Libby reached across the table to clasp her mother's hands. "I want you to fly to Anchorage with me for some tests at the hospital there. You don't look well. You've lost too much weight."

"The winters are always hard," Marie said. "Things will get better. They always do."

"We'll fly out tomorrow. I'll make reservations at one of the nicest places on the Seward Peninsula. We'll do some shopping, stay a couple of nights. Please, Mom. It'll make me feel a whole lot better."

"Hospitals are expensive and I don't need one. Now that you're home, everything will be okay."

"Hospitals are sometimes necessary, and besides, I'm a rich doctor now," Libby said, wishing with all her heart that it was true. She gave her mother's hands a gentle squeeze then pushed out of her chair and paced to the small window. She wished she was a rich doctor. Wished she could whisk her mother out of this dark and dreary place and give her the bright, sunny house and easy lifestyle she deserved. Wished she could afford to hire Carson Colman Dodge, who was crude and ill-mannered, but talked as if he knew his stuff. He certainly was expensive. Libby could see a small patch of the river between two other box houses. She watched the occasional ice floe drift past. Soon the salmon would start their run, and some of the villagers would move out to their fish camps. "Mom, is Tukey's fish wheel still up on the Kikitak?"

"No. I think it got washed away by high waters two winters ago. Now that Tukey's dead, I don't have anyone to make me a new one, but I sure miss fish camp."

Libby crossed to her mother and gave her a hug from behind. "Then we'll go to fish camp, just like the old days. We'll take the skiff and bring a net and catch enough fish to smoke for the winter. We'll pick berries when they come ripe and put them up in preserves. But first we'll go to the hospital in Anchorage. Okay?"

Her mother nodded with reluctance. "Okay."

"Good. I'll have Susan radio for the plane to come."

The fact that her mother relented so easily scared Libby even more. Forget Daniel Frey. Her mother was sick. There was time enough to pay a visit to the man who might have killed her father. She wouldn't let him kill her mother, too. She could wait a few days more.

THE MEDICAL TESTS TOOK most of the day, and were conducted on such short notice only because Libby, in her four years of medical school and two years of internship, had learned that the squeaky wheel got the grease. She squeaked loudly once in the emergency room, in professional terms that the doctors took note of. When they discovered she was a resident at Mass General, a slight twist of the truth on Libby's part, they took very good care of Marie and never again mentioned the medical center for Alaskan natives on the northern fringe of the city. At the end of a very tiring day Libby drove her mother to the waterfront resort in Homer, where they shared a room with a balcony overlooking Kachemak Bay, and where Libby sat until 1:00 a.m. listening to the tide rush in across the mud flats. The test results would take some time, though not as long as usual. Libby had stated in no uncertain terms that she expected some answers when she returned the following afternoon.

After breakfast the next morning, Marie and Libby half-heartedly browsed the string of shops in Homer, making small talk and walking arm in arm, then drove slowly back to the city where they checked into a hotel not far from the airport. Leaving her mother to a nap after lunch, Libby returned to the hospital. The staff didn't keep her waiting long. She was ushered into an office by a young resident who took his glasses off and opened the file on his desk, flipping through the pages as if trying to refresh his memory.

"Your mother has chronic lymphocytic leukemia," he said with a studious frown. "There's considerable enlargement of her liver and spleen and she's moderately anemic. She's also malnourished, probably because she hasn't felt much like eating lately. We'd like to start her on an anticancer drug we've had good success with. She should feel dramatically better after a couple of treatments, and she can take these drugs at home. She'll need to have periodic blood tests to monitor the medication levels, but this can be done at the clinic in Galena. That's close to where she lives, isn't it?"

Libby heard these words delivered over a dull roaring in her ears. She knew the diagnosis wasn't a death sentence. Chronic lymphocytic leukemia was very treatable, and many people who had it lived to a ripe old age, yet this was her mother they were discussing, not some stranger in the exam room.

She made arrangements to bring her mother in later that afternoon for the first treatment and to fill the prescriptions she'd need to take with her, then drove aimlessly around the city. She ended up in Spenard, sitting in the rental car which she'd parked in front of Alaska Salvage. "One bone," she said aloud, staring up at the neatly lettered sign. "One bone, and I can pay Carson Dodge whatever he charges to salvage my father's plane. I can put my mother in the finest house in Alaska and get her the best medical attention. All I need is some DNA."

The DNA in a single bone fragment would prove that Connor Libby had been her father, and it would be the kind of proof that Daniel Frey couldn't deny, no matter how much it would kill him to discover that half of his fortune belonged to a blue-eyed Athapaskan. The icing on the cake would be to somehow prove that Frey had caused Connor Libby's death by tampering with his plane, but the DNA was a damned good place to start. One step at a time.

Libby got out of the car. There was only one truck parked in front of the Quonset hut doors. She could only hope it belonged to Carson Colman Dodge. She stepped into the dim interior of the hut. The overhead lights were off, but the wreckage of the commuter plane was exactly where it had been two days ago. Everything was quiet and the office door was ajar. She peered inside, convinced that they'd all gone out to lunch, and was startled to see Dodge slumped over the desk, head pillowed in the curve of one arm. She watched him for a few moments, long enough to deduce that he was asleep and not dead, then she rapped her knuckles smartly against the door. "Mr. Dodge?"

He jerked upright and lunged half out of his chair. When he recognized her, he slumped back, unable to completely mask the grimace of pain his sudden movements had triggered. "Lady, let me give you a little advice," he said in that rough and borderline hostile voice. "Never sneak up on a man that way. It could get you into a lot of trouble."

"I didn't sneak," Libby said. "I walked in, knocked on your door and called out."

He eased himself in his seat and drew a few careful breaths as if the exercise were a tricky one. He looked even worse than he had on Libby's first visit, if that were possible. He gestured to the metal chair opposite his desk. "Have a seat."

Libby sat, glancing over his shoulder at the *Playboy* calendar pinned to the wall behind him, and felt the heat come into her cheeks before she could drop her eyes. She hadn't noticed that calendar last time. "I didn't mean to disturb you, Mr. Dodge. I just wanted to ask you a couple more questions."

He made a small gesture with his bandaged hand. "Fire away."

"You mentioned that you sometimes took salvage instead of money to cover the cost of a recovery effort."

"That's right, but usually that just defrays some of the cost. If you're talking about the de Havilland, fully restored it might bring three hundred grand. But selling the wreckage of that plane wouldn't come close to covering your expenses."

"Actually, Mr. Dodge, I wasn't talking about the plane."

Dodge studied her with a cynical expression. "You mentioned in your first visit it was something the plane was carrying."

Libby nodded. "That's right."

"Wait. Don't tell me." The faint trace of a wry grin mocked her. "The plane was loaded down with gold dust and nuggets from a secret mother lode, which is why it crashed. You know how many of those I get a year?"

Libby felt her flush deepen. This crude man definitely needed some lessons in business etiquette. "Obviously quite a few, from the way you talk." She pulled the *Forbes* magazine from her shoulder bag and laid it on the desk. "But how many of them involve this man?"

Dodge leaned forward and glanced at the glossy pictures for a few moments, his eyes scanning the captions. "Okay," he said, leaning back and giving her a calculating stare. "So tell me, what does billionaire Daniel Frey have to do with the wrecked plane you're looking for?"

"His godson was flying the plane when it crashed," Libby said.

"And what do *you* have to do with all of this?"

"Frey's godson was Connor Libby, the son of billionaire Ben Libby, and he was on his way to marry my mother."

Dodge slouched back in his chair, picked up a pen and tapped it on the desktop, eyes narrowing in thought. "So, let me get this straight. This superrich son of a billionaire crashes the plane into the lake and leaves your mother standing at the altar bereft of both a husband and his considerable fortune. And now, twenty-eight years later, you want to find the wreckage. Your mother must have been expecting a nice wedding gift from her fiancé, and she thinks it's still in the plane. Is that it?"

Libby leaned forward, her blood up. "Mr. Dodge, I have five thousand dollars in my savings account. I know that's only half of what you require for a deposit, and I'll tell you right now that if you don't find the plane that's all you'll ever get. But if you do find the plane, I guarantee I'll pay your company the full freight. What you stand to make on this job will be in direct proportion to how good you are at what you do." Libby rose to her feet, tucking the magazine back into her bag. "I'm staying at the Airport Hotel tonight and flying out first thing in the morning. If you should wish to discuss this further, please give me a call."

She was almost out the door when he said, "Lady, how the hell do you expect me to call when I don't even know your name?"

WHEN CARSON LIMPED DOWN the dock ramp that night and descended the ladder onto his old wooden cabin cruiser, he was carrying a six-pack of beer and a thick, bloody slab of steak. The two chili dogs he'd eaten on the drive to the marina had taken the edge off his hunger but he was still contemplating the possibility of a real meal. Real as in meat and potatoes. Real as in something that might build his blood back up and return his strength. First, though, he wanted to nurse his bruised ego with a cold beer. It galled him to be puttering around the office while his crew was off on a job. He knew Trig would see that things ran smoothly, and he also knew they needed the work and couldn't sit around waiting for him to come to the front. Big equipment cost big bucks, and banks liked to get their payments on time. He could've gone along with them, could've captained his vessel, but he was still so crippled up he knew he'd only be in the way, and worse, his crew would try to make things easy for him. He didn't want anyone to see him like this. Just climbing down the ladder to his boat had left him weak and out of breath. The doctors said his condition would slowly improve, but they all hedged when pressed for details. Punctured lung, lacerated muscles, abdominal wounds, torn tendons all take time to heal, they said.

No shit.

Carson hated doctors. Hated their rhetoric, their placid, professional expressions and their holier-than-thou condescending attitudes. Hated the fact that they'd saved his life because he hated being beholden to them. Hated having to follow their instructions and forgo salvage diving for some unspecified length of time…maybe even forever. Yes, they'd hinted at that, too. His injuries, the highly paid specialist said in her placid, professional tone, had been severe. No shit times two. It didn't take eight years of education and a fancy medical degree to figure that one out. He'd lost thirty pounds in those four weeks of hospitalization. He'd also lost his spleen, the use of one of his lungs and the tendons in his left shoulder and wrist, a big chunk of muscle in his left thigh, and almost all of his strength. The guys were all hush-hush about it but he knew they were talking, saying things like, "Old King Cole sure screwed the pooch this time. He'll probably never dive again."

Old King Cole… His crew had long since picked up on his mother's pet name for him and, knowing his dislike for it, used it when they wanted to get his goat.

His crew also called him "the old man." Maybe he was, to them. They were all young kids, the oldest was Trig at twenty-seven. Was thirty-nine *old?* It was only one year away from forty, and forty was definitely old. He sure as hell felt old tonight. He never used to notice things like aches and pains and cuts and bruises, and sure as hell he never used to get caught napping at his desk by a pretty young woman. Damn. How humiliating was that?

He crammed the six-pack, less two, into the little propane refrigerator in the galley and then went up on deck, breathless again after climbing the ship's ladder, and kicked back to enjoy the sunset. If he had the energy he'd take the cabin cruiser out and do a little fishing. Try for a halibut, maybe. Halibut was good eating, fit for a king...even an old and injured one. But he felt too run-down to cast off the lines and fire up the cruiser's engines. Maybe after a beer or two he'd feel better. Younger. More like his old self.

Old? Whoa. Poor choice of words.

He took a long swallow and gazed out at the looming snowcapped Chugach Mountains, aglow with a clear yellow fire in the late-evening sunlight. He thought about the unexpected visitor he'd had, and the offer she'd made. Libby Wilson had beautiful eyes and was quiet spoken. Didn't chatter. He liked that about her. Came right out and said what she wanted to say. He'd treated her a little rudely, but she was just too damned pretty. If she'd been ugly he'd have been nicer. Anyway, odds were he'd never see her again. A measly five grand wasn't even worth gassing up the plane for.

On the other hand, Evening Lake was mighty good fishing at the right time of year, and the right time of year was coming up quick. Still, finding a wrecked plane when one didn't know exactly where it went down would be time-consuming...not that he couldn't do it. She had a helluva nerve intimating that he might not be up to the task and that his skills might only be worth five thousand dollars.

What was in the plane that she wanted to get her hands on? Obviously something of value that the pilot had been bringing to Libby Wilson's mother on her wedding day. Something of *great* value, considering the girl's keen interest in recovering the plane. Wedding day… His own experience with such events was shallow at best, a whirlwind courtship with a student he'd met while teaching a dive school in New York City nine years ago, followed by a marriage that began in Las Vegas with a cheap gold ring and ended barely a year later. A bitter year it had been, too, a year of disillusionment, betrayal and hurt that had plagued every moment of their doomed marriage. Brown-eyed Barbara McGee with the sweet, pretty smile that had lured him into such an ugly hell of emotional bondage. Barbara, who loved the nightlife, loved to party and didn't know how to sit home at night alone when he was off working a salvage job.

Didn't know how to be faithful.

Lesson learned the hard way. Love is blind, deaf and very, very dumb.

Anyhow, it was pointless to reopen old wounds thinking about his own brief and ill-fated marriage. The wedding scenario Libby Wilson had described was completely different. She was talking billionaire groom on his way to marry his beloved. Flying his own plane to his own wedding. And in that plane he was ferrying proof of his undying love. Jewelry. That had to be it. A big diamond, possibly huge. Maybe an enormous diamond ring and matching necklace, bracelet and, what the hell, a tiara. Daniel Frey's rich godson could afford to go overboard on his bride. A veritable treasure trove could be sitting on the bottom of Evening Lake inside a de Havilland Beaver that crashed twenty-eight years ago.

Carson eased his bad leg out in front of him and took another swallow of beer. Finding the plane didn't have to be a full-crew job. He'd need to call Trig after he found the wreckage, but he could search for the plane himself. The search itself wouldn't be physically difficult, just tedious. He'd work the search pattern using the rubber boat with the side-scanning sonar and GPS and map out the bottom of the lake lane by lane, like mowing a giant lawn. He could do that alone, no sweat. He could pack up his tent, the rubber boat, some supplies and the sonar gear and fly up to Evening Lake. Worst-case scenario, he'd make five grand taking a working vacation and maybe get some good fishing in on the side. A big lake trout or two broiled over the coals would taste pretty good. And what the hell, it sure beat sitting around the office wishing he were out with the boys on the *Pacific Explorer,* that sleek, beautiful forty-eight-foot dive vessel that was the pride of his salvage operation.

Or wondering why Gracie hadn't been by. Not since the accident had that sultry, sexy bartender from the pool hall paid him a visit. She, too, was probably convinced he'd never be a whole man again and had sought out greener pastures.

He finished the first beer and cracked open the second. Halfway through it he went below to snag his cell phone. Back on deck, after he'd caught his breath, he called the Airport Hotel and asked to be connected to Libby Wilson's room.

"Dodge here," he said when she answered. "I've been thinking about your proposal and I have a counter proposal of my own."

"Go ahead," she said, cool voiced and calm, as if she'd been expecting his call.

"I'm teaching a deep-diving rescue-and-recovery course at the university this weekend. I can fly up and look the situa-

tion over on—" he glanced at his wrist watch "—June 15.
That's a Monday, five days from now."

"All right."

"If I like what I see I'll take the job and play by your terms
if we don't find the plane."

"And if we do find it?"

"You shell out one hundred and fifty grand minimum, and
it could shake out to be more if the salvage costs run high.
Odds are I'm going to end up with a huge loss I can't particularly afford right now. I'll want the five grand up front, and
I'll want the salvage contract in legalese, signed, sealed and
delivered into my hand upon arrival at the lake."

On her part there was no hesitation whatsoever, which re-
inforced his theory of huge diamonds. Millions of dollars'
worth of rare and priceless jewels. "Fine," she said. "Will you
be bringing your crew?"

"Until the plane is located, I won't be needing any crew."

There was a pause. "No offense intended, Mr. Dodge, but
are you sure you're up to doing this by yourself?"

"I'm up to anything you can throw at me," Carson responded,
inwardly bristling. "Where should I hook up with you?"

"There's a new fishing lodge almost directly across the lake
from Daniel Frey's place. I believe it's called the Lodge on
Evening Lake. That's where I'll be staying. I'll see you on
Monday the fifteenth, Mr. Dodge."

She hung up before he could, and he stuffed the cell phone
into his pocket with a silent curse and finished off his second
beer while nursing his twice-bruised ego.

LIBBY REPLACED THE PHONE in its cradle and then sat up in her
bed with a surge of panic that centered around a horrible

thought. What if Dodge found the wreckage, but her father's remains couldn't be found? What if she couldn't prove her paternity? She'd never be able to come up with the money to pay him off. It would take years. She reached for the phone to call him back and tell him the truth, then paused. She'd led him to believe that the plane held great treasures, and to her it did. But if she told Dodge he was looking for bones, what were the odds he'd take the job? She drew a deep breath and slowly exhaled. She had nothing to fear. Her father's bones wouldn't have dissolved, and they'd be with the plane.

Wouldn't they?

She glanced over at her mother. Marie was sleeping. It had been a long day for her, and while the medicine she'd received at the hospital had begun the process of making her feel better, in the interim she was far better off sleeping. Chronic lymphocytic leukemia. Marie Wilson deserved a whole lot better than that. She deserved to live the way she should have been living for the past twenty-eight years, and would have been if Daniel Frey hadn't sent her away, denouncing her claim that Connor was the father of her child when he knew Connor loved her and was on his way to marry her.

"I'm going to nail the bastard for what he did, Dad," Libby said. "I swear to you, I will."

Dad.

She'd lived with the idea of him all her life, but it had been an elusive idea. Nothing more than a picture on her mother's bureau. Not one he'd given Marie, but one an employee at Frey's lodge had stolen and passed to her after his death. That picture had been all Libby had to call Dad, and it was a military picture at that, one he'd sent his own father shortly after getting his wings. A picture of him standing beside his plane at some air base. The plane was a wicked-looking thing. Her father was grinning at the camera. Handsome, dashing. A boy, really, so young and sure of life.

Libby thought it ironic that Connor Libby had survived Vietnam only to die on his wedding day, but she was determined to prove that Frey had something to do with it. Tomorrow she'd fly with her mother back to the village and fill her empty cupboards with food. Then she'd pay a little visit to the eccentric billionaire Daniel Frey, as a guest of the Lodge at Evening Lake, who'd read the wonderful article about him in *Forbes* magazine. She'd gush. She'd flatter. She'd use all of her feminine wiles to draw him out, to get him to talk about Ben Libby. About Connor. And about the plane crash that had killed her father.

CHAPTER THREE

EARLY SUNDAY MORNING, Libby packed her bag in preparation for the trip to Evening Lake. In the past few days she had done much to improve her mother's living situation. She'd stocked up on food, had the propane tanks filled, dragged all the rugs out and hung them on the line to beat them clean and let them air. She'd arranged for a home health-care visitor daily who would make sure her mother had a good lunch and took her medications. This would happen on the days Libby was absent. The home health-care worker was a government employee trained as a nurse's assistant, who lived in the village and looked after the needs of the elderly. Marie, of course, wanted no part of this.

"I can fix my own meals and swallow my own pills. I don't need any help."

"Mom, you're still very weak. Soon, you'll start to feel much better but I'm going to be gone for a few days. I don't want to worry about you."

"You've been gone for years to those fancy schools back East and I was just fine. I'll be fine for a few days more."

"Please, Mom. You told me you liked Susan. She won't stay long. Just long enough to make sure you eat at least one good meal a day. You're too thin. That dress will look a whole lot better on you when you fill out. Besides, if we're going to fish camp, you have to be strong."

Marie remained unconvinced. "Where are you going, Libby? You tell me you're going away for a few days but you don't tell me where."

Libby had already resolved to keep as much as possible from her mother. Marie would only get upset, and now was not the time to open Pandora's box. "I'm going to visit friends. I've been away so long and there are so many people I want to see."

"You're going to Evening Lake, aren't you? After all this time you still can't let it go." Marie may have been weak from her anemia and sick from the anticancer medication, but her eyes were as piercing as ever and she knew her daughter well.

"Mom, please. Just promise me you'll let Susan check in on you while I'm gone. I'll be back as soon as I can. Promise me."

"I promise I will let Susan in the house if you stay away from Daniel Frey."

Libby gave her mother an impulsive hug. "Eat your food, take your medicines and don't worry about me."

As she climbed aboard the float plane she knew her mother wouldn't let Susan in the house. Out of sheer stubbornness Marie would make life hell for that poor woman, who had promised Libby to watch her mother closely. "Don't worry, Marie will be fine," she assured Libby. "Your mother is one of the toughest ladies I know. Besides, she should start feeling much better soon." Libby hadn't a doubt about that, but now she was worried about Susan, who took her job very seriously and hadn't a clue how ornery Marie could be.

THE FLIGHT TO EVENING LAKE took less than an hour. In all her years of living in the village, of knowing that her father had drowned there, Libby had never been to see it. Had never wanted to see it. Never wanted to put her hand in the water and know that her father's bones were hidden in the dark cold depths. Even now a part of her dreaded seeing the lake, and as the plane headed north and west she stared out the window with a heart that beat a painful rhythm. Then suddenly the plane skimmed over a ridge and she was looking at a huge body of water shaped like a giant horseshoe, the deep curve on the southernmost end and two parallel arms, divided by perhaps a mile of timbered forest, stretching north. Several small rivers fed the lake along both of the upper arms, and a big river flowed out of it in the curve of the southern shore, the same river where they'd found the plane's pontoons. She could see it snaking through the spruce and she could just make out the rapids where the pontoons had gotten hung up.

She studied the surface of the lake, but it gave up no secrets. The water looked black and cold near the outlet, while the west arm that stretched toward the glaciers was streaked a thick milky blue in places with glacial silt. There was still some ice in the deeper coves, but most of the lake was open. The plane lost altitude quickly, and soon she could see the buildings. Both lodges were on the southernmost end of the lake, near the outlet but on opposite shores and about half a mile apart. Which was Frey's? She didn't know. One lodge appeared much larger than the other, and she supposed this would be the place she was staying.

But she was wrong. The plane landed and taxied to the dock fronting the smaller property. She was greeted by the owner of the lodge, a stout friendly woman in her early forties. "I'm Karen Whitten." She smiled and extended her hand. "Welcome to the lodge. My husband, Mike, is guiding, but you'll meet him tonight. I'll have your bags brought to your cabin. Come on up. You're just in time for lunch, though most of the guests won't show up until supper time. Fishing. I swear, you'd think the world turned around fly rods and lake trout."

Libby followed Karen up the ramp. The main lodge was cozy and small, with four guest rooms, a big kitchen, a vaulted living room with a handsome fieldstone fireplace and a friendly dining room. There were three small guest cabins to one side of the main lodge, and two employee cabins to the other. Karen showed her to her little cabin, complete with a tiny bath and a woodstove for heat. "This is just perfect," Libby said.

Karen herself served up the lunch, and the two women shared it in the kitchen. "So, are you here to fish?" Karen asked, ladling Portuguese kale soup into big earthenware bowls and setting a fresh loaf of crusty bread and a knife on the table.

"Not exactly," Libby replied, having carefully thought out her story. "I read an article in *Forbes* magazine about Daniel Frey, Ben Libby's partner, and after reading it I thought, wouldn't it be nice to write something about Ben Libby and all the good things he did with his money to help other people, especially since one of my college scholarships was funded by the Libby Foundation." Libby paused. "My friends always teased me about that scholarship. They said I got it because of my name, which was a fortunate coincidence. Anyway, who better to talk to about Ben Libby than Daniel Frey? Since I was sick of Boston and it was time for a vacation, I put the three together and here I am."

"From what I understand, Ben Libby was quite a philanthropist," Karen said. "I just hope Mr. Frey will talk to you. He's pretty reclusive. We've been here for two years and have yet to meet him. Mike and I have gone over a couple of times, knocked on his door, left a pie once and a loaf of sourdough bread with the employee who answered it. But if he was home either time, he wasn't entertaining visitors."

Libby would have inhaled the soup if she'd been alone. She buttered a piece of the crusty bread and took a big bite. The warm yeasty flavor nearly brought tears to her eyes. Marie should be here, eating this food and getting strong. "Well, I guess I'll just have to hope that he'll want to give Ben Libby the accolades he deserves. All I can do is go over there and ask. Do you have guides for hire here?"

"Oh, yes. Three, not counting Mike. Joe Boone used to work for Frey and Ben Libby when they first built the lodge. You might want to talk to him, too. He's out guiding a couple of fishermen now but he'll be back around supper time."

After lunch Libby walked down to the dock again and stood looking out over the lake. The wind was blowing just the way Dodge said it would, through that high mountain pass and across the water. It was strong enough to put a pretty good chop on the lake's surface. She knelt on the edge of the weather-bleached dock and plunged her hand into the icy water. Within seconds her hand ached with the cold. *I'm here, Dad,* she thought. *Right here.*

Had he been conscious when the plane went under? Had he struggled to escape as the frigid lake water filled the cabin? Libby pushed to her feet and shoved her hands into her jacket pockets. According to the pilot who had flown her to the lake, all the planes took off up the west arm, heading due north into the wind that came through the pass. They used the west arm because there were no big rocks just beneath the surface, and if they had to crab their takeoff or landing, the terrain was

flatter to the east and west, making for a safer climb-out. Her
father would have taken off the same way. His plane would
have been visible from Frey's lodge for a long distance, until
the west arm curved enough to close it out of sight behind a
fringe of dark forest.

She had watched the pilot who delivered her to the lodge
take off. His plane had lifted into the air not a quarter mile
from the dock, but he'd been flying a turbine engine Cessna
206 with a very powerful motor. The de Havilland would
have required a longer takeoff run. Still, that gave her a
general idea of where the plane might be.

Sort of. She had exactly twenty-four hours until Dodge
arrived to look over the situation and decide if he was taking the
job. Twenty-four hours to find out as much as she could about
where that plane went down. A lot to do, and not much time.

She studied the lodge across the lake. From a distance, she
couldn't make out exact details, but she could see enough to
realize it was quite the place. The Rockefeller clan could have
lived quite comfortably in such a log mansion. Being a hermit,
Frey must have greatly resented the arrival of Karen and Mike
and the construction of their new lodge. That's probably why
he had refused to greet them when they came to introduce
themselves.

She wondered if Frey had eaten the pie and the bread Karen
and Mike had left behind.

LIBBY RETURNED TO HER little cabin and took a nap, something
she hadn't done in many years and hadn't intended to do at
all, but sitting propped up against the headboard, jotting down
the questions she intended to ask Daniel Frey, her eyelids
became so heavy that it was impossible for her to resist the

rhythmic crash of waves against the shore, the lonely sigh of wind through the spruce, the snap of firewood in the wood-stove. She set the notebook aside, slid down until she was lying flat and laced her fingers across her stomach. The next thing she knew she was being roused by the sound of a clanging bell. She sat up, muzzy headed and drugged with languor. Karen had told her that she'd ring the supper bell at exactly 6:00 p.m., and sure enough it was exactly 6:00 p.m. Libby had slept for four solid hours.

The guests were already seated at the table when she arrived. Eight wealthy middle-aged fishermen, temporarily escaping corporate America and their wives and families, leaped out of their seats like jack-in-the-boxes when she stepped into the room. Karen introduced her around, then brought her into the kitchen to meet her husband Mike, a genial forty something Willie Nelson look-alike who was helping her prepare the meal. Karen began bringing forth yet another gastronomic tour de force while Libby pitched in, and the two of them smothered laughter in the kitchen at the expressions on the faces of the eight corporate clubhouse boys.

"Whatever will they do with such a beautiful guest in their midst? It's too bad you don't fish," Karen said. "I'll introduce you to Joe after supper. He seems to think he can wrangle you an interview with that old hermit, Daniel Frey."

Conversation during dinner began like spurts of machine-gun fire then rapidly progressed to a nonstop barrage as her fellow dinner guests sought to outboast one another to gain her attentions. Bottles of wine circulated around the table, fueling the frenzy. Each had a story to tell, an important story about themselves. Libby concentrated as best she could, nodding and smiling her appreciation of their intelligence and importance, but she was relieved when the meal was over. She helped Karen clear the table and would have plunged into the task of washing the dishes except that her hostess led her outside onto the porch.

"Joe?" she said as a lean, wiry gray-haired man with a deeply lined and weather-beaten face pushed off the railing. "This is Libby Wilson. She's staying with us for a few days. Libby, meet Joe Boone. He's been guiding since he was seventeen years old."

Joe shook her hand. "Karen tells me you want to talk to Dan Frey. Dan and I go way back. He's a crotchety old coot, no doubt about that, but I bet I could soften him up for you."

"That would be great. I'd so appreciate any time at all he could give me. I'm writing an article about Ben Libby and all the philanthropic things he did with his money over the years before he died. I was hoping Mr. Frey could cast a more personal light on the man, having known him for so long. I'm sure you could, too."

"Oh, no doubt. You busy right now? I could run you over in my boat. This is a good time to catch him. He likes to sit on the porch with his whiskey and cigars. I'll hook the two of you up, and come pick you up in a hour or so. We can talk then, if you like."

Libby could hardly believe her luck. "I'll just grab my notebook and meet you down on the dock," she said.

SURE ENOUGH, AS THEY approached the opposite shore Libby could see Daniel Frey on the vast covered porch that fronted the log mansion and faced the lake. He watched their approach without moving, sitting in a recliner with a side table at each hand. Libby stayed on the dock while Joe

Boone climbed the steps onto the porch. After a few minutes he turned and motioned for her to come up. She drew a steadying breath and climbed the porch steps as Frey rose to his feet.

"Hello," he said, extending his hand. "I'm Daniel Frey."

All of her life she'd wondered what this moment would be like. She looked at Frey and was amazed that lightning didn't streak across the wronged heavens. She marveled that the evening could remain so calm in the midst of the emotional tempest that raged within her. She smiled and shook the hand of the man who had robbed her of her identity and may have had something to do with her father's plane crash. "Libby Wilson. Thank you for seeing me, sir."

Frey was even more imposing in real life than he'd been depicted in the pages of *Forbes* magazine. He was a tall, vigorous and handsome eighty-two-year-old man, with the hawklike eyes of a predator. His hair was thick and pure white, brushed back from the weathered, tanned brow. "Please, have a seat," he invited. It was obvious her name meant nothing to him. "Joe, will you have a glass of whiskey with me?"

"Thanks, but no. Have to guide a couple sports for the evening hatch. I'll return for Ms. Wilson in about an hour or so, if that's all right, or if I can't make it I'll send another guide along."

Joe Boone returned to his boat and motored back across the lake. Libby perched on the edge of the matching leather recliner and waited while Frey tried to light his cigar. At length an acrid stench flavored the air and he grunted with satisfaction. "I don't like people very much," he said, refilling his shot glass. "Normally I wouldn't talk to you, but Joe said you wanted to discuss Ben Libby."

"Yes, sir. I'm writing a story about him. I won a scholarship from the Libby Foundation and that helped pay for my education."

"*LUANNE!*"

Frey bellowed so suddenly that Libby jumped in her seat. She heard a little scurrying sound and the screen door of the log mansion opened to reveal a very timid-looking young woman, maybe eighteen or twenty, pretty, dressed in a maid's uniform that harkened back to the 1950s.

"Yes, Mr. Frey," she said, advancing with her eyes on the floor.

"We have company. Perhaps you could offer Ms. Wilson something to eat or drink. That's what I'm paying you for, isn't it?"

"Yes, Mr. Frey." The girl glanced questioningly at Libby. "Miss?"

"I'm fine, thank you, Luanne. I just had a wonderful meal at the lodge across the lake." Libby watched as Luanne rushed back inside. "She must be from one of the native villages?"

"Athapaskan," Frey said. "They're all I can get out here. Now, what do you want to know about Ben Libby?"

Libby poised her pen over the notebook. "Everything, I guess. I mean, I already know a lot about how he made his fortune. What I really want to know is what kind of man he was. What he was like. Did he have a sense of humor? Did he like animals? You know. Human interest stuff like that."

"Sense of humor?" Frey clearly thought this was an odd question.

"Well, maybe you could start by telling me how you met him. How you became partners."

"We were officers in the navy and we served on the same sub."

"Wow. I mean, I just can't imagine being in a submarine under all that water. So, what did the two of you do on the sub?"

"We played cards. Poker. Endless games of poker." Frey took a sip of his whiskey. "Ben always won. He won at everything. When the torpedo hit, that was the only time I thought he might lose."

"You were playing poker when a torpedo hit the sub?"

"It flooded the forward compartment. There were two men trapped inside. We could hear them shouting, screaming for help. Everyone else evacuated because our compartment was starting to flood, too, but Ben stuffed his cards inside his shirt and went to rescue the trapped men. He couldn't do it alone, so I helped him."

"That was courageous of you."

"On the contrary, it was quite stupid. Our rescue attempt could have lost the sub. But we were lucky. We got the two trapped men out and managed to seal off the compartment behind us. Afterward Ben showed me his cards. He had a full house. He said that was why he knew he'd make a successful rescue." Frey barked a humorless laugh. "He was a brave son of a bitch. Smart, too. We survived the war and when we were discharged he asked me if I wanted to go in on a business venture. He told me he'd found some weird patents he wanted to back. He thought they'd be big moneymakers. I had some money saved up so I said, sure, then went home to Maine. Ben took my little wad of savings and in less than two years he'd made me a millionaire."

"He must have been a genius."

"He was. I quit my job as a shift supervisor at the paper mill in Rumford, bought a better truck and went to work at a furniture factory making chairs. I'd always wanted to learn how to make furniture. A year later I was discovering that making it wasn't nearly as much fun as I thought it would be when Ben calls out of the blue and asks if I want to go on a fishing trip to Alaska.

"I said sure, and this is where we came. He'd been studying maps of Alaska for years but had never been here. We were flown in with all our gear and camped in a tent on this very beach. We fished and explored the country. At the end of the week Ben said he didn't want to leave, and neither did I. When the plane came to pick us up he told the pilot we'd be staying another week. Then he asked me if I wanted to go in on a fishing camp in this very spot."

"And you said 'sure,'" Libby said, scribbling like mad.

Frey barked another laugh. He lifted his glass in a gesture toward the lake and the majestic Brooks range beyond. "By 'fishing camp' I thought he meant a little log shack on the shore we could come to for a week or two every summer, but this is what he built."

"Have you lived here ever since?"

"Pretty much. I spend winters in Hawaii now. It's warmer."

"So your initial investment in Ben Libby's entrepreneurial genius made you a rich man."

"That's right."

"Can you tell me anything about Ben's wife? The article barely mentions her."

"Ben fell in love with a German girl he met while on leave. He married her after the war and when the lodge was completed, he brought her here. She was a nervous thing. Pretty, but high-strung. Definitely a city girl, born and bred. She didn't like living on the edge of nowhere. She was afraid of the dark. Ben thought she'd get used to it, and once the guests started coming she'd be okay. But I knew she wasn't right for the place. When she heard a wolf howl for the first time she ran inside and cried in fear."

Frey realized his cigar had gone out and paused to light it again. Libby caught up on her notes and when she smelled the rank odor she glanced up. "What happened to her?"

"She went nuts. Wacko. She left him, finally, and went back to Germany."

Libby paused and glanced up from the notebook. She'd half expected the omission of Connor Libby. "But wasn't there a son?"

Frey took another sip of whiskey, puffed on his cigar, gazed out across the lake. "Connor," he said. "Right after Ben brought her here she got pregnant and insisted that she had to be near a good hospital with good doctors. Ben kept her in Anchorage at this fancy town house he rented until she had the baby, then brought her and the boy back to the lodge."

"Whatever became of her?"

"About a year after that, she left the boy with Ben and returned to Berlin. Just as well she did. We later learned that she threw herself beneath a train as it pulled into a station."

"She killed herself?" Not even Marie knew about this. She knew only that Ben's wife had died. "How awful. She must have felt hopeless even after she returned to the place she loved."

"She was crazy," Frey said with a shrug. "I guess that proved it."

"What became of the boy?"

"Ben raised him, made me the boy's godfather. When the wife ran off, Ben hired people to manage his money and his properties and pretty much planted himself here. He loved this place."

"Did the boy like it, too?"

"Connor? This life was all he knew until he went off to college."

"Did he know about his mother?"

"We told him she'd gone to visit her family in Germany and got sick and died there. He never knew she'd abandoned him."

"What happened to Connor?"

"He graduated college and about that time the war in Vietnam was getting into high gear so he joined the air force and learned to fly."

"I remember the article said he was killed in a plane crash. Was that during the war?"

Frey gave Libby the first real stare since she'd arrived. She felt the dark malice in his flat gaze and dropped her eyes to her notebook while he took another sip of whiskey. "No. He survived two tours, got a bunch of medals, served out his enlistment and came back here."

Libby could sense the gathering tension in Frey as he spoke about Connor. "What did Ben Libby do during the war?" she asked, changing the topic in an attempt to relax him.

"He made another billion dollars on some sophisticated electronics they were putting into the same jets his son was flying. And then he was diagnosed with liver cancer. By the time the war was over, Ben was gone." Frey finished off his drink. "I still miss him."

I just bet you do, Libby thought, scribbling furiously. "The article in *Forbes* stated that Ben divided his estate between you and his son. Did that surprise you?"

"Yes. I thought he'd leave it all to his son."

"How did Connor feel about that?"

Frey shrugged. "He didn't give a damn about money. Maybe that's one of the reasons why Ben left me half of the estate, to keep an eye on the business end of things. That, and Connor was my godson."

"So, what happened to Connor?"

"When he came back from the war he was pretty depressed. Suicidal, I thought. He bought himself a float plane. Pretty plane, bright yellow."

Libby glanced up again and frowned to mask her outrage that Frey would imply her father had been suicidal, when in fact he'd been in love. "Oh, no. You're going to tell me that he crashed that plane, aren't you?"

Frey gave her another flat stare. "How long have you been freelancing?"

"Not that long, actually. I hope you don't hold that against me, sir."

Frey relaxed and gave her a thin smile. "No, not at all." He poured another glass of whiskey. "Connor crashed the plane. He hadn't had the thing for a month and he crashed it."

"That's terrible," Libby said. "I'm assuming he was an experienced pilot, after all that flying in the war. How did it happen?"

"LUANNE!" Frey belted out for the second time, causing Libby's heart to skip several beats. She heard the same soft scuffle and the young woman reappeared, eyes downcast. "Where are my medicines?"

"Coming, sir," Luanne said, retreating.

"No matter how many times I tell her, she always forgets. You can't train them. I don't know why I waste my time trying." Luanne made another appearance, bearing a glass of water and two tiny pills on a small tray, which she left on the table. Frey picked up the two pills, placed them in his mouth, and chased them down with a swallow of water, followed by a bigger swallow of liquor. He puffed on the cigar for a few moments, then gave her another predatorial glance.

"Who're you writing this story for?"

"Actually, sir, the Libby Foundation asked me to write it."

Frey grunted and seemed satisfied with her answer. "Ben did a lot of good things. He had people and organizations after him all the time with their hands out. He supported more damn causes and still felt like he wasn't doing enough."

"Was his son the same way?"

"Connor didn't hold a candle to his father."

"Were you here at the lodge when Connor…crashed the plane?" Libby asked.

"I was fishing up on the Kandik. The first I knew something had happened was when I saw the warden's plane buzzing up and down the lake."

"So they think the plane went down in the lake?"

"That's what they figure. Only thing they found were the two floats hung up about half a mile down the Evening River, just below the big rips."

"No other wreckage was found? No body was recovered?"

Frey shifted in his seat. His shaggy white brows drew together in a frown. "I thought this article was supposed to be about Ben."

"Yes, sir, it is, but the fact that he had a wife and child is a great human interest angle. Where do you suppose Connor was going when he took off that day?" Libby asked, fishing for some mention of Connor's wedding.

"*LUANNE!*" Frey belted out, startling Libby yet again. For the third time Luanne scuttled out onto the porch, eyes downcast. "Get down on the dock and tell that bastard he's not welcome here."

For the first time Libby noticed the canoe that was approaching the dock. "Who is it?"

"That damn Indian guide who works for those flatlanders

across the lake. He knows this place is off-limits to him. He tried to sic the Department of Human Services on me last summer for some alleged infractions of human rights. He told them I mistreated my employees, didn't house them properly or pay them their legal wages and overtime. Overtime, for cripe's sake. They actually sent someone out from Fairbanks to inspect their living quarters and check my books." Frey made a sound of disgust. "Overtime! They're lucky I pay them anything at all."

Luanne was speaking to the man in the canoe. She turned and walked swiftly back to the porch and stared at Mr. Frey's slippered feet. "He says he is here to take Ms. Wilson back across. He says Joe Boone is busy guiding two clients and couldn't come."

Libby stood, folding her notebook. "Thank you so much for your time, Mr. Frey."

Frey grunted and picked up his glass of whiskey as Libby started down the steps. She paused at the bottom and glanced back. "Were you surprised that Connor left everything to you in his will?"

Frey shook his head. "He didn't have anyone else."

"Did they ever find Connor Libby's plane?"

"They'll never find that plane. This lake is bottomless, part of an old volcanic cirque," Frey said with a shake of his head. "End of story."

"On the contrary, Mr. Frey," Libby said. "I haven't even started writing it yet."

CHAPTER FOUR

LIBBY WALKED OUT onto the dock to meet the canoe, and the man seated in the stern nodded to her. He was much younger than Joe Boone and stockily built. Black raven's wing hair was pulled back with a strip of red cloth that hung between his shoulder blades. He wore faded jeans, a red flannel shirt and a green wool cruiser. On his feet were a pair of moose-hide moccasins. "I'm Graham Johnson, one of Mike and Karen's guides. Karen thought you might prefer a canoe ride this time of evening."

"She's right. This is much nicer than a motorboat. Thank you for coming to get me," Libby said. She knelt in the bow of the canoe and picked up the paddle as he swung around and started along the edge of the lake.

"How did your interview with Daniel Frey go?"

"Okay." It was a beautiful evening. The wind had died, the lake was calm and reflected the majestic mountains upon its silken surface. "Actually, I didn't learn anything new. A plane crashed in this lake twenty-eight years ago and I came here to see what Daniel Frey might know about it." She spoke without turning, and the air was so still that she feared for a moment that Frey might have overheard.

"You're talking about Connor Libby's plane?"

"Yes. Do you know anything about the crash?"

"It happened before I was born, but there was a lot of talk in the village about it."

"What kind of talk?"

"My mother had a cousin who worked here at the time. Frey gave all the hired help the weekend off because Connor was getting married to a native girl from Umiak, who worked at the lodge and had invited them to the wedding. But Daniel Frey didn't come and never planned to come. So mostly the talk was about why he wouldn't attend his godson's wedding."

"Why wouldn't he?"

"Everyone thought it was because he didn't want his godson to marry a native girl. He doesn't like Indians much. That's common knowledge. And some thought he didn't want to be in the plane, either."

"Because Frey knew it might crash?"

"Maybe." Graham's answer was noncommittal.

"Is there anyone else at all who might know something about it, other than Daniel Frey?"

There was a long pause, just the sound of the paddle dipping into the water. "My father, maybe," Graham said.

Libby felt a jolt of surprise. "Was he living around here at the time?"

The silence stretched her tension to the limit before Graham spoke again. "My father lived out here most of the time, fishing in summer and running a trapline in winter. He only came home maybe once, twice a year. When I was old enough, I spent summers with him. He didn't talk much, but every once in a while he'd tell me a story. There was one story he liked to tell, to scare me and make me stay close. It was the story of a yellow three-legged dog. He said the dog howled in the night like its heart was broken and wandered like a ghost along the shores of the lake, looking for lost souls. He said if I wandered off into the woods, Windigo would get me. He told me the three-legged dog would carry my soul to the land of the forgotten. When I got older, the people in the village told me that dog belonged to a white man from the lodge, the one who died in the plane crash."

"Do you think your father would tell me that story?" Libby asked, turning to face him.

A brief pause followed, the length of three paddle strokes. "I don't know. You'd have to ask him."

"Where does he live now?"

"Where he's always lived, a few miles up the west arm."

"Could we go there now? It won't be dark for another three hours."

"He might not talk to you. He doesn't like whites much."

"I'll take my chances. I need to learn all I can about that plane crash." She waited with bated breath for his answer, because his expression wasn't promising.

"All right," he finally said. "We'll trade our canoe for a motorboat and take a trip up."

KAREN WAS WAITING on the dock when they arrived. "I hope you didn't mind coming back by canoe," she said as Libby climbed onto the dock.

"It was wonderful. Thank you for thinking of it."

"How did your meeting with Mr. Frey go?"

"He was more talkative than I expected." Libby glanced back to where Graham was already shifting his gear into a motorboat. "Graham is going to take me to talk with his father. He says he might have something to add to the story."

"How's Solly doing, Graham?" Karen asked.

"Not so good. He still has a cold, but he won't see a doctor. Doesn't trust the white man's medicine."

"I'll pack you some food to bring to him," Karen said, and Libby accompanied her up to the lodge. "Well, you've managed to accomplish two things in less than a day that I've been trying to do for several years," she said wryly while arranging food in a basket in the kitchen. "You've met Daniel Frey, and now you're going to meet Solly Johnson, though I don't know what light he'll be able to shed on Ben Libby."

"Actually, I'm hoping he'll know something about the plane crash that killed Ben's son," Libby explained.

"Ah. Well, it's possible. And if nothing else, you'll get a good boat ride with Graham. He's our best guide. He knows this lake better than any of the others, all the lore and legends, and he knows where the best fishing can be found. Our guests really enjoy being guided by him. They request him more than all the others."

"Does he have any family other than his father?" Libby asked.

"His mother lives in a village on the Yukon, and I believe he has several brothers and sisters," Karen replied. "I think he has a soft spot for a certain girl who works for Daniel Frey. Luanne Attla. He's brought her here a couple of times. She's a nice girl."

"Yes, I met her this evening. She has a tough job."

"I offered to hire her but she seemed determined to stay with Frey. He must pay his help a whole lot better than I can." Karen handed the basket to Libby and smiled. "Tell Solly he's welcome here any time. And good luck."

CARSON WAS TOO TIRED TO EAT after the dive class at the university adjourned late Sunday afternoon. He'd thought the class would've been an easy teach and scoffed at the dean's suggestion that he reschedule it for a time when he was "feeling better." All he had to do was show some slides and film clips on the AV equipment, talk a while, answer questions, draw some stuff on the blackboard. The students in the class were all experienced. There would be no need for long explanations or simple kid talk. But in retrospect, teaching beginners would have been a helluva lot easier. The way the divers had studied him had put him off. It was as if they were looking for cracks in his armor. Waiting for him to collapse onto the floor. And then, not an hour before the class finally ended, he'd given them what they'd been waiting for. He stumbled into a desk and all fourteen experienced, young and physically fit divers had leaped to their feet as if to catch him before he fell.

Ironic, that he'd been scheduled to teach this class long before his accident, but it was his experience with being rescued that had been the source of multiple questions from the divers, who all feared the same fate. He told them what he could, but mostly he was relating facts that he'd been told by Trig, who'd made the actual rescue. He personally had little recollection of anything at all after the cable had tightened around him and dragged him into the wreckage.

After the conclusion of the second day one of the students walked with him to his truck on the pretext of asking a few extra questions, but Carson had the distinct impression that he was being chaperoned. At the truck, the young man had stuck out his hand and then realized that Carson's hand was swathed with bandages and instead had patted him awkwardly on the shoulder. "It was a great class and I learned a lot. You're a legend amongst us divers. You're the king, man, the best of the best."

A washed-up and crippled legend. An old king. Hell, he couldn't even play pool anymore. He'd gone to the pool hall the night before because Saturday night was traditionally pool hall night. He thought he'd have a few beers and shoot a few games with the guys after teaching the first day of the diving course. It had seemed like a good idea at the time. After all, nearly six weeks had passed since he'd last stopped in, but Carson realized after his second beer and during his first game of pool that he was in no way ready to take up where he'd left off before the accident. In fact, halfway through the first game, while taking an easy rail shot, he'd collapsed over the table in a fit of coughing brought on by both bending over the table and the movement of his arm, which somehow combined to aggravate his lung. Which had brought Gracie rushing to his side, but not the way he'd envisioned. He'd wanted her to sidle up to him the way she used to, when she was feeling playful and kittenish and thinking about spending the night with him on his boat. He'd wanted her to act as though he was still man enough for a hot-blooded woman like her, and then he'd wanted to prove her right.

Instead she was helping him straighten up off the pool table, taking the stick out of his hand, her face a mask of concern. "Oh my God, Carson, sit down. Are you all right? Should we call an ambulance?"

An ambulance? Shit!

Twenty minutes later he gave up all pretense of playing pool and was pulling on his coat. Gracie was serving drinks when she glanced up and caught his eye. She came around the bar and gave him a brief, motherly peck on the cheek. "Are you sure you're all right to drive?" And then, reading his expression, she reached out and touched her fingertips to the only place on his face that didn't have a scar. "Carson, please, if there's anything I can do, let me know," she said.

He limped out to his truck and sat for a while in the cab. Stupid idea, coming to the pool hall. Ridiculous, to think that he could walk through those doors and act as if nothing had changed. Foolish, to think Gracie would be loyal enough to volunteer to warm his bed. After all, he'd been the one who was so adamant about a casual relationship. No strings. No commitments. But even if she'd hinted at coming to the boat after getting out of work, what then? What if his performance was no better between the sheets than it had been at the pool table?

That was it for him. No more playing pool, and until he got back up to speed, no more thoughts of carnal lust with Gracie. The entire weekend had left him feeling demoralized, and now he had to pack his gear for the trip to Evening Lake. Most of it was already stashed in the back of his truck. He'd drive to the float plane base tonight and load it into the Otter. He wanted to get an early start in the morning. Maybe he'd feel better about things once he got out of Anchorage and started looking for the plane and the treasure it held. A week or two out in the Alaskan bush would give him time to come to the front. Even if he wasn't quite as appealing to women as he had been before the accident, he still knew how to run a salvage operation. He'd prove to Libby Wilson that he could find the plane wreckage she was so keen to recover, and when he did, maybe he'd recover some of his self-esteem.

Still, Gracie's peck on the cheek had rankled.

GRAHAM WASTED NO TIME on the trip up the west arm to take Libby to meet his father. For thirty minutes they traveled in silence, unable to talk over the sound of the outboard motor until they reached the place where the Yaktektuk River emptied into Evening Lake and Graham beached the boat. The river water was a thick milky blue that diluted visibly in an ever-widening delta into the darker lake water. "The Yaktektuk is full of glacial silt from the spring runoff," Graham explained in response to Libby's question about the color. "Bad fishing, right here. In a month or so the water will clear, but the silt settles at the mouth of the Yaktektuk and makes the lake water too rich in minerals for the fish. It's good in a way. Keeps the whites away from my father's place." He helped Libby to shore, tied the boat to a nearby tree and shouldered a fully laden pack basket while Libby retrieved the small cooler holding more of Karen's food and donned her own pack.

"We walk from here," he said. "There's too much white water up ahead. Keep your eyes peeled for bears. We're in their territory now."

They started up the faint trace that Graham's father had worn along the banks of the Yaktektuk in all his years of living in this country. "Frey told me that you'd caused him a lot of grief with the DHS over the way he treated his employees," Libby said as she fell in behind him.

"The DHS slapped him with a big fine. So did the Department of Labor."

"He omitted that information," Libby said, struggling to keep up. "But the fine didn't change his attitude. He doesn't treat Luanne very well. I felt sorry for her."

"Don't. Luanne might come across as browbeaten, but she's not. She's a college student. Berkeley. Majoring in social science. She's been working for him for two summers now.

He pays great wages, almost twice what the Whittens can pay. She's also working on her thesis paper and Frey's providing her with all sorts of ammunition. The information she passed along to me is why Frey got fined."

"She's certainly dedicated to the cause of enlightening the world."

"Yes, she is. I just wish the world would listen to her."

"How long has your father had a cold?" she said, beginning to gasp for breath.

"Too long."

"I know about medicine, and I'm half Athapaskan. Maybe he'd let me help him."

"Maybe," Graham said. "But if it's white man's medicine you're practicing, you'd better have Athapaskan ways."

"I'll be as diplomatic as I can be with a medical degree from Tufts," Libby said, her lungs starting to labor for air. "Frey told me this lake was bottomless. How deep is a bottomless lake?"

"Deep enough to keep its secrets," Graham said.

"You think the plane that crashed can't be found?"

"I think the lake is deep. You're a real doctor?"

"Yes. The Libby Foundation helped pay for my schooling."

Graham traveled swiftly and within minutes Libby was so out of breath that had she wanted to ask more questions she would have been hard put to voice them. Soon the day pack she was shouldering and the small cooler became like a leaden weight, and she wondered, as the seconds and minutes and seeming miles passed, how much farther it would be. City life had softened her, made her weak. Eight years of living in steel-and-concrete buildings, surrounded by artificial light, had changed her into something that was now alien in this land she used to know so well.

About ten minutes later it became apparent why they'd left the boat on the beach. A steep drop of high water and big rocks turned the Yaktektuk into a boiling cauldron of rapids for a good hundred yards. Just above the rapids, where the river opened into a wide calm pool and the turbulent air became quiet again, Graham stopped so abruptly that she ran into him with a jarring bump. "That's not so good," he said, staring ahead. Libby peered over his shoulder and saw the log cabin that huddled beside the deceptively placid stretch of river.

"What's not good?" she said.

"It's a cool evening and there's no woodsmoke."

Libby felt a twinge of unease as Graham began walking even more quickly toward the weather-beaten old cabin. He opened the door, bent to clear the lintel and disappeared inside as a pack of skinny sled dogs tethered to one side of the cabin sprang to attention and howled a belated warning.

Libby followed Graham into the cabin's dim interior. He was bent over a bed in the corner. He'd taken his hat off, holding it in one hand while the other closed on his father's shoulder. "Dad? Dad, it's Graham."

There was a hoarse muttering in response, and Libby moved up beside the bunk. A very old man lay beneath a plain wool blanket. His shoulder-length hair was pure white and his face as brown and wizened as a walnut shell. Libby could hear the fluid rattling in his lungs as he breathed.

She shrugged out of her day pack. "It sounds to me like pneumonia," she said, trying to hide her shock at the old man's critical condition. "Could you build a fire in the stove and heat some water?" She unzipped the pack on the edge of the bunk and removed her medical kit. It was compact but fairly comprehensive. Libby knew what life in the bush could be like and she wasn't about to travel anywhere unprepared. "Does your father understand English?"

"When he wants to," Graham said, crumpling a wad of old newspaper and shoving it into the firebox along with several generous handfuls of dry spruce twigs. He struck a match and before Libby could don her stethoscope the fire was off and running. In moments the metal stovepipe began to tick with heat, the cabin began to warm and a pot of water was heating.

"Help me sit him up," Libby said. "I'd like to listen to his lungs."

The old man was too weak to protest Libby's ministrations. She didn't have to be diplomatic as she took his pulse, and then his temperature. "I'm going to give him an injection of a powerful broad-spectrum antibiotic."

Libby raised her voice as she filled the syringe with antibiotic. "Solly, you have a bad sickness in your lungs. The sickness is keeping you from breathing and making you very weak. This medicine is very powerful. It will sting a little when I give it to you but it will make you feel better and help you get strong again." She swabbed the site on his arm with alcohol and injected the antibiotic. The old man didn't flinch. "Can you heat up the soup that Karen packed? I'll try to get some into him," Libby said over her shoulder in a voice tight with anxiety. "But IV fluids and oxygen at the hospital in Fairbanks would be a thousand percent better."

Graham shook his head. "He won't go. He would tell his spirit to leave him if you tried to take him away from here."

Libby realized the futility of argument. She knew how the traditionalists could be. Her own mother was the same way. She might not agree with their beliefs, but she respected them. "Solly, I'm going to have you sit up. I think it will be easier for you to breathe." When the old man was as comfortable as she could make him, she motioned to Graham and together they stepped outside the cabin.

"Your father really needs to be hospitalized."

"I've had this argument with him before. He won't leave here," Graham repeated. "He says when he dies to burn the cabin to the ground with him in it. That's what he wants."

"Okay then," Libby said, "like it or not, he's going to have to put up with a half-breed Athapaskan cleaning his cabin and fixing him something decent to eat." She glanced around the corner of the cabin to where five scrawny sled dogs watched intently from the ends of their chains. "You'd better tend those poor neglected huskies. I'll heat the soup."

By 10:00 P.M. LIBBY had gotten a bowl of beef broth into Solly one patient spoonful at a time. He dozed while she scrubbed and cleaned and swept the dingy little cabin. He never roused when she changed the bedding on his bunk, sliding him onto the freshly made bed as gently as she could. He didn't weigh much at all, and she wondered aloud how long he had been so sick.

"Last week he had a bad cough," Graham said. "But he was up and about. I spent the night and he ate a good breakfast before I left. He's lost a lot of weight in the past year or so. I don't think he eats too good."

"It's going to take some time for the antibiotics to kick in," Libby said. "I can leave pills for him to take, but if he doesn't take them, they won't help. What he really needs is a good nurse."

"I'll come back here after I drop you at the lodge and stay with him," Graham said. "I can borrow a motorboat, be at the dock at sunrise to take the clients fishing, check back here at lunch, be back at the dock for the evening crowd. In a motorboat I can get back and forth quick."

Libby straightened the blanket over Solly. She crossed the small room to the woodstove and looked at Graham. "I don't have to be anywhere until tomorrow morning. Your father needs a doctor right now and if he won't go to one, then I really think I should stay."

Graham glanced to where his father lay on the bunk and lowered his voice. "He's that sick?" Libby nodded. He stared at her with those dark, unreadable eyes. "I'll go back to the lodge and tell them where you are, and bring the motorboat back tonight. If he's that sick, we'll both stay."

IT WAS A LONG, SLEEPLESS NIGHT for Libby. She lay in the top bunk, wrapped in a sleeping bag that Graham had brought back from the lodge, and listened to each labored breath that his father drew in the murky light of the midnight sun. Graham slept on the floor, between the woodstove and the door. No mattress, just the sleeping bag. He lay flat on his back and breathed so quietly she didn't know if he was awake or asleep, but as long as the little cabin was filled with the sound of Solly Johnson's breathing, the straining of his fluid-filled lungs and the deep rasping coughs, she knew that the old man was alive and struggling to stay that way.

At 2:00 a.m. Libby slipped out of the top bunk and built up the fire in the woodstove. She boiled water and laced it with dried sage. She made a tent of a blanket and held the pot of water under it, so the old man breathed the steam. He roused only briefly while she did this, then slipped away again. She kept the stove stoked against the chill night, kept the water boiling, kept the steam vapors trapped beneath the blanket so the old man breathed them.

At 5:00 a.m. Graham rose and made coffee. He handed her a cup. "He's breathing better," he said.

It was true. Solly's breathing was improved. He was resting easier. Libby sipped the coffee slowly, savoring the strength it gave her. "I'll give him more broth before I leave, and make sure he takes his pills."

"I'll come back at lunch time and feed him again, and spend the night, too," Graham promised.

By 6:00 a.m. they'd returned to the lodge, and Graham was soon back out on the lake with three clients who had been waiting on the dock. Libby retreated to the warmth of the kitchen and sipped another cup of coffee while placing an indecently early call on the lodge's satellite phone to her mother's caregiver. Susan's voice was thick with sleep.

"Your mother's fine, Libby," she said, "but she refused to let me in the house. She told me she ate a good lunch, one of the meals you prepared before you left, and she promised me she took her pills."

"Susan, when you go over today, ask if she likes to play cribbage. That might get you through the door."

"How's Graham's father?" Karen asked when she was off the phone.

"Very sick with pneumonia. He should be in the hospital, but Graham says if we try to take him away from his cabin, he'll die out of spite." Libby paused. "Karen, I came here to talk with Daniel Frey, but I'm not a journalist. Making up that story was the only way I could think of to get to see him. I'm actually a doctor, but the real reason I'm here is to find the plane that Connor Libby crashed in this lake twenty-eight years ago, and I didn't think Daniel Frey would want to talk about that. I'm sorry I deceived you, but I'm glad I brought my medical kit."

This confession didn't seem to phase Karen at all. "And I'm glad you took care of Solly."

Libby finished off her pancakes and reached for her mug of coffee. "I'm expecting a visitor today. His name is Carson Dodge and he runs a salvage company out of Anchorage. He'll be flying in sometime this afternoon. I've hired him to look for the wreckage of the plane but I'm not sure he's going to take the job. I was hoping Mr. Frey might know the location of the plane, but he said he didn't. In fact, I didn't find out anything from him at all. And Solly's too sick right now to tell me anything even if he wanted to. The only other person I haven't talked to yet is Joe Boone. Is he guiding today?"

"Yes, but he should be back in around lunchtime. I'll hook the two of you up." Karen pushed to her feet with a weary sigh. "I suppose I'd better get back to work. The two Fairbanks girls we hired a month ago to work for the summer quit last week. It's hard keeping employees way out here. Hard getting them and hard keeping them."

"Do you provide room and board as part of the pay package?" Libby asked.

"Yes, and boat privileges, as well. We have two cabins for employees. Since most of the guides are men, they stay in the guides' camp. The cooks' camp is for the women."

Libby thought about her rapidly dwindling bank account. "I'd be happy to pitch in for a while," she offered. "I'm not working at the moment, and if Mr. Dodge decides to take on the salvage operation, it would be handy if I could stay in the area at least until he finishes the job."

Karen gave her a skeptical frown. "You mean to tell me you'd clean cabins after going to medical school?"

"I wouldn't want to make a career out of it, but if I could get three square meals and a roof over my head while Mr. Dodge looks for the plane, I'd think I was a lucky woman."

"Yes, but…"

"At least think about it. One other thing. If you decide to hire me on a temporary basis, I'd like to bring my mother here. I'd work for nothing if you fed and housed us both."

Karen shook her head. "I couldn't ask that of you. I mean, you're a doctor, for heaven's sake."

"Doctors and their mothers have to eat, too, and I could keep an eye on Graham's father. He's very weak. But my guess is his odds of a fast recovery would improve considerably if I could ferry him one of your meals every day."

"Well, I…" Karen shook her head again, clearly astonished. "I don't know what to say. If you're serious, I'd love to have you stay. You and your mother can share the cook's cabin. It's empty now and lord knows the way things are going it might very well stay that way all summer, but—"

The sound of an approaching plane interrupted their conversation. Libby glanced at her wristwatch. "That might be Mr. Dodge. This meeting will either go well, or not at all. Either way, I'll help you clean rooms and fix the meals. You've treated me like a sister, and made me feel like this place is home. I'm sorry I told you that story about being a journalist."

Karen reached out and squeezed her arm. "I know the story about Connor Libby and the plane crash. If there's anything I can do to help you out, just let me know. In the meantime,

I'll get started on the rooms. Will Mr. Dodge be needing a place to stay?"

Libby shook her head. "I have no idea."

"Well, if he does, tell him we have vacancies."

CHAPTER FIVE

LIBBY WAITED DOWN on the dock as the plane taxied in. It was a beefy red-and-white Otter, and she wasn't surprised to see that Carson Dodge was the pilot. He seemed like the kind of man who would fly his own plane. He climbed out and lashed the plane to the dock while Libby looked on, hands shoved in her pockets. Dodge looked a little better for having had a few more days to recuperate. He straightened and gave her a curt nod.

"So, have you found the exact location where the plane went down?" he said.

Was that sarcasm she detected in those oh-so-casual words? Libby studied the bruises and scars on his face, noting that in spite of them, he was a handsome man. The scars only seemed to enhance the aura of virility he radiated as he stood gazing at her with that cryptic and borderline arrogant expression. "Not exactly," Libby said. "But I've narrowed it down." She swept one of her arms out in an all-encompassing gesture. "It's somewhere in this lake. Have you had breakfast?"

Another curt movement of his head, this time a shake. "Left early. Don't usually eat breakfast."

"Coffee, then?"

"I could stand a cup," he said.

Libby brought him up to the lodge, introduced him to Karen,

sat him beside the still-glowing embers of the living-room fireplace and delivered to him a big mug of coffee along with three of Karen's huge blueberry muffins. For a man who didn't eat breakfast, he made short work of the muffins. Libby brought him three more. "I don't know much more than I did when I first spoke to you," she admitted as she topped off his mug. "I spoke with Daniel Frey shortly after I arrived here, and he told me the plane must have gone down near the outlet. He also said he wasn't here when it happened, he was off on a fishing trip." Libby set the coffeepot down on the side table and took a chair near his. "The thing is, Mr. Dodge, I've been studying how the planes take off from here. There haven't been a whole lot, maybe two or three, but they all take off the same way."

"And?" he prodded.

"And I don't see how Connor Libby's plane could have crashed near the outlet. By the time the planes are airborne, they're at least a quarter mile up the west arm."

He was eating another muffin, pulling it apart, feeding big chunks of it into his mouth and chasing it down with coffee. He acted as if he hadn't eaten a decent meal in a dog's age, and Libby knew just how he felt. She'd felt the same way when she'd first sampled Karen's cooking.

"You told me the plane's pontoons were recovered in the Evening River," he said.

Libby nodded. "They were. Do you think the pull of the river's current could have been so strong it moved them into the outlet from a quarter mile out?"

"Against that wind? Doubtful," he mumbled around another mouthful. The sixth muffin rapidly disappeared as Libby refilled his mug for the third time. "But maybe on that particular day, for some reason, the wind died completely. I suppose they could've moved toward the outlet. Depends on how long it took for a search to be launched. Do you know anything about that?"

"My mother told me the wardens were called three hours after the time Connor was supposed to have shown up at her village. So presumably, four hours after the plane had crashed, the authorities were alerted. But it took them another three hours to arrive from Fairbanks. They made the initial flyover at approximately 8:00 p.m. on the day the plane went down. No wreckage was spotted between the village and the lake, and there was no wreckage on the lake itself. The following morning a search plane spotted the pontoons a quarter mile down the Evening River, hung up in the rapids."

"Huh." He took a swallow of coffee. "That's not much to go on, but I wasn't really expecting much."

Libby flushed. "I haven't finished asking around. There's a guide who works here who has known Daniel Frey for a long time. I'm going to talk with him at lunchtime. And there's an old Athapaskan who lives a few miles from here and was around at the time of the crash. He knows something, I'm just not sure how much." She paused, eyeing his empty plate. "Would you like more muffins, Mr. Dodge?"

He shook his head. "No, thanks. What I would like is for you to stop calling me Mr. Dodge. Carson's my name. Where can I park my outfit?"

"Excuse me?"

"My plane. I can't leave it at the dock. I'll need to set up a base camp, get my gear unloaded and the boat inflated. I don't want to be in the thick of things. I imagine this lodge is a busy place."

"I'm sure you won't bother anyone no matter where you

set up your camp," Libby said. "You could even stay here if you like. They have vacancies."

"No thanks. I like my privacy. I saw a point of land about two hundred yards north of the dock with a sheltered cove on the far side," he said, rising to his feet.

Libby stood. "That would be a good place. I can walk there easily."

"No reason for you to walk there," he said.

"I thought I could give you a hand setting up your camp."

"I won't be needing any help."

Libby's cheeks grew hot. "I just thought—"

He gave her a warning look. "I have two hands and that's all I need. I'll get situated and get out on the water as soon as possible."

"Mr. Dodge...Carson," Libby said as he turned to leave. "You may not need my help, but I need to know what's going on. I hope that doesn't offend you. If it does, I'm sorry, but I have a vested interest in this search."

"Then I'm sure you'll understand that the less time I have to spend answering your questions, the more time I can spend out on the lake. My crew is working a tight schedule on another project and I can only give you one week, Ms. Wilson."

"One week?" she said, feeling a tight burn of anger at his rudeness and her stupidity. She'd never broached the subject of how long he was supposed to look in order to get his five-thousand-dollar retainer. "If that's all the time you can give me, you'd better get started."

LIBBY'S FRUSTRATION WITH Dodge carried her through a morning of cleaning rooms. She helped Karen with two of the rooms to familiarize herself with the routine, then cleaned two more on her own. Periodically she would peer down the lakeshore to the point of land where Carson had been planning to set up his base camp. She couldn't see his plane because he'd taxied it beyond the point, and she could detect little activity on the point itself. By noon all the guest rooms were cleaned and she walked down onto the dock. She had thought that by now he'd be out on the lake starting to search near the lake's outlet, but no rubber boat plied the waters.

Karen served up lunch when the hungry fishermen arrived with their guides but Libby wasn't able to speak with Joe Boone because he stayed out with his clients and didn't come back to the lodge for the midday meal. "That's not unusual," Karen said as they carried dishes to the kitchen. "If the fishing is really good, they'll beach the boat somewhere and Joe'll cook up a quick feed. The guides always bring along lunch, just in case. You'll be able to talk to him tonight at supper." She paused by the window and glanced out. "I'm surprised your salvage operator isn't out on the lake yet."

Libby confessed her anxiety over the same matter. "He told me he could only search for a week and he hasn't even started yet."

"Something must be holding him up. Why don't you bring him some of that leftover fried chicken and potato salad. My guess is he won't bite your head off if you come bearing food. Most men like their chow."

"No doubt most men love yours," Libby said. "Thanks. I'll take him some right after we get the kitchen cleaned up."

Karen shook her head. "I'll take care of that. You go light a fire under Carson Dodge." She grinned at Libby as she ran hot water into the sink. "Believe me, if I were single, I'd go myself. He's quite the hunk, even if he does look like he just lost a major battle with seven samurai."

Ten minutes later Libby was carrying a picnic basket along the edge of the shoreline. The walking was fairly easy, the afternoon sun felt good, and a pleasant breeze blew the bugs away. As she approached the point, she inadvertently eavesdropped on some of the foulest profanities she'd heard in quite some time. When she finally spied Carson's camp site she understood why. He was surrounded by a mountain of gear and in the midst of trying to assemble some sort of high-tech piece of equipment using a tool Libby didn't recognize with a bandaged hand that clearly wasn't cooperating. A green canvas wall tent was in the beginning stages of being set up and the rubber boat on the beach near the plane was only half inflated. It looked to her as if he'd started several projects and had to give up on each one.

When he spotted her he stood, still holding the tool in his good hand. His face flushed a darker shade with anger or embarrassment or some combination of both as he fixed her with an accusing stare. "What the hell are you doing here?"

"I was wondering why you weren't already out on the lake, but I can see you've been having some problems."

"Nothing I can't handle," he said, gruff as a grizzly. Even his scowl looked as if it hurt him. His bandaged hand showed signs of blood seeping through the cotton gauze, which was badly soiled and needed changing.

"I brought you some lunch." She held up the picnic basket.

He eyed the basket and his scowl deepened. "Not hungry and don't have time," he said, crouching back down beside a piece of equipment that resembled a small streamlined black-and-yellow torpedo with fins.

"I could help," Libby offered.

"I can manage," he said, not looking at her but not managing too well, either. The tool obviously required two-handed dexterity and there was no way on earth he was going to be able to use it on his own. Libby set the picnic basket on the ground and moved closer.

"What are you assembling?" she asked, kneeling beside him.

"Nothing. I'm fixing the towfish's cable connection," he muttered, concentrating on the hopeless task. "And if you don't mind, I'd prefer not to have an audience."

"Look," Libby said, her patience wearing thin. "Just this morning you told me you could only give me one week of your time, and already half a day is gone. I was told you were the best salvage operator around and that might be true, but right now you're recovering from some pretty serious injuries and like it or not, you could use a little help. I could screw that thing in there for you. I can see what you're trying to do, and I can do it. I have two perfectly good hands." Libby held them out, turned them over then back again, though he didn't bother to look. "Please, let me help. Helping you helps me. I really need you to find that plane."

He glanced up at her, and their eyes held for several long moments before he looked away. He stared out at the lake, heaved a sigh, then handed her the tool and pushed slowly to his feet. "Okay then, I'll put the motor on the boat."

"Karen's fried chicken is the best I've ever eaten," Libby commented as he started away. He paused and glanced at the picnic basket. "Best potato salad, too, and if you're an apple pie fan, you'll think you've died and gone to heaven. Better make it disappear, Mr. Dodge, before the bears get wind of it."

BY THE TIME HE'D FINISHED off every last morsel of the enormous lunch, Libby had tightened the connection on the towfish, whatever that was, finished putting up the wall tent and assembled the little woodstove that went inside the tent. She'd pumped the rubber boat up to maximum inflation and affixed the motor to the transom. He watched her silently as he ate, and when he was done he packed all the wrappings into the basket, drained the last of the lemonade, and stood.

"Good?" Libby asked.

He nodded grudgingly. "So are you. Not many women would know how to do all that stuff."

Libby gave him a wry smile. "Not many women would want to know. I guess you're ready."

He nodded again. "I'll work until dark. That'll make up for the time I wasted."

"If you stop by the dock before quitting time, I'll rebandage your hand," Libby offered. "I have a good first aid kit, and that dressing really needs to be changed."

He gave her a strange look, as if he hadn't a clue how to treat her after she'd helped him out. "Thanks, but I can take care of it."

"Suit yourself." Libby picked up the empty picnic basket. "How will I know if you find the plane?"

"*When* I locate the plane, I'll be sure and communicate that to you directly and in person," he said.

"And then what happens?"

"Then we mark the spot and purchase the salvage rights from the state."

"Do you think you'll be able to find the plane in one week's time?"

"I'll stand a better chance if you let me get back to work," he said, the gruffness returning as he turned his back on her and shut her out.

Libby left the camp so swiftly she caught her toe in a tree root, stumbled and nearly fell. She was fuming as she skirted the shoreline back toward the lodge. Carson Dodge might be the best salvage operator going, but his insolence was intolerable. The best thing she could do was give him the space he asked for, which wouldn't be hard.

Not at all.

CARSON HAD NEVER FELT less like working than he did after consuming the contents of that huge hamper. Without a doubt it was the tastiest lunch he'd ever eaten, but now all he wanted to do was crawl inside his tent and sack out for a day or two. He was relieved when Libby Wilson finally left the camp. Bad enough that she'd had to help him get set up, but when she'd offered to fix his bandage it brought back with painful clarity all those days he'd spent lying flat on his back in the hospital while doctors and nurses prodded and poked and made notes on clipboards. He'd take care of his own damn hand. He didn't need or want anyone fussing over him ever again.

He headed the rubber boat toward the inlet to begin the search pattern, reflecting that the only thing he hated more than doctors was being dependent on anyone for anything, especially a woman. The fact that he hadn't been able to operate a simple hand tool to tighten the towfish connector was galling. Of course, his condition was only temporary. He *would* get his strength back. His hand *would* function normally again, no matter what those damn doctors had told him. Doctors were experts at delivering worst-case scenarios, but they weren't gods, and they didn't know how determined he was to prove them wrong.

As he motored steadily into the pattern, adjusting the tow-fish's depth, scanning his monitor, checking the GPS, perusing his charts of the lake, his feelings of frustration gradually faded. It was hard to brood on dark thoughts when surrounded by water, be it the Atlantic, the Pacific, or a glacial cirque just shy of the Arctic Circle. Besides, this search was something he could do even while he regained his strength. All he had to do was work the pattern and keep his eyes peeled. He'd find the plane, and when he did he'd bank the hundred and fifty grand in his private account...just in case those doctors were right.

LUANNE HAD SPENT BETTER DAYS, and worse, too, though working for Daniel Frey made every day a challenge. She kept telling herself that in the end this summer would be the best summer of all, for what she learned from working for Frey, and for the relationship she was building with Graham Johnson, but today, finding the silver lining was hard.

"LUANNE!"

She flinched as she heard Frey's shout. How many times today had he shouted her name? Too many to count. She found him out on the porch. It was after supper, and he sat there as always with his liquor and his cigars, in his reclining chair, looking out at the lake through his binoculars.

"Yes, sir?" she said, slipping through the screen door.

He didn't lower the binoculars. "Who's that man out on the lake?" he said.

Luanne followed his gaze and saw the rubber boat moving

slowly toward the outlet. She shook her head. "I've never seen him before, Mr. Frey."

"He flew in this morning. That's his plane, moored up on the point. Why is he here?" He lowered the binoculars to give her a hard stare.

"I don't know," she said.

"He's not fishing," Frey stated, eyes narrowing with suspicion as he leaned forward, raising the binoculars again. "Why isn't he fishing? He just sits in that boat and drives it in the same pattern over and over, across the lake by the outlet. He's been out there for hours. Why? What's he doing?"

Luanne watched a few moments more, then shrugged, thinking how pitiful it was that all Frey could find to do was be nosy about other people's affairs and critical of everything she did. He was a bitter, miserable old man. "I don't know, Mr. Frey. Can I get you anything?"

"You can find out who he is," he said. "Find out from that no-good friend of yours. Johnson."

Luanne felt herself tense when he mentioned Graham. Masking her dislike for Frey was becoming increasingly difficult. "I'll try, sir."

She turned on her heel to leave him to his evil ponderings but his voice arrested her. "You'll do more than try," he advised in an ominous tone of voice. "Take the boat and go find out. If you expect to keep your job and rake in that easy weekly paycheck, you'll bring back some answers for me."

Little did Frey know that she worked for him not solely for the money, but also for the experience, and for what she could gain in credibility when she wrote her thesis paper about bigotry being alive and well in the workplace.

LIBBY'S CONVERSATION with Joe Boone was tightly sand-
wiched between supper preparations and actual service of the
meal and left her feeling no more enlightened about the relationship between Daniel Frey and Connor Libby. "I only
guided for them when they had a full house," Boone said,
leaning against the counter while Libby prepared vegetables.
"Ben would fly me out, I'd work for as long as he needed me,
then he'd fly me back to Fairbanks. It was good money, and
the clients tipped me well. But after Ben was gone, there was
no guiding. Daniel liked having the place to himself."

"Would you consider Mr. Frey a hermit?"

"He's always been pretty reclusive, but he gets lonely, too.
He used to fly me in occasionally on the pretense of having
me guide him on fishing trips, but I think it was really because
he wanted company. That's how I got to know him. He'd
invite me to take meals with him, and we'd sit out on the porch
the way he does now, smoking cigars and drinking brandy or
whiskey, whatever tripped his trigger that night."

"Did you know Connor Libby at all?"

"Oh, sure. Connor was a good kid. Easygoing. Loved the
outdoors, and loved living in the wilderness. Talked about
going to college, getting a degree in wildlife biology or
zoology or something, then coming back here. I was kind of
surprised to hear he'd joined the air force. I mean, he wasn't
a gung ho fighter type, you know? He wouldn't even hunt
unless he needed the meat. But I think he felt like he had to
join up, to live up to Ben's expectations. Ben felt that every
able-bodied citizen owed military service to their country."

"Do you think Ben Libby pressured Connor to enlist?"

"No. I think Connor just wanted his father to be proud of

him. Like I said, he was a good kid. You'd never guess, talking to him, that he was a rich man's son."

"Did Mr. Frey talk about Connor at all?"

"Not really. I asked him if he heard much from the boy after Ben died, and Daniel said he'd gotten a few letters. He was sure that when the war was over Conner'd meet a girl, get married, and settle near her folks somewhere in the lower forty-eight."

"Did that eventuality seem to make Mr. Frey sad?"

Boone shrugged. "When Ben and Connor were there, Daniel played by their rules. Never said much. Stayed in the background and deferred to them in all matters. When they were gone, he transformed into the lord and master of the kingdom. He demanded constant service and was pickier than all get-out. Seems like he had a plane flying his mail and provisions in every other day. Of course, he could afford to. It was no big deal. If he wanted the daily paper delivered daily, he got it delivered daily. Didn't matter to him if that newspaper cost five hundred bucks in air-mail charges."

"Did he ever mention the plane crash that killed Connor Libby?"

"Sure. Daniel was Connor's godfather. The boy was the only family he had."

"Did he mention why he wouldn't attend Connor's wedding?"

"No. But Daniel didn't like Indians and didn't approve of the marriage. He was pretty up-front about that."

"Why did Mr. Frey dislike Indians?"

Joe shrugged. "Why do some people dislike blacks and Hispanics? Who knows."

The dinner bell clanged. Libby thanked Boone for his information and hurried to help Karen. After supper had been served and the kitchen cleaned up, she called Susan to check on her mother.

"Marie's feeling pretty good. She beat me three games straight at cribbage, which made her feel even better," Susan said, "and her appetite's getting better by the minute."

"That's great news. Tell her I miss her and I'd like her to fly out tomorrow to stay with me for a little while. And Susan? Be forewarned. She'll probably put up a fuss about leaving her house, but this is such a beautiful place, the food's out of this world and there's a cute cabin for us to share."

"Sounds like just what your mother needs. Don't worry. If you send a plane for her, I'll make sure she's on it."

Libby went down to the dock and shaded her eyes against the sun, searching for Carson and the rubber boat. Yes, he was still out there, motoring slowly along near the mouth of the river. Although the sun was still high above the horizon, the air was already starting to cool. She thought about the wood-stove in Carson's wall tent, and the fact that no firewood had been cut for it. She remembered seeing the blood seeping through the bandages on his hand and felt a twinge of guilt at the not-so-nice thoughts she'd been having about him since their last conversation. No way would he be able to cut firewood, and without it, the inside of that tent would be a cold and miserable place come morning. She knew he'd resent her help, but she also knew he'd burn the wood if she cut it, and it was in her best interest to keep him as healthy as she could.

She was shrugging into her jacket and preparing to walk back up the shoreline with another hamper of food, a bucksaw and her first aid kit when she spotted Graham Johnson getting ready to take two clients out fishing and headed down to the dock. "How's your dad doing, Graham?"

His expression answered her before his words did. "Much better. I made sure he ate some lunch. He's breathing a lot easier and eating pretty good. He's also taking the medicine you left."

Libby nodded. "Glad to hear it. Tell him I'll be by to check on him very soon." She caught a glimpse of a motorboat approaching the dock, and Graham glanced over his shoulder.

"That's Luanne," he said, sounding surprised. "Frey doesn't usually let his hired help use the boat. He doesn't think we indigenous peoples can handle motors."

Graham's clients were still settling their gear into the boat, trying to decide what flies to take from an unimaginably large selection when Luanne reached them. She throttled down and put the engine into reverse at exactly the right moment, easing up to the dock like a pro. She gave Graham a quick, shy smile, then looked up at Libby. "Mr. Frey sent me," she explained. "He's wondering about the man in the rubber boat, the one who flew in this morning. Mr. Frey has noticed that this man isn't fishing."

Libby shoved her hands into her jacket pockets. She wasn't about to offer up any information. "Oh?"

"I asked him myself on the way over, and he told me he was measuring the water depths in the lake for the state maps."

Graham turned to his clients. "You ready?" They nodded, and he cast off the lines and started the motor. "I'll see you later?" he said to Luanne, and she answered with another quick, shy smile. She watched Graham motor away from the dock then turned again to Libby.

"Graham told me you came here to look for a plane that crashed in the lake a long time ago," she confided.

"Then no doubt you know why that man is really out there in the rubber boat."

Luanne nodded. "Yes, I do, but Mr. Frey doesn't, so he sent me here to find out."

"Did he appear to be interested in what was going on?"

Luanne nodded again. "Very."

"Good," Libby said.

"What do you want me to tell him when I go back?"

Libby realized that eventually Frey would find out why Carson was here. What was the point of trying to keep it secret? What could Frey possibly do to foul up the search? "Tell Mr. Frey that the owner of Alaska Salvage is here on a little fishing expedition, and he isn't trolling for lake trout. If he wants to know more, Libby Wilson will be happy to speak with him again."

For the third time, Luanne nodded. "All right." She started the motorboat. "Will you be a writer from Boston if he invites you back?"

"No," Libby said. "I'll be an Athapaskan born in the village of Umiak."

Luanne smiled as she backed the boat away from the dock. "Good."

CHAPTER SIX

CARSON WAS FULLY AWARE that he was being closely watched by the man he assumed was Daniel Frey sitting on the porch of the lodge not far from the lake's outlet. He had the distinct impression that Libby didn't like Daniel Frey. Didn't trust him.

He glanced at his gas gauge. Nearly empty, but he had enough to make it back to his campsite, where he had two spare gas cans stashed. He made a mark on the chart to keep his place in the search pattern, plugged the data into the GPS, reeled in the towfish, then decided to have a word with Daniel Frey. Maybe the old man could shed some light on the mystery of the plane crash, and he was obviously wondering what Carson was up to.

Wondering? Hell, if his reactions were any indication, Frey was fairly frothing at the mouth. The old man was standing at the top of the porch steps when Carson climbed out of the boat. Carson tied the lines off and stood for a moment, staring up at the eccentric billionaire.

"Come on up here, goddammit!" Frey ordered, motioning with one arm and scowling darkly.

Friendly bastard, Carson thought. He climbed the porch steps with as much energy as he could muster, willing his bad leg to work normally, but the effort cost him. He was sweating long before he conquered the last step. He stuck out his unbandaged left hand. "Carson Dodge, owner of Alaska Salvage."

Frey's bushy white eyebrows framed sharp, predatorial eyes. He paused, then shook Carson's hand in a clasp that felt as sharp and bony as an eagle's talons. "Daniel Frey. Sit," Frey said, indicating one of the chairs. "Have a brandy."

The old man was supposedly in his eighties, but didn't act or look it. He poured two glasses and handed Carson a big snifter with a generous slug of what had to be fancy stuff. "I've been watching you out there," Frey said, settling himself back in the recliner. "It looks to me like you're searching for something, and if you're the owner of Alaska Salvage I can assume you are."

"You assumed correctly," Carson said, tasting the brandy. Just as good as he'd expected from a billionaire. "I'm looking for a plane," he said, swirling the rich, honey-colored liquid in the snifter. "A de Havilland Beaver. Maybe you know something about it."

"That's very interesting," Frey said. "A young woman was here just yesterday. Said she was writing an article for the Libby Foundation. She asked a lot of questions about that very same plane."

"What did you tell her?"

"There was nothing to tell." Frey took a swallow of brandy. "I wasn't here when the plane went down. I was fishing up on the Kandik. In any event, that crash happened nearly thirty years ago. Why would you be looking for the plane now?"

"It's what I do," Carson said.

"Not without a reason," Frey countered. His eyes glittered like shards of ice as he leaned forward in his seat. "For your information, Mr. Dodge, my godson died in that crash. I'm guessing you want to salvage his plane to make a few bucks and that journalist wants a good story, but I don't give a damn about her article or your greed. I'm asking you to let the boy and the plane he died in rest in peace."

Carson took another sip of brandy. "This is very good," he said. "Courvoisier XO, isn't it?"

"Who hired you?" Frey asked, the suspicion in his sharp eyes deepening.

"Nobody. I just happen to collect old Beavers," Carson responded.

"Bullshit. That journalist's in on this, too, isn't she? The reporter from Boston. I was right about her. She's nothing but trouble."

Carson drained his snifter, set it down on the side table and stood. "I appreciate the cognac, Mr. Frey, but it's time for me to be getting back to work."

"What kind of story is she really after? How much is she paying you?" Frey was clearly agitated.

"I'm not at liberty to discuss my client's business," Carson said. Make the old bastard sweat. Carson hadn't known him ten minutes and he already disliked him, in spite of the brandy.

"Then I'll discuss some of my own with you. It's worth a lot to me for that plane to remain undisturbed. This lake and that wreckage have a deeply spiritual significance to me. I don't want you digging up Connor Libby's grave. I consider that a desecration."

"I'll be sure to pass that information along," Carson said.

"Mr. Dodge," Frey said when he was halfway down the steps. Carson paused and glanced back. Frey was on his feet, and he spoke very carefully. His words were as chilly as his eyes. "Let me repeat myself. It's worth a lot to me for you, and whoever hired you, to give up this salvage project. I'm fully aware that a restored de Havilland Beaver in flying condition is worth well over a quarter of a million dollars. I realize how much this salvage project is worth to you. I'm a very wealthy man. I can afford a big kill fee. A fee that would be worth twice what you'd ever recoup for the plane."

"I'll be sure to pass that information along, as well."

"One more thing, Mr. Dodge. If you pass up my offer, I can guarantee you won't get a cent for the time you put in searching for the plane. Even if you find it, you'll never get the chance to bring it to the surface. You'll never be able to purchase the salvage rights to that plane. I'll make sure of it."

Carson nodded before continuing down the steps. "I'll take that into consideration."

A few minutes later he crossed paths with the slender young Athapaskan woman who had queried him on the lake. She was just docking the beautifully restored vintage Chris-Craft as he prepared to depart. She cast him a questioning look as she jumped onto the dock. He was about to introduce himself when Frey let out a bellow from up on the porch.

"LUANNE!"

The girl bent to secure the Chris-Craft to the dock cleats, then stood and flashed him an apologetic glance before walking swiftly up the dock to where Frey waited.

Carson took his time puttering back to his campsite to refill the rubber boat's gas tank. The wind had died, leaving the surface of the lake as still as glass and reflecting the soaring grandeur of the snow-clad Brooks Range. He kept up just enough head speed to outrun the horde of mosquitoes that gave chase and pondered Frey's reaction to the search for the missing plane. He didn't strike Carson as the type to wax sentimental over a dead godson, but then again he certainly didn't need the money from salvaging the plane itself. Maybe he really did want to keep the site sacred.

How much more would Frey offer them for a kill fee? How much would it be worth to an aging billionaire to keep the ghosts from the past buried for yet a few more years, and keep the story out of the press? A fortune might be sitting on the bottom of Evening Lake, and it would take a mighty hefty kill fee for him to walk away from this project.

LIBBY CARRIED THE HAMPER, her first aid kit and the bucksaw with her when she returned to Carson's campsite. Since he refused to let her tend his hand, she would at least leave the proper supplies so he could do it himself. The camp looked pretty much the same as when she saw it last except that Carson was absent, out searching the lake bottom for her father's plane. She set the hamper and first aid kit inside the wall tent, noting that he'd tossed his sleeping bag and gear together in a careless heap. Curious, she peeked inside the cooler, which was full of beer, then took stock of his food supply, which consisted of at least forty packets of dried noodles, beef and chicken flavor, two loaves of white bread and several cans of baked beans. She then walked the shore-line long enough to gather up a goodly amount of driftwood. She made a big pile of it near the tent, then commenced cutting it to stove-wood length. The bucksaw Karen had lent her was sharp, and the work was easy and would have been almost pleasant except for the mosquitoes. After the wind died and before the cold air from the high places seeped down and rendered them dormant, they attacked with a vengeance. Unfortunately, she'd forgotten to bring bug spray.

For a while she worked without pausing, but when the attacks intensified beyond tolerating she threw the bucksaw aside and went into the wall tent for temporary relief and to hopefully find some insect repellent. She was sifting through Carson's gear when she heard the muted sound of an engine approaching the shore. Libby froze, her heart skipping several beats. She hadn't expected him to return so early, and the last thing she wanted was to be caught inside his tent. Could she slip out unnoticed and disappear before he beached the boat? She peeked out the tent's door.

Not a chance of it. He was already ashore, pulling the boat up onto the gravel strand and turning toward the camp site. For a few moments he didn't notice her or the firewood she'd stacked. He grabbed one of the five-gallon gas cans and refueled the boat, and while his back was turned Libby edged out of the tent. He was perhaps twenty feet away, and preoccupied. With a little bit of luck she could sneak into the brush and...

He caught her movement out of the corner of his eye and jerked abruptly upright, sloshing gas from the can. She froze again, and for a few silent moments they stared wide-eyed at each other. She waited for him to ask her what she was doing there, but instead he said, his rough voice dark with accusation, "By damn, I thought you were a bear." Then his glance dropped and took in the pile of wood she'd gathered and cut. His expression became even stonier. "I could've done that."

"I brought you some supper. I left it inside the tent," Libby said, having regained her wits.

"I have my own food."

"Yes, I saw it. I think you'll find what I brought to be a little more nutritious, not to mention better tasting. Did you find anything yet?"

He stared at her for a long moment, as if contemplating whether or not to answer, then shook his head. "No, but I met Daniel Frey. He was watching me with binoculars the whole time I was out there and sent a girl to ask me some questions, so I went over and introduced myself. He had a few things to say about the salvage operation."

Libby didn't quite know how to react to this unsettling information. She had expected that Frey would be curious, but had thought his seclusiveness would keep him at a safe distance, at least for a little while. "Oh?"

"He wants the wreckage left alone."

Hot anger boiled up and she shook her head. "No way in hell is that happening."

"He offered a generous kill fee if we pulled foot. He told me the pilot of the plane had been his godson and he doesn't want the place disturbed."

"I'll just bet he doesn't," Libby snapped heatedly. She clenched her fists and blew her breath out sharply. It wouldn't do to fly off the handle. She might reveal things she really didn't want Carson Dodge to know. "What did you tell him?"

"I said I'd pass the information along. He also told me there was a young woman asking about the plane a couple of days ago. A journalist from Boston. Any idea who that might be?"

"That would be me." Libby drew a shaky breath. "I interviewed him for a supposed story I was writing for the Libby Foundation."

"Huh." He eyed her calculatingly. "In that case, he believes you hired me to find the plane to give your story drama, and he thinks I'm in on the scheme for what I can get for the plane."

"Does he still believe that after your little chat?" Libby asked.

Carson shrugged. "I didn't enlighten him, if that's what

you're asking. I told him I'd run his offer by you. He was
hinting at half a million dollars, but I'm guessing you could
up the ante and he'd pay."

"Even if he offered three million dollars, I'm not letting this
go," Libby said.

"He threatened that if we didn't take the money, he'd make
sure we'd never get the salvage rights to the plane even if we
found it."

"I'm sure he'll make a lot more threats before this week is
through. You agreed to find the plane and I trust you're a man
of your word."

His eyes narrowed and his shoulders squared. "If that plane
is in this lake, I'll find it." He set the gas can down and turned
back toward the boat.

"You better eat something first," Libby called after him.
"Some real food. And I brought along a first aid kit so I could
rebandage your hand."

He paused and glanced down at the swathe of wet, dirty
bandaging. "My hand's fine."

"I disagree, and you'll be of no use whatsoever if it gets
infected. This won't take but five minutes, and I can assure
you that will be five minutes well spent. If you try to tend
to it yourself it's going to take a whole lot longer and be a
much sloppier job, and if you do nothing at all, maggots will
be crawling in that bandaging before too long, if they aren't
in there already." She reached for the first aid bag and
opened it on top of the little table he'd set up under the tent
awning. "This'll go a lot faster if you cooperate." She
arranged the items she needed on a clean cloth and picked
up a pair of bandage scissors. "You're wasting time," she
said, glancing up.

"You have a high opinion of your first aid skills."

"I've had lots of practice," Libby returned. "Could you possibly step a little closer? My arms aren't quite that long."

He hesitated, and she sensed the churning turmoil within him before he grudgingly moved near and held out his hand. It took her several minutes just to cut away the layers of soiled and bloodied bandage.

"I suppose the doctors told you not to use this hand until the wounds had healed up and the stitches were removed," she commented as she laid aside the scissors, carefully peeled away the bandaging and gently swabbed his hand with surgical scrub. She'd expected to see abused injuries hidden beneath but was dismayed at the extent of the damage. She wondered if he'd ever be able to use it normally again. His right hand was laced with deep lacerations, several across the palm itself and it looked as if his last two fingers had nearly been sheared off. "I see you've been busy ripping out some of these stitches," she commented as she worked. "The more you abuse this hand, the longer it's going to take to heal, but I'm sure you realize that."

He gazed stonily out across the lake while she finished cleaning up and began bandaging with fresh supplies. Her ministrations, though careful, had to be hurting him, but his expression never changed. "I suppose the doctors also told you it would take a long time for your hand to heal properly, and that you'd need to undergo lengthy physical therapy before you regained full use of it." She wrapped the elastic gauze around and around as she spoke. "No doubt they also told you to keep the bandaging clean and dry."

"Doctors like giving orders," he said.

"There's usually a reason behind all of them." Libby cut the gauze, then applied several strips of tape to secure it.

"There. That's a little better," she said, gathering her supplies back into the bag. "I'd recommend changing that bandage daily if you insist on ignoring their advice. I'd be more than happy to do that for you." She closed the bag and glanced up. "Did any of your doctors prescribe something for the pain?"

"They did, but I don't need anything," he said, dropping his hand to his side.

"Tough guy, huh?"

"Tough enough." He started to turn toward the boat then paused and gave her a guarded look. "Thanks," he said.

"You're welcome."

He turned away once again, and she stood on the shore and watched while he pushed the boat back into the water and climbed aboard. "Keep that bandaging dry," she ordered.

His expression was still guarded as he picked up an oar to push into deeper water. "What are you, some kind of nurse?" he asked.

Libby shook her head. "Some kind of doctor," she replied.

"I thought so," he said as if suddenly her behavior made a dark kind of sense to him. "That's why you like giving orders."

"That's right. And I expect them to be obeyed," Libby returned.

"You, and all the rest of 'em."

He dropped the oar, lowered the motor into the water and settled himself in the stern. He started the motor with one quick pull using his left hand and headed back down the lake toward the outlet. Libby shook her head as she watched him depart without a backward glance. "And you be sure and have a nice evening, too, Mr. Dodge," she muttered. She shoved her hands deep into her pockets as she turned and began the short walk back to the lodge.

LIBBY WILSON.

Carson watched her walk along the shore, head down, dark hair blowing in the wind. Why had she told Frey she was a journalist from Boston when she was "some kind of doctor"?

Connor Libby.

Libby Wilson.

Was the name just a coincidence?

Maybe, but Libby wasn't exactly a common name, was it?

She had a strong, determined walk. She strode along as if she was mad as hell about something; mad at him, no doubt. He didn't blame her. He'd behaved as if his mother had never taught him basic manners. But there it was again. She was just too damned good-looking. She knew the power she held over him. All beautiful women were aware of that power. If he'd treated her rudely, it was only in self-defense. His ex-wife had destroyed him effortlessly, and he still felt the hurt of that betrayal. He kept it buried deep down inside but felt it, nonetheless.

Never again would he let himself become that vulnerable. Women were to be used for physical pleasure and kept at extreme arm's length all other times. That was the only way for a man to stay sane and retain his freedom and independence.

She'd reached the dock now, stepped onto the weather-bleached boards and turned to look toward him, as if she knew he was thinking about her. She stood there for a long moment. Was she going to stand there on the end of the dock and watch him work the search the same way Frey had? Minutes passed while the boat drifted on the still waters. Then, quite abruptly, she walked away in that same head down, determined manner. Carson was relieved that she'd left, but for some reason even though he had no more distractions he couldn't concentrate on the search pattern. Couldn't focus on the job at hand.

A loon called somewhere out on the glassy, golden waters of the lake as the sun set, and he felt a tug of loneliness at the wild, haunting sound. He searched the shoreline for the young woman with blue eyes and hair the color of a raven's wing, but she was gone.

CHAPTER SEVEN

"LIBBY?" KAREN WHITTEN poked her head around the cook's cabin door. "Sorry to wake you. I know it's early, but your mother's on the phone."

Libby pushed onto her elbows and blinked the sleep from her eyes. She felt as if she'd just gone to bed. Could morning be here already? And what had Karen just said? That her mother was calling? Why would her mother be calling at this hour? Was something wrong? Panic galvanized her into action and her feet hit the floor even as she reached for her blue jeans. "Oh, God. I'm coming!"

Dressing herself as she followed Karen, Libby reached for the phone in the lobby of the lodge. She was barefoot, her blue jeans unfastened, flannel shirt half buttoned and hair a wild tangled mane. "Mom? Mom, are you all right?"

"Libby, I want you to know that I'm not coming on the plane. Susan cannot force me to come. Call the air service and cancel the flight."

Her mother's voice was firm and clipped. Libby gripped the phone. "Are you feeling okay? Mom? Tell me the truth. Are you all right?"

"I know where you are, Libby," her mother said in an admonishing tone of voice. "You're at Evening Lake, and I am not going there."

"Mom, do you have any idea what time it is?"

"I can't sleep knowing you're there. I want you to come home."

"Mom…"

"I will not come there. I never want to see that evil man again."

"You don't have to see him. He lives across the lake."

"Come back home, Libby."

Libby sighed with frustration. "I can't, Mom. Not for a little while, anyway. I was hoping you'd come here. The food's great and you'd love Karen. We'd have our own little cabin to stay in. It's beautiful here, and I miss you."

"Then come home. Why are you there? What are you trying to prove? Libby, the past is behind you. Leave it there. Let it go. Come home!"

Libby closed her eyes and slumped against the wall. "I can't. Try to understand that this is something I just have to do. I can't go forward with my life until I can understand the past. I need to find the plane, Mom. I need to find my father."

There was a long silence on the other end of the line, and then Libby heard a faint sigh. "I felt that way once, too," her mother said. "I looked and looked, but I never found him. Neither will you. You have to let him go."

Tears stung beneath her eyelids and her throat tightened. "I can't," Libby repeated. "Try to understand. I just can't."

Another long silence followed. "Well," her mother said. "I'm not going back there. I swore I'd never go back and I won't. I'll wait for you here."

"You'll take your medications and listen to Susan?"

"I'll take my pills," her mother said.

"You'll eat the food I left?"

"Libby, Daniel Frey is a dangerous man."

"I'll be careful, Mom. I promise."

"The old man who lives in the woods will tell you how dangerous he is."

"The old man?" Libby opened her eyes and blinked back the tears. "Do you mean Solly Johnson?"

"Frey shot the old man, years ago. You ask him about it, if you can find him. He knows many things, but he keeps his secrets."

"Mom? You listen to Susan. I'll be home in a week. I love you. Do you hear me?"

"I hear you," her mother said in that same stern voice. "Do you hear *me?*"

"Yes," Libby said, even as her mother hung up the phone on her end.

DAWN CAME AT 4:00 A.M. in the arctic summer. The sun lifted over the rim of mountains to the east, a great reddish-orange orb rising over a wilderness so beautiful it made the heart ache, and Libby was wide-awake to greet it, sitting on the edge of the dock with her knees drawn up to her chest and her arms curled around them, bundled in a jacket against the morning chill and drinking a cup of hot black coffee. Her mother's phone call had banished all thoughts of returning to her bunk for another hour of slumber. Instead she sat and gazed across the lake to the lodge where Daniel Frey lived…and where her own father had grown up.

She wondered if Frey had kept any of Connor's things. In her imaginings she pictured Connor's room exactly as he might have left it, the drawers and closet full of his clothing, knickknacks on the bureau, pictures he had held dear still hanging on the walls. A journal, maybe, secreted away in a bookshelf that contained his favorite novels. A shoe box full of letters he'd kept while in the air force, written to him by his father, perhaps, or Frey himself, or old girlfriends. His air force uniform. The medals he'd been awarded. A baseball bat and glove. His collection of favorite rock music. His fly rods. Maybe a hand-carved canoe paddle and the pack basket he'd used when he went camping.

She dreamed that she'd walk into his room and touch his things and somehow be connected to him. Simply by standing there, surrounded by all his paraphernalia, she'd absorb the essence of the boy he'd been and the man he'd become. Somehow she'd come to know the father she'd never meet.

Libby sighed and shifted her gaze up the lake's west shore, to the timbered point where Dodge had set up his camp. She could just make out part of the tent from where she sat, but most of it was hidden by the spruce. Mist rose from the still coves, glowing gold in the early sunlight. It was so quiet she could hear a loon at least a mile up the lake. She saw a curl of woodsmoke from his campsite and on impulse pushed to her feet and walked back to the lodge. Karen was in the kitchen baking muffins. The first tray was just coming out of the oven when Libby made her appearance.

"Blueberry again, by request of the guests," Karen said, sliding the muffin tin onto the counter. "Help yourself."

"Could I bring a couple to Carson? I'm not sure what he has for breakfast, or if he can even cook with his hand wrapped up like that."

Karen brushed a stray lock of hair off her forehead and grinned. "For a man that size I'd highly recommend six muffins, a stick of butter and a thermos of fresh coffee. You can't go wrong." Even as she spoke she was plucking six big piping-hot muffins out of the tin and bundling them in a clean dish towel that was tucked inside one of the lunch hampers used by the guides. She filled a thermos with coffee, nestled it beside the muffins, and lastly added the butter and a knife. "Tell him he's welcome to keep his boat at the dock if he wants," she said, handing Libby the hamper. "There's plenty of room and he'd be closer to the food source."

"I will, thanks. I'll be back shortly to help with breakfast."

Karen waved her out the door. "Take your time. From the looks of him, that man could use some TLC."

Libby gave a laugh. "He doesn't want it. I tried that yesterday and he was as bristly as a porcupine."

"What happened to him, anyway? Was he in a car accident?"

"He was salvaging a plane that went down off Anchorage and got caught up in the wreckage."

"Oh! I read about it in the newspapers a month or so ago. That was awful, both the plane crash and the salvage accident. The article said all the passengers and crew had been killed, and the diver was in critical condition."

Libby nodded. "He only got out of the hospital a week ago. He was probably ordered to take it easy for a couple of months, but he's the type that can't stand sitting still."

Karen shook her head. "Men can be stubborn creatures."

"True enough, though he doesn't complain about his circumstances, and that's rare." She hefted the lunch hamper. "Thanks again, Karen. Maybe this'll soften him up."

But as she walked along the shoreline toward Carson's camp, she doubted he would receive her warmly, and she was right. If anything, he was more surly than he'd been the previous evening. He was shaving when she arrived, standing in front of a little mirror he'd hung from a spruce branch, next to where he'd hung his kit. He didn't turn when she entered the camp, making no effort to be quiet, but she saw his shoulders stiffen. He was wearing the same faded blue jeans and flannel shirt he'd been wearing the day before, and she wondered if he'd bothered to get undressed or if he'd slept in his clothes.

"Good morning," she said. "I see you're up."

He caught her eye briefly in the mirror, grunted and continued shaving.

"I brought you some blueberry muffins and coffee. The muffins are still warm, just came out of the oven. I wasn't sure if you'd had breakfast yet."

He stuffed the razor into a pocket on the side of his kit, plucked a hand towel from yet another handy branch and wiped the last of the shaving cream from his face before turning. "It's not even 5:00 a.m.," he pointed out.

"And the sun is already high in the sky," Libby said. "I knew you'd be wanting to make an early start. I saw the woodsmoke from your stove and figured you were up and about. How's your hand feeling?"

"Just like new."

"Would you like me to pour you some coffee?"

"I can pour my own coffee," he said, moving past her and stepping inside the tent. Libby stood outside, still holding the hamper, and wondered for a moment if she'd just been dismissed, but he reemerged after a few long minutes, day pack dangling from his good hand. "And I don't need a babysitter."

Libby flushed. "I was only trying to be helpful."

He rounded on her, standing so close that she felt threatened by the sheer power he radiated. He may have been at his most vulnerable after suffering that terrible accident, but she had no doubt that he was still stronger than most men she'd ever encountered.

"Look," he said. "I'm here to do a job. I don't need to be supervised or watched over or nagged and goaded."

"Fine." Libby set the hamper at her feet with a thump. "I'm sorry I bothered you. I promise I won't do it again." She turned and started out of his campsite, willing herself to walk carefully and not stumble as she had before.

"Who are you, really?" he called as she moved away. "And why is finding this plane so important to you?" he said, his words so unexpected that it took Libby a few moments to process them.

She stopped and turned to face him. "I already told you who I was, and why I want to find the plane."

His eyes were so clear and keen that she felt threatened. It was as if he could see right through the thin veneer that hid her soul and innermost secrets from the world. "You're not telling me the whole story," he said. "Frey's offered a big sum of money for us to quit this project, more than the cost of the plane, maybe more than what it might be carrying, but you're not biting. Hell, you didn't even rise to the bait or consider making a counteroffer."

Libby drew a deep breath to steady her nerves. "You agreed to give me one week. Are you trying to back out of your commitment?"

"You agreed to pay me one hundred and fifty thousand dollars if I found the plane. Frey is hinting that he'd cough up a whole lot more than that for us *not* to find the plane. Why?"

"Who knows what motivates that man, and what difference does it make? You're working for me now. You don't need to know why, do you? Why did you salvage that downed commuter plane?"

"Because the relatives of the victims wanted the bodies recovered, the FAA wanted to study the wreckage to discover the cause of the accident and I wanted the money they were willing to pay. I don't risk my life in a hazardous occupation because I enjoy living dangerously. I do it for the money. To tell you the truth, nobody's ever offered me money *not* to risk my life, and I kind of like the idea of it."

The deep breath she'd taken had failed to calm her. She felt her hands close into tight fists. "You bastard," she said. "You told me yesterday you were a man of your word."

He took a step toward her and once again she became aware of his sheer power. "I am," he said. "I'll find the plane for you. But at least consider this possibility. If we waited until after Frey dies of old age, we could pocket a chunk of change now and salvage the plane in a few years. He's in his eighties and he can't last much longer. You're a very young 'some kind of doctor' who rakes in the big bucks. You can hold off for a few more years, can't you?"

Libby struggled to control her temper. "If you don't want to salvage the plane, I'll find someone who does. I doubt Frey will pay you one cent if he knows I'll just hire someone else to find the wreckage, someone a whole lot more honorable than you!"

"What if his threat to block purchase of the salvage rights is real? You have to consider that possibility. The man's a billionaire. He certainly has the power to influence more than a few politicians, and it's the state that grants salvage rights on inland waters that don't fall under the realm of the admiralty laws. One phone call from him could shoot this project down." He loomed over her, and as angry as she was, Libby was nonetheless impressed and a little intimidated by the sense of power he exuded. "Look," he said, "all I want is for you to be aboveboard with me. I want some honest answers. Is that asking too much?"

"Find the plane, Mr. Dodge, and you'll have your answers." Libby spun around and fled the camp, forgetting to be calm and composed. She was furious, both with Dodge and herself. She was halfway back to the lodge when she realized that she hadn't told him about Karen's offer to keep his boat at the dock. She kicked a small rock aside, satisfied by the way it shot into the water and threw up a plume of spray.

To hell with Carson Colman Dodge. He was not only rude, he was greedy, and she hadn't a doubt that he'd take Frey up on that kill fee...if he could. It was up to her to squelch that possibility as soon as possible. She was going to have to pay the intimidating Daniel Frey another visit, this time as the rightful daughter of Connor Libby, and lay all her cards on the table. As frightening as the prospect was, she could see no other way to stop Frey from undermining the salvage operation.

CARSON WAS SO STEAMED UP when he left his camp that he forgot his day pack and left the hamper sitting on the beach. He forgot the spare gas can, forgot his parka, forgot the bug spray. He motored past the Otter, giving it his standard critical appraisal, even as he seethed over his encounter with the maddeningly testy Libby Wilson.

To hell with her. He'd go talk to Frey again and find out just how much money the old bastard might be willing to cough up for a kill fee. If he could get Frey to cut Libby out of the deal, she wouldn't be able to afford to hire anyone else to salvage the missing plane. The nearest good salvage

operator was based out of Seattle and would require an exor-
bitant amount of money up-front, more than anyone would
pay to salvage a de Havilland Beaver out of a remote lake, no
matter what it held or how much it would be worth when
restored to flying condition.

As Carson neared the search area his anger slowly cooled
and he realized if the plane did in fact hold a fortune, all
Libby would have to do was whisper about it and all the
treasure hunters in the lower forty-eight would be heading
for the Brooks Range at top speed. She knew that, too, of
course, which is why she was keeping quiet. Or was there
some other reason? Hell, she'd hired *him* to take on the
salvage job. Why wouldn't she tell him the real reason she
wanted that plane found? What was she hiding? What was
Frey trying to hide?

He fumbled his maps out of the waterproof case, damning
his bandaged hand for not cooperating, damning his useless
fingers for not moving. The numbness scared him more than
any pain ever would. He worked it at night, using his other
hand to move the fingers within the limitations of the bandaging, flexing everything back and forth, over and over,
willing the sensation to come back. The fact that it hadn't was
ominous. The doctors had said it would take time for the
severed nerves to regenerate, but they also said the nerves
might not regenerate at all. Or he might only regain partial use
of the hand. Already six weeks had passed since the accident.
That was way too long, as far as he was concerned. Something
should have happened by now.

He spread the maps, turned on the GPS, returned to the
search pattern. At his present rate of speed, scanning a hun-
dred-foot swath each time he crossed the lake, it would take

him all week just to search the outlet area and the area used by the pilots for their takeoff runs. There was a good chance the plane would be outside of the search area, in which case he was going to run out of time and the mystery would remain unsolved. All the more reason to talk with Frey, but maybe he'd wait and give it another few days. He might get lucky and find the plane, and if he didn't, Frey might get antsy and up the kill fee on his own and by then, with the one week deadline looming on the horizon, Libby Wilson might be more amenable to accepting it.

Good plan.

He'd wait, work the search pattern, and hope for the best possible financial outcome.

LIBBY WAS VACUUMING HER last room when Karen poked her head around the door frame, her face flushed from working in the laundry. "Meet me for a glass of iced tea when you've finished beating up that rug!" she invited before ducking out of sight. Libby straightened and paused, vacuum still running, then laughed. It was true enough. She'd assaulted her rooms this morning, taking out her anger and frustration on the beds, the bathrooms and the floors. It was good therapy and she'd finished her rooms in record time, but a tall glass of iced tea sure did sound tempting. She switched off the vacuum cleaner, wrapped up the cord and put her cleaning things away. Karen was already in the kitchen, two tall glasses of iced tea sitting on the table.

She dropped into a chair across from Karen and lifted her glass. "Thanks. I'm sorry I've been in such a mood."

Karen picked up her own glass and regarded her for a

moment. "I take it the muffins and coffee you brought to Mr. Dodge's camp didn't have the desired effect."

"No. My appearance at his campsite this morning put him in a worse mood than ever. He seems to take offense at everything I do and say."

"Maybe his ego can't stand the idea of needing TLC."

"That's putting it mildly." Libby took a sip of the lemony iced tea. It was delicious. She held the sweaty glass to her hot brow for a moment. "He promised me a week, but I think he's going to try to welsh on me. It seems Mr. Frey doesn't want the plane found and has offered a big kill fee if Carson abandons the project."

"Hmm," Karen said.

"The thing is, I'm investigating the death of Ben Libby's son, and finding the plane is key to that investigation. I wish I could tell you more, Karen, but right now I can't."

"I understand."

"I'm very grateful to you for letting me work here."

Karen smiled and reached across the table to give Libby's hand a squeeze. "Do you have any idea how much help you've been to me? In just two days I feel like a new woman. You've cut my workload in half. I'm already dreading the day you leave."

"It won't be till the end of the week, if I have anything to say about it. You said that boat privileges came with this job?"

Karen nodded. "We have an old outboard that we keep as a spare. Runs okay but looks pretty awful. You're welcome to use it, if you want."

Libby nodded. "Thanks. I'd like to go check on Solly Johnson after lunch." She paused. "I don't suppose you know anything about Daniel Frey shooting Solly a long time ago?"

Karen frowned and shook her head. "You'll have to ask Graham about that, or Solly himself. I'll pack up some food for you to bring along. I know Solly doesn't like us white folk much, but I betcha he wouldn't refuse my food."

CARSON SAW LIBBY LEAVE the lodge in the old aluminum boat and head up the west arm of the lake. She looked like a woman on a mission, and neither glanced in his direction nor acknowledged his existence. For someone who had earlier been very interested in his progress, he got the feeling he was now being pointedly ignored. Snubbed, in fact. Fine by him, and good riddance to her. He watched her until she had disappeared out of sight behind a point of land, neglecting the sonar long enough so he'd have to repeat an entire leg of the grid to make sure he hadn't missed anything. He cussed a bit, then realized he was actually hungry and decided to put off the search for the wreckage long enough to return to his camp and break into the basket of muffins Libby had brought early that morning. He folded up the maps, returned them to their waterproof case, shut off the GPS, reeled the towfish aboard, waved to Frey, who was watching through his binoculars from the porch and had been all morning, then headed for camp.

Back at his site he tied the rubber boat to one of the plane's pontoons and waded ashore to exercise his leg. The cold water felt good, but his bad leg didn't particularly enjoy the physical exertion of wading through it. Nor did his burning lung or the rest of his aching body. It was barely twenty feet to the beach, but it felt more as though he'd just climbed one hundred vertical steps at high altitude shouldering a heavy pack. He had to start pushing himself harder.

The basket was sitting right where Libby had dropped it,

but he noticed that the dish towel had been pulled halfway out, the butter was on the ground beside the basket and pecked to shreds, and upon closer inspection he saw that all the muffins were gone. Every last crumb had been eaten by the gray jays, who swept in while he ate and begged scraps from his plate.

Damn! After an entire morning of anticipating how good those muffins were going to taste, he was going to have to settle for a can of cold beans. No time to fire up the little stove and heat them. Good thing he liked them cold. Even better thing that gray jays couldn't open cans.

Five minutes later he was still trying to open the can himself, holding it clamped between his knees and cursing heatedly with every unsuccessful turn of the can opener's key with his left hand. After five minutes of struggle all he'd managed to do was puncture the seal. He couldn't make the can opener work from either direction. He gave up finally and broke into one of the loaves of cheap white bread, stuffing a slice into his mouth and chewing it in foul humor, thinking about those huge warm muffins loaded with blueberries and slathered with sweet creamery butter. The black flies plagued him as he ate, and by the time he'd polished off four slices of bread he was ready to return to work. He heard a boat approaching and stood, his heart rate accelerating at the thought of another visit from Libby.

It would have pleased Carson greatly if his first and only thought was that she might be bringing another hamper of food, but it wasn't. He was also thinking that he ought to apologize for his poor behavior and that he ought to make a greater effort to be polite and civilized in her presence. It wasn't her fault that she was so damn beautiful and he was a washed-up wreck of a salvage diver. He was revving himself up to make amends when he saw that his visitor wasn't Libby Wilson.

The approaching boat was the same vintage Chris-Craft he'd encountered the evening before piloted by the slender dark-eyed Athapaskan girl called Luanne. This time, however, it was Daniel Frey who motored up beside the Otter and shifted the boat's engine into reverse, bringing the boat to a gentle halt before throttling the engine down to a low idle.

"We need to talk," Frey said over the sudden crash of big waves breaking onto the pebbled beach.

Carson walked to the edge of the water, damning the burning limp he couldn't quite mask and the audible wheeze of a lung that hadn't yet recovered from wading ashore. "So talk."

"I brought along some papers for you to look over. I can fly a notary in tomorrow to make them legal and binding. These papers are worth half a million dollars to you if you sign them."

"To me alone?"

"To you, and whomever hired you," Frey replied. "You can split it however you like."

"What do these documents state?"

"They stipulate that from this day forward you will cease and desist to search for the plane and Connor Libby's body. That you will leave this lake and not desecrate my godson's grave. And that you will never return, not even after my death."

Carson thought about the four slices of cheap white bread he'd just eaten to thwart his hunger because he couldn't open a goddam can of beans. He thought about the medical bills that he was fighting with his insurance company over. He thought about the constant pain that gnawed and stabbed and robbed him of his strength. He thought about his useless hand and his gimpy leg and the lung that didn't draw breath without causing him agony and might never function properly again. He thought about the fact that he was almost forty years old. He thought about all the nights that Gracie hadn't come to his boat after the pool hall shut down. He was beginning to think that signing those documents might not be such a bad idea.

And then he thought about Libby Wilson.

Big mistake.

Dammit all, she'd already begun to destroy him, even after he vowed he would never let such a thing happen to him again.

"I'll pass that information along," he said.

Frey wasn't about to be put off that easy. "Sign the papers, Dodge. Don't be a fool. I know all about the injuries you suffered when you attempted to salvage that commuter plane. I know exactly how bad off you are right now, both physically and financially. It was an unfortunate accident, but the odds are you'll never dive again, and your diving skills were the heart and soul of Alaska Salvage. I'm sure your crew is competent, but without your hands-on skills and expertise the company will fold. You owe too much money for all that fancy equipment you use, especially your ship, the *Pacific Explorer,* which already has a hefty lien against it, as I understand, and right now your bank account is dead empty."

Clearly, Frey had done his homework. A billionaire could pull some strings, and Frey had pulled them all, including the loan officer's at Anchorage Trust. So much for the Privacy Act.

"My crew is highly skilled. Even if I never dive again, Mr. Frey, my company will continue to exist."

"Teetering day to day on the verge of bankruptcy." Frey held out a sheaf of papers. "Would you like to read the agreement?"

Carson shook his head. "Not for a measly half a million bucks. It's not worth my time, thanks just the same."

Frey's smile was mirthless. He set the papers on the dash. "No, perhaps half a million wouldn't interest you. That won't even cover what you owe the bank, will it? Of course that measly amount wouldn't interest you. Silly of me to think it would. I'm sorry I wasted your time."

"Don't be," Carson said. "It makes me more determined than ever to find that plane."

"And if you do find it, Mr. Dodge?" Frey said. "What then?"

"I get half of what's recovered," Carson said, hoping for some reaction, hoping to get some answers to his questions before he even found the plane. "We're splitting the spoils."

Frey shook his head and gave Carson a look of condescending pity. "Then you'll be splitting absolutely nothing and desecrating the grave of a brave young man who served his country well. The bad publicity alone will ruin your company. I'll make sure it does. And as I said before, the salvage rights to that plane will never be granted. It's your choice, Mr. Dodge."

"My choice," Carson nodded. "I've made it, and I'll stick by it."

"Then you really are a fool," Frey said, starting up the Chris-Craft. "Tell that journalist she's making a big mistake."

"I'll be sure to pass that on, along with everything else," Carson said as Frey backed away from the shallows, turned the boat and headed back toward his lodge.

CHAPTER EIGHT

THE OLD MAN WAS SITTING on a splitting stump outside the cabin door when Libby walked into the clearing. He was leaning against the weathered log wall and soaking up the sunshine, and the very fact that he was up and about was a positive sign. The sled dogs out behind the cabin alerted him to her arrival, and he pushed to his feet as she approached.

"Hello, Mr. Johnson," she said, easing the pack off her shoulders and setting it on the ground. "I'm Libby Wilson. I was here two days ago, when you were pretty sick."

"I wasn't that sick," Solly Johnson said. He was giving her the same kind of look Carson gave her when she had tried to help him. Libby sighed. Karen was right. It must be a guy thing.

"You certainly look like you made a good recovery. I brought you some food, and some more medicine."

The dark eyes glittered in the wizened face. "I don't need the white man's medicine. I got my own and it fixed me up pretty good."

Libby flexed her shoulders to ease a muscle cramp. She wasn't used to carrying a heavy pack up a steep trail. Her legs were tired and she was tired of dealing with stubborn-headed men. "Shall I take the food away, too? A white woman fixed it." He made no response to this, so Libby picked the pack up and went inside the cabin, where she deposited the contents on the small wooden table. Solly had followed her in and was watching her with a grave expression. At the bottom of the pack were the antibiotic pills. She lifted the bottle and shook it so the pills rattled sharply. "There's a five-day supply of medicine in here, Mr. Johnson. Swallow one pill with each meal for five more days. Three pills a day. This will help make sure the sickness in your lungs goes away."

Again, he remained silent. Libby glanced around the cabin. Everything seemed in order. Graham was still spending nights here to keep an eye on Solly, and he was also keeping things neat and tidy. Good.

She picked up the pack. "Before I go, I was hoping you could tell me something about the old white man who lives at the big lodge. Daniel Frey. My mother used to work for him, years ago. She's a villager from Umiak. She said to ask you about how dangerous Daniel Frey was. She said you would tell me. She said he shot you long ago."

The dark eyes glittered but Solly remained silent, keeping his secrets. Libby had to resist the impulse to scream her frustration aloud. Instead she nodded to the food on the table. "This should last a few days. I'll bring more before I go back to my mother's village." She paused by the door to gather her resolve. "There's one more thing I have to ask you. I know you don't like whites, but there was a white man who used to live with Daniel Frey at the big lodge. He flew a yellow plane and had a three-legged dog named HoChi. The plane crashed in the lake twenty-eight years ago. You were living here then. Graham says you used to tell him stories about the three-legged dog. He says you used to say that the dog howled in the night like its heart was broken and wandered like a ghost along the shores of the lake, looking for lost souls. You told Graham if he wandered off in the woods, the three-legged dog would catch him and carry his soul to the land of the forgotten."

The old man was studying her as she spoke, as if trying to decide something very important, but he remained silent.

"Mr. Johnson, I came here to look for that plane because the young man flying it when it crashed was on his way to Umiak to marry my mother. That man was Connor Libby, and he was my father. Do you know anything at all about that crash, or where the plane might have gone down? It's very important that I find it."

The silence stretched out long enough to put Libby's teeth on edge. She blew out an exasperated breath. "If you should remember anything, anything at all, I'll be at the small lodge for a few more days. You can send a message to me by way of your son. Take your medicine, Mr. Johnson. There are some things the whites do that are good. The food on the table is good, and that medicine is very powerful."

She was out the door when she heard him speak. He stood in the open doorway and the breeze lifted the tangle of gray hair from his shoulders. His expression was thoughtful. "When I first came here, there were no flying canoes in the sky. It was quiet, in the world before this world. Only the ravens talked and the sky belonged to them and they shared it with the eagles. Now those flying canoes are everywhere, and it gets harder and harder to find a quiet place."

Libby waited for what seemed like five minutes after he

sat back down on his stump to take in the sun, but that was all he was going to say.

"Goodbye then, Mr. Johnson," she said, and started down the steep path.

BY THE TIME SHE RETURNED to the lodge, Karen was already beginning supper preparations. Libby could see Carson puttering along near the lake's outlet as she docked the aluminum boat. She wondered if he'd found anything. She wondered if he was even looking. Maybe he was just pretending to search, hoping she'd change her mind at the end of the week and accept Frey's offer of a kill fee.

She felt a twinge of unease. As rude as he was, she'd like to think that he was a man of his word, yet there was no doubt that he'd been tempted by Frey's offer. Could she really blame him? Most men would still be lying in a hospital bed after what he'd been through, but Carson was pushing himself to prove that he was as good a man now as he'd been before the accident. She was partly to blame for that, walking into his office and hinting that if he was able to find the plane, he'd make a good deal of money. In her quest to prove her paternity, she'd deliberately played on his greed and ego to lure him to search for the missing plane.

Karen glanced up from making a big salad when she came into the kitchen. "We had a visitor while you were gone," she said with a bemused expression. "Mr. Frey himself drove his boat to the dock and asked to speak with the journalist from Boston."

Libby felt a stronger twinge of unease. "What did you tell him?"

"I told him we had someone staying by that description a

few days ago, but she wasn't a guest here anymore. It wasn't exactly a lie, was it? How was Solly?"

"Much better. I'm sure he'll appreciate your food, though he's about as prickly as Carson Dodge when it comes to accepting help. Did Mr. Frey say what he wanted?"

Karen rested the knife for a moment. "Only that he wanted to talk with Libby Wilson again and he asked for your address and phone number. Of course, I couldn't give it to him. I told him that was privileged information and when he left he wasn't too pleased with me." She smiled. "At least we finally met, after two years of sharing the same lake, so to speak."

"I'm sorry I missed him," Libby said, which was true. She would much rather have spoken to Frey in the safety of Karen's lodge. "There were a few more questions I needed to ask."

Karen glanced at her watch. "Why don't you run over there right now? He only left about half an hour ago. On your way you might invite your salvage operator to have supper with us. The other guests are dying to ask him all about his adventures."

"No way am I broaching that subject with him," Libby said. "Besides, he wouldn't come. He's hiding out like a wounded animal. I don't think he wants to see or talk to anyone until he looks and feels like his old self again. Are you sure you can spare me for a half hour or so?"

"I'm all set here. Are you going over to Mr. Frey's lodge as a journalist or a medical doctor?"

Libby didn't pause. "No more deception. I'm going to tell Mr. Frey who I really am and why I'm really here. Connor Libby was my father, and the reason I've hired Carson Dodge to find his plane is to prove that to Mr. Frey."

Karen's expression never changed and Libby realized that

she'd already figured everything out. "How do you think he'll take that news?" she asked.

"Poorly."

"Then maybe you should wait until you have proof. Wait until the plane is found. And even then, maybe you shouldn't go over there alone. I mean, if he shot Solly Johnson…"

"Solly didn't confirm that, Graham isn't around to ask and I don't want to wait any longer, Karen. Besides, what can Frey do? He's an eccentric old billionaire who doesn't treat his help very well, but I don't think he'll hurt me. There are too many people around for him to get away with anything like that now. He might rant and rave and call me crazy, but he turned my mother away twenty-eight years ago when she went to him for help and I strongly suspect he may have caused my father's plane to crash, and it's high time he faced the consequences, whether he wants to or not."

Karen nodded thoughtfully. "Go ahead then, but if you're not back in an hour, I'm sending in the troops."

IN SPITE OF HER BRAVE WORDS to Karen, Libby was scared as she headed the aluminum motor boat across the lake toward Frey's dock. Her heart was pounding, her palms were damp and her mouth was dry. She was very aware of Carson's long stare as she passed within a hundred yards of his boat, but she didn't glance in his direction. For all she knew, he'd already been to see Frey again himself to find out how high he was prepared to go. Maybe they were dickering over the kill fee. Well, let him wonder why she was paying a visit to the bitter old man.

Let him wait and wonder.

She approached the dock cautiously, filled with apprehension. The beautiful old Chris-Craft was tied to the cleats, and she parked across from it and jumped onto the weathered boards, lashing the painters fore and aft to secure the boat. She tried to act as if she had every business being here as she straightened and began striding up the porch steps. Mr. Frey wasn't sitting on the porch, which took her aback when she reached the top step. For a moment she faltered, her momentum losing steam, but before the fear could paralyze her completely she marched to the screen door and rapped loudly.

"Mr. Frey?"

She heard footsteps within and tensed, but it was Luanne who came to the door looking as apprehensive as Libby felt. "Mr. Frey is eating his dinner," she said, her voice lowered as if she was afraid her boss would overhear. "Would you like to wait out here on the porch?"

"No, I wouldn't," Libby said bluntly. "I need to speak with him immediately."

Luanne cast a wary glance over her shoulder, then opened the screen door and stepped out. "Mr. Frey doesn't like to be interrupted when he's eating. He has certain rituals that he observes and he becomes very upset when his routine is disturbed."

Libby stepped around the younger woman and opened the door. "I'm sorry, Luanne. I know you're just doing your job, but if I don't do this right now, I never will."

She entered the big lodge for the first time, gazing around at the vaulted great room. The fireplace was enormous, taking up most of the far wall, and the sheer size and gloominess of the room intimidated her. She mustered every last ounce of resolve to force herself to cross the room toward what she supposed was the entry to the dining room.

It was.

She paused in the doorway, taking in the huge expanse of glass overlooking the lake, the long table that was set between the fireplace and the wall of windows, and the man who was seated at the far end, regarding her in scowling silence.

"Mr. Frey, my mother worked at this lodge when she was a young woman. Her name is Marie Wilson. I'm quite certain you don't remember her, but Connor Libby was on his way to marry my mother when his plane crashed."

Frey pushed his chair back and stood. He was wearing a pair of brown slacks and a white shirt with a green tie and a cardigan. Apparently getting dressed for meals was one of his rituals. "I am eating my dinner," he said, clearly outraged at her audacity for interrupting. "I would ask you to leave."

"You told Karen Whitten you wished to speak with me," Libby continued, ignoring Frey. "Well, I'm here. I'm not a reporter, and I'm not writing a story for the Ben Libby foundation. I'm the daughter of Marie Wilson and Connor Libby, and I've hired the owner of Alaska Salvage to find my father's plane. I was hoping you might tell me where it went down, but of course it was foolish of me to think that you would. Obviously you don't want it found, and I think I know why. There's more to it than just losing half of your fortune, isn't there?"

Frey's growing anger was clearly visible on his tight, pale features. "If you don't leave at once, I'll have you thrown out."

"You don't want it found because if the FAA ever got their hands on it, they might discover that the plane had been tampered with, isn't that right, Mr. Frey? They might suspect foul play. And if they did, others might question why you weren't planning to attend your godson's wedding. Why *weren't* you going to the wedding, Mr. Frey? Was it because you couldn't stand the thought of Connor Libby marrying a native woman and bringing her back to share this lodge and the Libby fortune with you? Is that why you tampered with the plane and caused it to crash?"

"This is outrageous!" Frey flung his napkin down on the table. *"LUANNE!"*

"Mr. Dodge has informed me about the kill fee you offered if we stopped the search for the plane. I just want you to be aware, Mr. Frey, that even if you pay him a million bucks to stop looking, I'll have another salvage company in here before you can blink an eye. No amount of money is going to protect you now. No power on earth is going to prevent me from finding that plane. Not only am I going to prove that Connor Libby was my father, but I'm going to prove that someone tampered with his place and caused it to crash. If I have to go to the Supreme Court to overthrow any road blocks you put in my way, I will. You can bet on that. You may think your money will buy you out of this mess, but I'll fight you, and I'll win."

"LUANNE!"

"You're going to spend the rest of your life in prison, Mr. Frey, where you should have been for the past twenty-eight years."

Libby spun on her heel and left the dining room, left Daniel Frey standing in ashen-faced shock at the end of the huge table, left the big gloomy lodge that her father had grown up in and descended the porch steps while her heart pounded in her ears. She was so wired that she didn't remember getting into the boat or starting the outboard motor, but once she was back out on the lake she remembered the look in Frey's eyes, the burning hatred that radiated clear across the big dining room at her as she spoke, and she found herself wishing she'd heeded Karen's advice. There was a powerful malevolence in Frey that transcended any limitations of his age, and she had the distinct impression he would kill again to protect his kingdom.

FOR A FEW TENSE MOMENTS, when Libby sped away from Frey's dock and started across the lake, Carson thought she was planning to ram him as a result of whatever had transpired within the big lodge. She bore down on his inflatable boat at full speed, but at the last moment she swerved and throttled down. Her blue eyes blazed at him as his boat rocked wildly in the wake thrown up by the bigger aluminum craft.

"What the hell do you think you're doing?" he said. "You damn near swamped me!"

"I just spoke with Frey," she snapped.

"So I gathered."

"I told him who I was and why I was looking for the plane."

"Then he's a lucky man. He knows a helluva lot more than I do."

She leaned forward intently. *"You have to find that wreckage!"*

"Yes, ma'am, anything you say. I don't suppose he pointed out to you the exact spot where it went down?"

"I told Frey that even if he offered you a million dollars to fly out of here, I'd just bring someone else in to find it."

Carson shook his head and uttered a derisive laugh. "If he knows half as much about you as he does about me, he'll know that was an empty threat."

She drew back, eyes narrowing warily. "What do you mean?"

"I mean, he can find out exactly how much is in your bank account and how much spare change is lying on top of your bureau. He has connections. He knows how much I owe on my boat, my plane and my gear. He knows just how deep in the hole I am, and he's going to find out mighty quick that you can't afford to bring in another salvage crew."

"How do you know I don't have the funds?" she challenged.

"Hell, you could barely scrape up the five thousand bucks to get me out here. In fact, you still haven't coughed it up, I'm not even sure you have it, and when I quoted my rates to you, you nearly fainted in my office."

If anything, her eyes blazed with greater fury than before. "I have *plenty* of money, Mr. Dodge," she said. "Your rates seemed high, that's all, and I wanted to strike a better bargain with you. That's why I misled you as to my financial situation."

"If that's the case, then you'll have nothing to worry about if I decide to take Frey's kill fee and pull foot, will you?"

"You'd do it, wouldn't you? You'd go back on your word just to make a few extra bucks without having to work for them!"

Carson tugged the brim of his cap lower. Damn, but this woman rubbed him in all the wrong ways. "I said I'd find the plane."

"You told me you could only give me one week. You've spent two days out here and you've only covered a fraction of the lake's outlet!" she said with a frustrated gesture of her arm.

"Working a search pattern takes time," he said, bristling at her criticism. "With one person, it takes twice as long. You have to steer the boat and watch the monitor at the same time. You can't go as fast or you might miss something. The towfish sonar I'm using has a shorter range than a lower frequency sonar would and I have to work a tighter pattern because of that."

"Then I'll help you look. I'll drive the boat or watch the screen, I'll do whatever you tell me to do. We can bring lights and work at night, after supper. It hardly gets dark this time of year, it wouldn't be that hard for us to work straight through if we have to. Pick me up on the dock after supper. I'll help you look!"

Carson stared as his warning bells began to ring. She was so tightly strung she appeared on the verge of bursting into tears, and moody, emotional women had always made him very uncomfortable. He hadn't figured Libby Wilson to be the moody, emotional type. "No way," he said with a curt head shake, knowing that if she were aboard he'd be more distracted than ever. Even as he spoke he could see the tears shining in her eyes. She was about to cut loose and get hysterical. He held up a placating hand, hoping to calm the irrational storm. "Now listen…"

"No, *you* listen!" she interrupted. "You took me up on my offer of five thousand dollars and you told me you'd play by my rules. That was *before* you got here. It was only *after* you arrived that you changed your story and said you could only give me one week! If you had no intentions of doing the job in the first place, you should have said so, right up-front, instead of stringing me along like that!"

She was so mad she was hanging half out of the boat to confront him. If she leaned forward any farther, she'd be in the lake. So, Carson realized, would he. His blood pressure had hit an all-time high. "I told you I'd find the goddam plane, and I will!" he thundered. "I haven't gone back on my word! I have *never* gone back on my word!"

"What if you haven't found it by the end of the week? What then? You'll take Frey up on his offer, won't you, because it's a whole helluva lot better than mine!"

"What if Frey kills the salvage rights to the plane? If he gets the state to designate the crash site as some kind of monument to Ben Libby's son, which he has the power and influence to do, we won't be able to bring the wreckage up."

"He'll never be able to do that. I can guarantee you."

"How in hell can you guarantee something like that?"

"Just find the wreckage and let me worry about the rest!"

"Look, I'll keep searching for the plane, but the very least you could do is tell me what the hell it is I'm looking for."

For a few moments she glared at him, sparks shooting from her eyes and shoulders heaving around ragged breaths. Carson could see that the tears were about to spill over and her chin was trembling as she fought for control. She'd told Frey everything. Why the hell was she so reluctant to tell him? Why was it such a big secret?

"You're not looking for jewels. You're looking for bones," she blurted out abruptly, as if speaking the words aloud pained her.

Carson shook his head, perplexed. Had he heard her correctly? "What am I looking for?"

"*Bones!*" she shouted as if he were deaf, the tears finally brimming over. "*My father's bones!*"

The words hung in the air, arcing back and forth between them, electric and shocking. Carson could only sit in silence as he assimilated this overload of information. As soon as she'd spoken the word *father*, all the pieces of the puzzle had clicked together.

Of course. He should have guessed. She was about twenty-eight years old. She had blue eyes, was of native descent and her name was Libby. He'd already wondered about the strange coincidence of the name. He should have guessed the rest long ago, but he'd been too fixated on finding that planeload of fist-sized diamonds.

"If we can find just one bone in that wreckage, the DNA will prove my paternity and Frey will never be able to stop us from recovering the plane." Her eyes were wide, fixed on him, riveting him in his seat. The silence stretched out again. "Well?"

"Well, what?" he said dumbly.

"I suppose now you're going to want to charge me more money."

Carson stared at her for a moment and then shook his head. She really thought that he was in this just for the money. And why shouldn't she? He'd given her no reason to believe otherwise. Yet the truth was, he was already hooked. He'd help her out even if she couldn't pay the retainer fee. Hell, he already was. "You have a really high opinion of me, don't you?" He started the motor. "Tell you what. I'm going to take a quick break, gas the boat up and grab something to eat. I'll be back out in an hour."

"Pick me up at the dock at seven, Mr. Dodge," she said. "And don't tell me no. I have way too much at stake for you not to let me help."

Before he could respond, she started her own outboard and veered around his boat, heading at top speed for the lodge where she was staying. He watched after her for a few moments, rocking in the bigger boat's wake, then muttered, "Yeah, I guess maybe you do at that. Several billion dollars is a pretty big stake."

CHAPTER NINE

LIBBY HARDLY HEARD the conversation that went around the supper table that night as she helped Karen serve up the meal. She was scarcely aware of what it was she was serving. At one point, in the sanctity of that wonderful kitchen, Karen touched her arm and brought her to a halt.

"Are you all right?" she said.

Libby nodded. "Fine." Then, noting Karen's genuine concern, she forced a smile. "Really, I'm fine. It's been a long day, that's all. And I was hoping to talk to Graham about Mr. Frey, but he'd gone back to Solly's place."

"Why don't you get some rest? I can handle the rest of this, no problem. Go lie down and get a good night's sleep. Things will look better in the morning."

For an awful moment, Libby thought she was going to burst into tears at Karen's kindness. She blinked hard and swallowed around the lump in her throat. "Actually, I think it's better if I keep busy," she said. "And Karen? Thank you."

"For what?"

"For being who you are, and being in this place, right here and right now. If it weren't for you, I think I'd drown in all the darkness."

Karen gave her an impulsive hug. "You've certainly been a great help to me. And if you need anything at all..."

Libby hugged her back. "Thanks for everything. After we finish up with supper I'm going out on the lake to help Carson look for the plane."

"Is there anything I can do to help?"

Libby wiped her cheeks with the palms of her hands. "Actually, I was hoping I could bring another basket of food with me. I have a feeling he hasn't been eating all that well, except for what he's gotten from you."

"You got it, kiddo," Karen said, squeezing her hand.

CARSON STOOD ON THE SHORE at his campsite, gazing out toward the mountains, eating another piece of white bread straight out of the bag and pondering all the implications of Libby Wilson being Connor's daughter. No wonder Frey was offering a big kill fee. He stood to lose half of his fortune. But he was an old man. What difference did it make at this stage of his life? Why wouldn't he want to right all the wrongs before he died?

Were there wrongs to be righted?

Had Frey known about Libby's mother being pregnant?

He took another bite of bread and watched a loon fishing a hundred yards offshore. Going down into the deep. Coming up, swimming parallel to the shoreline, going down again. Over and over. All day long. A loon's life.

Not so very different from a man's, come right down to it. It was all about survival. Catching the fish, cooking it, basic stuff. Simple.

But not always easy. Sometimes there were just no fish to be found. Sometimes the loon went hungry, as did the man. Carson stared at the last fragment of bread in his hand. He was getting too philosophical, which meant he needed to get busy. Get back to work. Find the plane. He flung the bread out onto the waters. It would feed a fish better than it would feed him.

Goddammit.

Libby Wilson would be a billionaire if he found that plane for her. Not only would she be beautiful, she'd be megarich, and few combinations could be any worse than that when it came to a woman.

She was waiting on the dock when he got back out onto the lake. Standing there like an eager little girl, clasping a hamper in front of her and anxiously awaiting his arrival. Would've painted a pretty picture except for the fact that she wasn't a little girl and this wasn't an innocent evening jaunt on the lake.

"I brought something for you to eat while I drive the boat," she said as he pulled up to the dock.

"What makes you think I'd let you drive the boat?" he said, more gruffly than he should have, probably, being as she might soon become a very wealthy young woman.

"Because I'm a good boat driver, and you're far more experienced at reading that computer screen," she said, handing him the hamper and climbing aboard. It was awkward, maneuvering out of the stern and letting her take his place. His awkwardness instantly plunged him back into a dark place. He sat where he could watch the monitor and tried to squelch his bad mood by opening the hamper. He was ravenous.

"Okay," she said, settling into his seat and backing the boat away from the dock. "I'll take us down to where you were, and you tell me where to go from there."

Inside the hamper were three thick roast beef sandwiches. They were made with homemade bread, of course, and he knew they'd be good. This was the stuff he needed to build back his strength. Slices of white bread just didn't cut it. "Right," he said.

"I figure we can work until midnight. That'll let us get four hours of sleep before the dawn."

"Right," he repeated, selecting and unwrapping one of the sandwiches.

"That'll give us four more hours of search time per night."

"Right." He wrapped both hands around the thick slabs of beef and bread, feeling his mouth start to water.

"But what if the plane didn't go down near the outlet?"

"Huh?" He tore his attention away from the sandwich.

"When you fly your plane out of here, how are you planning to take off?" she asked, giving him a pointed stare.

"Same way the other pilots did. Into the wind and up the west arm."

"Supposing my father did the same. Supposing he made a fairly routine takeoff in the Beaver. Where would that put the plane when it lifted off?"

Carson looked down the west arm. "Maybe a quarter, a third of a mile out from Frey's lodge, depending on how much the plane was carrying."

"Suppose he was hauling a lot of supplies. It makes sense that he would be providing most of the food and drink for the wedding reception. Marie's family was and still is dirt-poor. So where would that put him? Anywhere near us? Anywhere near where you've been searching? Anywhere near where *Frey* told everyone the plane must have gone down? Frey, who doesn't want that wreckage disturbed?"

Their eyes met and held. Carson felt his ego sink even deeper into that dark abyss. "If the plane was heavily loaded, the pilot would need to throttle up to the max on his takeoff run. The pontoons exert a lot of drag on the surface of the water, and it takes a lot of rpm's to overcome that drag. The de Havilland's engine is a 450 horsepower Pratt & Whitney R985 Wasp Junior. Big beautiful radial motor, perfectly capable of the job, but the takeoff at full throttle carrying a heavy load would heat the motor up, so the pilot, as soon as the pontoons cleared the water, would throttle back to cool the engine off. He'd execute a slow climb, maybe, depending on weather conditions. On a good day the west arm is perfect for a long skim above the surface of the lake to let the engine cool down before going for any real altitude."

Libby cut the boat's motor abruptly and they drifted along in silence while she gazed up the west arm with a thoughtful expression. "So basically you've been searching the wrong area for two whole days," she mused aloud. "We're way off base, by at least a half mile. We need to start up beyond where your plane is tethered. Up beyond the point."

Carson glanced over his shoulder toward Frey's lodge, wondering if the old man was watching, and sure enough he was sitting on the porch, as was the norm this time of evening. He wondered what Frey and Libby had discussed that afternoon, what had made her drive that damn aluminum boat away from Frey's dock as though she were being pursued by demons. He wondered if an old man in his eighties could pose a threat to a determined twenty-eight-year-old woman.

"Yeah," he said, looking back at her. "I think we need to start a new search grid up beyond the point. And I also think you'd better steer clear of Frey."

"Don't worry," she said grimly, restarting the motor and turning the boat around. "I've had my last conversation with that man. I believe he somehow caused that plane to crash, and he knows when the wreckage is found I'm going to prove that to the world."

THREE HOURS LATER, LIBBY was fighting to stay awake. It had been an endless and emotional day, exhausting in every way. She could only imagine how tough it was for Carson to keep going, but he never said anything about quitting, just gave succinct hand signals for her to navigate by and kept his eyes on the screen. Earlier, she'd asked him what he'd see if they passed near or over the wreckage.

"The side-scanning sonar profiles the lake bottom directly below us and about a hundred feet to either side. It sends sound pulses down and receives echoes back in fractions of a second. This sonar is high frequency, which gives us better resolution," he'd said, indicating with his finger objects on the screen that were obviously large rocks, "but less range, which in this instance isn't so good. If we were searching for a drowning victim, we'd want this setup. Searching for a downed plane we could use a much lower frequency scanner with a far wider range, but as it turns out that scanner is on the *Pacific Explorer* right now. I had to bring what was at the shop, which is the towfish we used to recover the victims of that commuter plane crash."

"I thought you said you didn't dive for bodies."

"Normally we don't, but with the riptides in that inlet, time was of the essence. We did what we had to do to recover the victims as quickly as possible. So anyway, with this high resolution imagery, when we find the plane we're going to get a great picture of whatever there is to see. Trouble is, that might not be a whole lot after twenty-eight years."

"Why? The plane won't have rusted away."

"When the plane crashed it would have hit the water nose first because the engine is so heavy, and it would have sunk the same way, but the wings would probably have kept it level and upright when it bottomed out, assuming it wasn't already flipped over when it hit, which would be unlikely. That plane is as steady and stable as they come. After twenty-eight years of silt and sediment settling out, the plane could be pretty well buried so what we'd probably see is just the tail section of the plane, sticking up from the lake bottom."

"Do you think the plane was airborne when it crashed?"

"Absolutely. If it weren't, the pilot could've just aborted the takeoff."

"If you were going to sabotage a plane and cause it to crash, how would you go about doing that?"

He flashed her an odd look before continuing. "There are a bunch of ways, I guess. I never thought about it much. But whatever happened to that plane, it had to have happened suddenly. Most crashes occur during takeoffs and landings, usually they're related to changes in throttle settings, but by all accounts Connor Libby was an experienced pilot. If he'd run into any engine trouble shortly after takeoff, he'd have had plenty of room to set the plane back down. So I'm thinking even if the engine cut out completely, he could easily have made an emergency landing on the lake. If he'd lost his engine over the land, he'd have had to put down on the taiga, and they'd have found the wreckage there, but the pontoons turned up in the river. So that puts the plane somewhere in this lake."

"But how did it get there? What did Frey do to make it crash?"

Carson shrugged. "Plant a bomb in the box of champagne, maybe?" He shot her another brief glance. "Why would he want the plane to crash? Why do you think Frey was involved?"

"Because Connor Libby was on his way to marry my

mother and bring her back to live at the lodge. I believe Frey would have done anything to prevent that from happening because of his unwillingness to share the Libby fortune with an Athapaskan. The warden in charge of the search believed this, too. I read his journal. He thought the plane had been tampered with."

That was the last of their conversation. The hours dragged on and the sun hovered ever lower, swelling in size as it did, and at ten-thirty finally melted into a golden glow behind the mountains. The wind through the pass gradually died off and the surface of the lake turned a smooth molten violet, reflecting the poignant beauty of the arctic sunset. A loon gave a wild territorial call that echoed hauntingly in the thickening twilight. Libby followed Carson's hand signals as he studied the GPS and the sonar screen and struggled to keep her eyes open. The monotonous drone of the boat's engine and the gentle lap of waves against the rubber hull soothed her the way riding in a car lulls a newborn baby.

"Coffee?"

The word came out of nowhere and startled her awake. She blinked. "What?"

"We have to put ashore to refuel. There should be some coffee left in that thermos you dropped off this morning."

"Isn't it midnight yet?" Libby said.

"Nope. We have another hour to go."

Libby had to refrain from moaning aloud. Her body was cramped from sitting in the same position for the past two and a half hours. She wanted to tell him that she was too tired to continue, but since she was the one who had insisted on this extended search, she couldn't. Instead, she headed the rubber boat back toward the point and parked it next to his float plane. He tied it off to the pontoon and then lowered himself over the side of the boat into the knee-deep water. "You can stay there. I'll bring the gas can and the thermos."

"No way," Libby said, standing. "I have to find the ladies' room and stretch my muscles."

She jumped over the side, gasping at the icy shock of the water, and followed Carson as he waded ashore. "Couldn't you just beach the boat in front of your camp?" she said.

"Yup," he said, not looking back. "But the wading is good exercise for my leg and I didn't think you'd be coming ashore. Sorry."

She noticed he had developed a pronounced limp by the time he reached shore and decided she wouldn't complain about her wet jeans and waterlogged sneakers. He was suffering a lot worse than she was. While she ducked into the bushes, he lit a gas lantern that had been hung outside the wall tent and by the time she returned the murky clearing glowed with a bright golden light. Libby immediately noticed the can of beans lying on its side with the can opener still attached, and the open hamper on the ground right where she'd left it, brightly checked muslin dishcloth dragged half out. "Looks like you've had company," she said.

"The gray jays ate the muffins you brought this morning," he commented, retrieving the thermos from the hamper. "Every last one of them."

"Lucky birds." Libby picked up the can of beans and finished opening it, leaving the lid on and setting the can on the small table. She accepted the enamelware cup Carson handed her with a murmured thanks and was surprised and grateful to find that the coffee was still hot. She sat on a stump, glad for the parka she was wearing, especially after that icy wade to shore. "How's your hand?"

"Never better," he said, raising his own cup for a swallow.

"I'm sorry I yelled at you today. I guess I was a little stressed after my visit with Frey."

"You did seem a little stressed," he agreed.

"I probably should have explained the situation to you right from the start."

"That would have been nice."

"I should have trusted you more."

"That would have been nice, too."

She gave him an exasperated look. "You don't have to agree with everything I say."

"As soon as you say something that I don't agree with, I'll argue the point."

Libby smiled in spite of herself. "Fair enough. But you have to understand the position I'm in."

"I do, and I think it's a dangerous one." He was standing with his back to the lantern, casting his face in shadow. Libby couldn't read his expression.

"I would have described it as desperate," she said. "What makes you think it's dangerous?"

"Daniel Frey makes me think it's dangerous."

"He's just a bitter old man," Libby said.

"He's a very rich and powerful old man who doesn't want you to find that plane." Carson slatted the dregs of his cup onto the ground. "You don't know what lengths he might go to, to try and stop you."

"What *can* he do, other than try to block the salvage rights?"

"Just a little while ago you were telling me you think he sabotaged that plane and caused it to crash on your father's wedding day. That's about as low as it gets, wouldn't you say?"

Libby felt a chill of fear and huddled more deeply into her parka. "There was nobody around back then. He was all alone and there were no witnesses. All the hired help had been flown out the day before the wedding to attend the party. Frey wouldn't dare try anything like that now."

"Maybe not, but he has a helluva lot to lose if we find that wreckage."

Libby set her cup on the table, not relishing the idea of wading through that ice-cold water to the rubber boat. "We'd better get back out there."

CHAPTER TEN

WHEN LIBBY OPENED HER EYES several hours later she closed them again instantly, wanting to shut out the fact that morning had indeed arrived. Too early! She lay in stillness, listening to the drip of night water off the cabin eaves and the slowly gathering birdsong swell of sound that heralded the new day. She gave a tentative stretch and moaned aloud. She'd worked long, long stints as an intern and was used to getting by on very little sleep, but the stress of the past few days had taken its toll, and the stressful days weren't over yet.

Would Carson stay if he didn't find the wreckage in the one week he'd promised her? He'd said he was working a tight schedule on another job, but he'd also said he'd look until he found the plane. Which would it be? And how long could he afford to search? The lake was huge. The plane could have gone down anywhere along the west arm, which stretched for ten or so miles to the north. It could take months to find the wreckage, or it might never be found at all. The familiar gnawing tension built within her as she lay in silent contemplation of all the unknowns and uncertainties and the dark imaginings of her ultimate failure.

Marie had lived for nearly three decades in abject poverty, knowing that her daughter was the rightful heir to half of the

Libby fortune. She was willing to live the rest of her life without pursuing it any further than she had when she'd gone to Frey all those years ago, young and scared, pregnant and penniless, and been turned away. She hadn't even known about such a thing as paternity testing, and thirty years ago using DNA to prove a person's identity was a technology that was still in its infancy. It simply wasn't practiced back then.

It wasn't until Libby went to high school in Anchorage, then to college back East and dived into premed courses that the mysteries contained in a fragment of flesh, bone or blood were revealed to her, and it wasn't until she started working in forensic pathology that all the pieces finally fit together. It was as if all of her life she'd been moving toward the day when she could use everything she'd learned to prove her paternity, but the five-thousand-dollar retainer she'd promised to pay Carson would effectively wipe out her savings account, and payments still had to be made on her school loans. In fact, they were already overdue.

Her mother's medical bills were also piling up. Good medical care was expensive and insurance companies typically did everything they could to avoid paying up on claims.

The churning in Libby's stomach intensified. She sat up and brushed her hair back from the sides of her face. It was all so overwhelming. She couldn't look at the whole picture right now. She had to take it one day at a time. One moment at a time. She'd get up, help Karen with breakfast, call Susan to check on her mother, clean guest rooms, get lunch out, then assist with the search for the plane until it was time to help Karen with supper preparations.

She wondered how Carson was feeling this morning. She was lying here feeling sorry for herself and he couldn't even open a can of beans. That had to be galling to a man as physical as he was. Yet, he hadn't sniped at her last night when she'd taken it upon herself to finish the job he'd started. She'd opened the can of beans and he hadn't said a word. Maybe he was getting better about accepting help when he needed it. Maybe he was learning that it was okay to need somebody once in a while.

Maybe they were both learning, little by little, to trust each other.

THE MORNING WAS COLD enough that Carson could see his breath inside the canvas tent. Frost coated the interior. He fed the last of the wood Libby had cut up into the tiny box stove and huddled over it for warmth, feeling sick and cold and weary to the bone. He made a little pot of coffee on the tiny propane stove and drank every last drop of it hot and black. His clothes were still damp and clammy and the bandage on his hand stank of gasoline from the awkward spill he'd had while refueling the night before. No doubt his boots would squelch like cold sodden sponges when he pulled them on.

What a nice restful and recuperative vacation he was having, here on Evening Lake. And he'd thought it would be easy money. Ha!

The camp jays watched intently from nearby branches as he pried the lid off the can of beans Libby had opened. He forked a mouthful out cold and chased it down with a piece of white bread. Breakfast of champions. He ate this humble but filling repast staring out across the lake, watching while the snowcapped mountains changed from a cold blue hue to a burnished red glow, yellowing as the sun rose behind them.

The wild, rugged beauty of his surroundings only served to intensify his melancholy mood and he wasn't, by nature, a melancholy man. Yet ever since the accident he'd been re-thinking his entire life, wondering if maybe he'd been missing out on something. His career had always been very satisfying to him. Planning and working the salvage jobs, ramrodding his crew, captaining the *Pacific Explorer*...all those facets of his life had occupied almost all of his time and had been enough. More than enough.

But when Libby Wilson had walked into his office, the encounter had triggered a restlessness inside of him that not even his focus on keeping Alaska Salvage afloat could quiet and calm. In fact, he'd be pacing right now if his leg wasn't so gimpy. That was the hell of it. If he could just *do* something, something purely physical, like cut and split twenty cords of wood, he knew he'd be able to work through this strange inner turmoil. But he couldn't even draw a deep breath without wanting to cough his bad lung up. Couldn't even wade out to the boat without feeling weak as a kitten afterward. Couldn't even feel his right hand, let alone move it.

She, on the other hand, radiated youthful vitality, making his own inadequacies all the more painfully noticeable. No man wanted to appear weak in front of a woman, especially a beauty like that. A beauty who was about to become a billionairess...but only if he got his ass in gear and found the damned plane.

He set the half-eaten can of beans on the little tabletop next to the remaining few slices of bread and reached for his wet leather boots. Pulling them on wasn't going to be the most unpleasant thing he'd ever done, but the way he was feeling right now, it'd come pretty close.

FISHERMEN, IN THE EARLY morning, were very easy to deal with. All they wanted to do was have their breakfast and get out on the lake. In spite of the fact that they'd spent every moment of the previous day on the water, they couldn't wait to get back at it. Fly rods and fishing gear in hand, they made for the boats. Libby stood in the doorway of the lodge, watching them move en masse toward the dock, when Graham Johnson spoke at her side, startling her.

"Karen said you wanted to talk to me. Luanne told me what happened between you and Frey yesterday," he said in his deep voice. "She says to be careful. She thinks Frey could be dangerous."

Libby studied Graham's expression. "What do you think?"

"I trust what Luanne says. My father told me to stay away from him ever since I was a little boy. He told me never to go near the big lodge on the warm shore."

"So being a typical boy, you went there the first chance you got," Libby guessed. "Graham, did Frey ever shoot at your father?"

He nodded. "One day, when I was ten years old, I took my father's canoe and fished my way down toward the forbidden warm shore. Nothing happened. I didn't see anyone. It was like the place was deserted. So I paddled to the dock and when nobody came out I decided the old man must be gone and I went to look inside the big lodge."

"And?"

"And Frey caught me snooping around. I was holding a piece of carved ivory, one of those Yupik fish lures. It was a beautiful thing and I was admiring it. Suddenly he was there. He looked huge to me. He shouted and his voice shook the logs. He took the lure from my hand and then he thrashed me."

"He hit you?"

"Beat me bloody. Drove me out of the lodge and told me if I ever came back he'd have me arrested and put in jail for stealing. So now I had to go back with my father's canoe and explain why I looked the way I did. I told him I fell out of a tree, but he didn't believe me. I guess I don't lie too good. So I told him the truth."

"I bet you never went there again."

"No, I didn't, but my father did. He went back there that very day. He stood on the dock and called Frey out of the lodge but the old man didn't come. I guess it was a good thing he didn't. My father was pretty mad. When my father came back home his arm was covered with blood. I asked him what happened and he told me that Frey took a shot at him from the lodge. He said Frey was a coward and wouldn't come out to face him. He told me if I ever went there again Frey would probably shoot me, too."

Libby was shocked. "Was this shooting ever reported?"

Graham shook his head. "I doubt Frey told anyone about it. Besides, no one was killed."

"Did Frey's employees know about it?"

"No doubt it kept them on their best behavior that summer."

"That must be how my mother heard about it. That episode sounds like something out of the Wild West. Graham, do you think Luanne is safe there?"

He shrugged. "Karen offered her a job. I told her to take it. The Whittens are good people and the food is great. But she's stubborn. She needs the money he pays. She's determined to stick out the rest of the summer."

"Stubborn seems to be the ruling word around here," Libby said. "I went to see your father yesterday."

"He told me, but I would have guessed by the food on the table. He said the bossy blue-eyed girl came by and told him to take more white man's medicine."

"Is he following my orders?"

Graham nodded again. "Reluctantly."

"He wouldn't talk to me about the story of the three-legged dog."

"He doesn't talk much. He needs to warm up to you first, and that can take a long time."

"Great," Libby said. "I have a few more days to work my way into his heart."

"You might make it," Graham said, preparing to head down to the dock. "You blazed a pretty good trail into his stomach with that basket of food."

After the fishermen and guides had departed, Libby placed a quick phone call to Susan. "Your mom's doing wonderfully," Susan assured her. "Feeling better by the moment and beating me daily at cribbage. She's worried about you, though."

"Tell her I'll be home soon," Libby said. "Give her my love."

Halfway through cleaning the guest rooms Karen surprised her by bringing her a glass of iced tea. "Thought you could use some refreshment. You were out pretty late last night."

"Too late. I feel like I'm moving in slow motion this morning."

"I don't see your salvage operator out there. He must be sleeping in."

"We're working above the point now," Libby explained, taking a swallow of the cold iced tea. "We think that's where the plane might have gone down. You wouldn't be able to see him from here, but I'm sure he's out there."

"Are you going out again?"

Libby nodded. "The more I can help him, the faster the search will go. It really takes two people, one to drive the boat and the other to watch the sonar readout. But it sure is tedious work. I didn't think an hour could possibly last two hundred minutes, but they do out there when you're working a grid pattern and studying the lake bottom."

Karen gave a sympathetic laugh. "Sounds like you're having some fun, but at least you're sharing the tedium with a handsome companion. Why don't you invite him to dinner tonight?" she urged again. "His presence at the supper table would be a welcome diversion from listening to all the fishing stories."

Once again Libby shook her head. "He'd never come. I'll just keep bringing him leftovers and hope he doesn't starve to death in the meantime."

"Suit yourself, but all work and no play…"

"Trust me, Karen. Carson Dodge isn't the least bit playful, unless romping with a pit bull is up your alley."

"Is he married?"

Libby gave her blank stare. "I don't think so."

"Does he have any kids?"

"I'm not sure."

"So, forgive me for asking, but what did you talk about last night to while away those long hours?"

"Nothing. We were both too tired to carry on a conversation."

Karen sighed, shook her head and turned away. "Hopeless," she muttered as she walked back toward the kitchen.

CARSON HAD ONLY INTENDED to stop briefly at his camp to refuel and take a short break, but he sat down at the base of a spruce to stretch out his bad leg and the warmth of the sun felt so good as it seeped through his still-damp blue jeans that he thought maybe a few minutes of sunbathing might loosen up his muscles and ease the pain. A few minutes soon became a few more minutes. The breeze was pleasant. It kept the bugs away. He liked the sound of the wind blowing through a stand of spruce, the high-pitched lonesome whisper it made over the wash of waves against the lakeshore. He closed his eyes and rested the back of his head against the tree trunk. Quiet here, with the noisy and demanding gray jays absent. They probably knew by now that the good stuff came in baskets from the lodge.

Carson opened his eyes and glanced toward the tent. A couple packages of those dried noodles would go down pretty good about now. Fill his empty stomach. Trouble was, he couldn't make himself move. Couldn't will himself to get up and cross the clearing. He closed his eyes again and let the sound of the wind and the waves fill his world with peace. When he opened them again it was with a start. He blinked, rubbed his face with one hand and was shocked to see that the sunlight had shifted so that his legs were now in full shadow. He heard a twig snap and the sound of approaching footsteps. No doubt that was what had wakened him.

Before he could stand up a woman came into view, skirting the shoreline. She stopped when she spotted him. "Hello," she said. "I didn't mean to startle you. I'm Karen Whitten. We met on Monday, when you flew in to meet with Libby. I brought you some lunch. Libby would have come herself but she's still cleaning rooms."

He must be hearing things. He pushed to his feet. "Did you say Libby was cleaning rooms?"

Karen nodded. "I told her to take a break but she refused.

She wanted to get done early so she could go back out and help you look for the plane. I hope you like tuna salad sandwiches, they're the flavor of the day."

"You mean, she's *working* for you?"

Another nod. "Just temporarily, for her room and board. She wanted to stay nearby while you were here."

Carson was certain his mind had been muddled from the nap he'd taken. He couldn't be hearing this correctly. "She told me she was some kind of doctor," he said.

"Crazy, I know, but she knew I desperately needed the help. She's way overqualified, no doubt about that, but I'm sure glad she's here. Summers may be short in Alaska, but when you have no help, they're endless. Mr. Dodge, are you married?"

The question took him completely by surprise. "Not anymore," he said.

"Have supper with us tonight. We eat at 6:00 p.m. Libby told me you wouldn't come but I'm guessing you might like my cooking and her company enough to show up. All you have to do is put up with a lot of long-winded fishing stories."

Carson shook his head. "Thanks, but I'm pretty busy." As soon as the words were out he realized how ridiculous they sounded. She had, after all, just caught him napping.

"I'll set a place for you, just in case you change your mind. Good luck with your search."

She set the basket on the table and left as swiftly as she had come. Carson watched her, baffled by the information she'd just given him. All this time he'd thought Libby was lounging about the way vacationing or off-duty doctors must do, reading thick novels and sipping white wine, or maybe martinis, after the sun had crossed the yardarm. And all this time she'd been working. Cleaning rooms, no less.

He waited until Karen Whitten was quite a way from camp before hefting the basket and lifting the dish towel that covered the contents. He shook his head again, marveling at the bounty within, then glanced up and narrowed his eyes in thought. Would she have invited him to supper if he'd told her he was married?

Women were strange creatures, no doubt about it. But they could cook, and at this particular moment, when his belly felt as if it was permanently plastered to his backbone, that's all he cared about.

"FOR YOUR INFORMATION, CARSON Dodge isn't married," Karen told Libby as they prepared a quick lunch for the guests. "But I didn't get around to asking him about kids, or if he had a girlfriend he was really serious about."

Libby froze in the act of spreading tuna over twenty slices of homemade bread. "You actually asked him if he was married?"

"I thought you'd want to know and figured you were too shy to ask." Karen gave her a bland, innocent look. "I also asked him to join us for supper."

"You didn't!"

Karen was putting lettuce on top of the tuna, then the second slice of bread, and cutting the sandwiches in half. She worked swiftly enough that Libby had to jump back into action with the sandwich knife and bowl of tuna salad. "Not only did I ask him, but I think he'll come."

"When did you have this little conversation?"

"I walked down to his camp a few minutes ago to leave him some lunch. He happened to be there."

"He was in camp? What was he doing?"

"I think he was having a nap, actually, which wasn't a bad idea. He looks like he could use a lot more sleep than he's been getting. As well as food. I'm sorry I interrupted him."

Libby glanced up, knife poised over the last slice of bread. "Did he look…sick?"

"He looked tired and beat-up. I think he's trying to do too much too soon."

Libby dropped her eyes back to the bread and spread it with the last of the tuna. She nodded. "You're right, and it's my fault. I'm pushing him because I'm so desperate to find that plane and he can only stay one week."

"You told me it took two people to search," Karen said. "Does he have to be one of them?"

"Reading that screen is a highly trained skill. What we're looking for is a plane that might be in a whole bunch of pieces and covered with three decades of sediment. There's a good chance that I could look right at those pieces of wreckage and not recognize them for what they were," Libby explained. "So yes, I think he needs to be the one interpreting the images." She paused. "Do you think he looks in worse shape now than when he came here?"

"Personally, I don't think four hours of sleep is enough for someone recovering from injuries that severe, but you're the doctor. Am I wrong?"

Libby felt a great weariness mire her thoughts. "No, you're not wrong." She set the knife down on the counter. "I'll tell him I'm not feeling well and that we can't go out tonight."

Karen's expression brightened. "Good. I know you're anxious to find the plane, but if he comes for supper I would recommend walking him back to his camp afterward, maybe building a cozy little campfire and sitting around it in a friendly, social way. Who knows? Maybe you could even try talking to each other. I've heard that works pretty good for getting to know someone. And to make that plan even more attractive, I'll give you the rest of the day off so you can help him search right up until supper time. That way you won't be losing any ground even if you do knock off early. How does that sound?"

"More than equitable."

"If you go over there right now, he'll probably still be working on the lunch I brought."

Libby frowned. "Are you playing matchmaker?"

"You bet I am. It isn't often that I get the chance, way out here. How'm I doing?"

"I'll be sure to let you know," Libby said with a grudging smile.

CHAPTER ELEVEN

IF CARSON WAS GLAD to see her he certainly didn't show it, but neither did he growl at her, which she took as a good sign. He was stuffing some things into a day pack when she came into the clearing and he paused to give her a questioning look.

"I have the rest of the day off," Libby announced. "I'll drive the boat again so we can cover more ground."

He nodded as he slung the pack over one shoulder. "Works for me, if it works for you. Are you really a doctor?"

"I really am. I graduated from Tufts Medical School, interned at Mass General and specialized in forensic pathology."

"Then why the hell are you cleaning rooms at that lodge?"

"Because I'm broke. I gave up a very lucrative residency to come out here and find this plane."

"Why now? Why'd you wait all these years?"

"Believe it or not, it took all those years for me to be in a position where I could actually afford to do something about it. Maybe I should have waited until my savings account was a little healthier, but when I read that article in *Forbes* magazine I guess I went a little ballistic. So here I am, cleaning rooms and helping you look for a plane at the bottom of the lake."

His eyes narrowed. "What happens to you if we don't find it?"

"You said you would, and I trust you. We'd better get out there."

He studied her a few moments longer. "Isn't forensic pathology where you cut up dead bodies looking for clues to their death?"

"Something like that," Libby said.

"Huh. Must be frustrating to be a doctor and not be able to boss your patients around, but at least they can't talk back."

Libby gave him a steely look. "Don't think for a minute the dead can't talk. They tell all kinds of stories in their own way. They talk the same way my father's bones will talk when you find his plane, and the whole world is going to sit up and listen to what he has to say. Now let's get going, shall we?"

This time she took off her sneakers and rolled up her jeans before stepping into the lake. As she waded out to the rubber boat, Libby reflected that Karen's efforts at matchmaking were definitely wasted on Carson Colman Dodge. He was so prickly a porcupine would run from him. Not that she cared. Theirs was strictly a business relationship. It was his professional skills she was banking on, not his sadly lacking social skills. Once he found the wreckage, they would go their separate ways.

LUANNE HEARD FREY MUTTERING aloud long before she came out onto the porch. He was leaning forward in his chair, binoculars raised, watching the point of land where Dodge was camped. "She's with him!" she heard him mutter. "She's with him. That's good!"

And then the screen door banged behind her and he jerked around, lowering the binoculars. "Don't sneak up on me like that!" he barked.

"You told me to bring your medications at noon, Mr. Frey. It's noon," she said, setting the pills and the glass of water on the side table. "The cook would like to know if you prefer an artichoke salad with your broiled fish, or a garden salad."

His scowl deepened. "I don't give a damn what kind of salad she fixes. It's all inedible. You tell her I don't give a damn."

"Yes, sir." Luanne turned to go.

"Wait!" he said. "Tell her I want the artichoke salad."

"Yes, sir."

"She can't possibly foul that up. It comes out of a jar."

"Yes, sir."

"Tell her to serve it right in the jar. Just open the top and put the jar on a plate. Tell her to do that."

Luanne nodded.

"And tell her not to burn the fish this time. Broiling doesn't mean burning. Tell her!"

She nodded again. Frey was becoming uglier by the day. She wondered if maybe Graham wasn't right. Maybe she should leave this place and go to work for Karen Whitten. It would be such a relief to escape Frey's bitterness and hostility, but she'd vowed to stick out the summer. College was expensive and the money Frey paid was good. And so she went to tell the cook how to prepare Frey's salad and broiled fish, and tried to keep her thoughts from straying too often across the lake, to the friendly place where Graham worked.

THE LOON HAD FOLLOWED THEM all afternoon, swimming just abaft their starboard beam, diving and surfacing, watching them closely for a while and then diving again. Carson was aware of the loon even as he concentrated on the monitor, but he was far more aware of the young woman sitting in the stern of his boat. He squinted against the bright sun, tugged his hat brim lower and eased his bad leg trying to find a comfortable position. He gave Libby a hand signal and she obediently altered course. He gave another short signal and she obligingly adjusted. She read him well. Too well. That was beginning to irritate him. It also irritated him that she drove the boat with such skill, took direction without questioning, was quiet when most women would have been yapping away endlessly about trivial things. It irritated him even more that she was a doctor, and it baffled the hell out of him that as a doctor she would choose to specialize in cutting up dead people. That was just plain weird. Women doctors should gravitate toward warm and fuzzy motherly stuff like pediatrics.

Although he kept his eyes on the sonar screen, he was aware of her presence and it was driving him crazy. She'd worn jeans again, and the cuffs were rolled up high enough so he could catch a glimpse of those slender and incredibly feminine ankles and equally graceful feet. Ankles and feet weren't supposed to be that beautiful. When she'd taken off her fleece pullover to pare down to a T-shirt, he became aware of her arms. Same story. Slender yet obviously packing some strength, probably from moving those talking corpses around on the slab. She had a pair of hands that would have made Michelangelo weep, and the curve of her neck as she turned her head to watch the loon would inspire a poet's imagination to lofty heights. The thick dark eyelashes that fringed those vivid blue eyes, that oh, so kissable-looking mouth, the way the T-shirt clung to the soft swell of her breasts…he was aware of all of these things without even looking at her, and all of them were driving him mad.

He had to force himself to concentrate on the screen, check

the GPS, motion to her for a course change, all without letting her see that she was causing a rapid meltdown of his defense system. If she even guessed what was happening, if she even suspected the effect she was having on him, he was doomed. She'd destroy him effortlessly.

He had to concentrate. Had to find that damned plane, get his money and go his own way before she got into his blood any more than she already had. Once she became heiress to the immense Libby fortune she'd no doubt beat a hasty path out of the Alaskan bush, take up residence in some California beachfront mansion and read thick romance novels and drink martinis while the surf crashed at her feet. She'd have servants, lots of them, and bell pulls in every room that she'd summon them with. And a pair of those ridiculous long haired Afghan hounds that she'd walk on her private beach at sunrise, wearing one of those sexy thong bikinis and pair of dark sunglasses, her long black hair blowing in the Santa Ana winds.

Well, maybe she wouldn't change that much, but when he found that plane she'd become a very rich woman with no use at all for a washed-up salvage diver. Not that she had all that much use for him now, but he liked to think he was earning his five-thousand-dollar retainer. Assuming she ever paid it.

LIBBY WAS ALREADY STIFF and sore and they'd hardly been out for an hour. Karen was right. Even though this job just entailed sitting in a boat, it was borderline torturous for her. She could only imagine what Carson must feel like, cramped over the sonar screen in a craft that was too small by half for his six-foot, broad-shouldered quarterback build. She studied the way he watched the screen, studied his profile, the strong, masculine planes of his face, bronzed after four days on the lake, the last pale vestiges of his long hospital convalescence erased by the sun reflecting off the water and burning him in spite of the long-billed cap he wore. He hadn't shaved that morning, and the dark stubble made his features appear even more rugged and helped to hide some of his injuries.

The scars on his face would fade, but they'd always be visible. Every time he looked in the mirror he'd be reminded of his close brush with death. She doubted his hand or his leg would ever function normally again, yet he pushed himself and persevered and refused to accept his limitations, and she admired that about him. So many people would have collapsed into a wheelchair and sunk into the depths of a black depression. So many would have given up, but Carson was too full of arrogance and anger, and anger was a great motivator. She had a feeling that Carson would go down fighting, no matter how desperate the circumstances or how high the odds against him were. He was the type that would fight to the end.

"Graham Johnson's father was shot by Daniel Frey when Graham was just a boy," she said, speaking the first words in well over an hour. Carson's head jerked toward her and his eyes locked with hers. She felt the electric jolt clear to the soles of her feet. "Apparently Graham sneaked into the lodge after his father told him never to go there. Frey caught him inside and beat him bloody. Solly Johnson took offense at that and went to see Frey. He stood on the dock and called Frey out. Frey stayed inside the lodge and shot him in the arm. The incident was never reported."

"Huh." Carson looked back at the sonar screen, checked the handheld GPS and gave Libby a signal. She adjusted course. The silence stretched out. Minutes passed. Another half hour of searching and not finding. And then, without glancing back, he said, "So, we know Frey is capable of violence. Did you ever talk to Solly Johnson about the plane crash?"

"Yesterday. He never answered me. I told him if he remembered anything at all to tell Graham. According to Graham, Solly's pretty reclusive and doesn't talk much."

Carson rounded his shoulders then rotated them around, easing stiff muscles. He shifted his bad leg, something he did frequently, and then reached his good hand into the day pack in the bow of the boat. "I brought some food," he said. "Tuna sandwiches and a thermos of tea. Your boss delivered it to the camp before you came."

Libby accepted a sandwich. "Thanks. Karen told me you were coming to supper tonight."

He flashed her another quick glance beneath the brim of his cap. "I told her I couldn't."

"She must have misunderstood." Libby unwrapped the sandwich with one hand, balancing it on her knee as she held the tiller. "She'll be disappointed if you don't come, and you'll miss out on some great food."

Carson made no reply, just kept his eyes on the sonar screen while he ate a sandwich. He finished a second one before she was halfway through her first, then handed the flask of tea to Libby, who opened it and poured him a cup, handing it back to him because the lake was too rough to set it on the seat.

"You can't live on packages of dried noodles and canned beans," she finally said.

"I've done all right up to now."

"Well, I wish you'd come. I'm getting pretty sick of listening to all those fishing stories."

No comment.

Lunch over, they shared an awkward silence that seemed

to build on itself as they got back to the tedious business of working the search pattern and looking for an elusive de Havilland Beaver.

THREE ENDLESS HOURS LATER, Carson dropped Libby off at the lodge's dock. She had a hard time climbing out of the boat and he heard her stifle a moan. Carson shifted into the stern to take her place at the tiller and prepared to depart. "Tell Karen thanks for the lunch," he said. "I'll drop her basket off when I go back out on the lake."

"Come to supper," Libby urged him, rubbing her leg muscles. "It'll be ready soon. Come up now and I'll fix you a drink. You can sit in the living room in one of the leather recliners and veg out. Life doesn't get any better than that."

He shook his head with a faint grin. "Thanks, but that sort of living would make me soft. I'll have to pass."

"Suit yourself, tough guy," she said, "but you're missing out on a great meal."

She turned and walked up the dock, hands shoved in her pockets, hair blowing like black silk in the late-afternoon breeze. Carson watched her for a few very painful moments. He was acutely aware that he was missing out on a whole lot more than a great meal. He started the motor and backed away from the dock, and as he headed for his camp he felt the gnawing aches in his leg and side and lung spread through him until there wasn't a single part of him that didn't hurt, but he wasn't sure the pain was real. He thought maybe it was all in his mind. He thought maybe his increasing agony had something to do with leaving Libby Wilson behind.

But that was foolish.

He tethered the boat to the plane's pontoon, secured the

towfish on board and waded ashore with the empty gas can and his day pack. He threw the pack inside the tent and stood for a moment, catching his breath and contemplating supper. He'd eat some noodles, maybe. He'd lived for years on those cheap twenty-cent packets of noodles and canned beans. Libby might think they were poor vittles, but they kept a man alive and they were an easy fix.

Easy being a relative term. Right now he was wondering if he had what it would take to boil the water and put the noodles into the pot. Not to mention going back out on the lake after supper for another four hours. How the hell was he going to manage that? She'd be bright-eyed and ready to go and he'd be hobbling around wheezing for breath and groaning in pain like an old man...which is why she'd suggested the break, no doubt. To spare him. Yepper, he was already practicing for the life of a washed up salvage diver.

Aspirin. He'd take a few before boiling up the noodles. Aspirin and a beer. Yeah, that'd help. Carson rummaged in his kit for the bottle of aspirin but instead came across the bottle of painkillers the doctor had insisted on prescribing. When Carson said he didn't need them, the doctor had given him that patronizing stare and said, "It's ridiculous to beat yourself up in this day and age when you can be comfortable."

Ridiculous.

Carson tossed the bottle back into his kit, looked for the aspirin a while longer, then gave up. He tried to open a package of noodles and couldn't, which aggravated him more than it should have. Why did they make those packages so impossible? He flung the noodles aside, feeling uglier by the moment. Then he got back into his kit and retrieved the bottle of pain pills. He'd take one and rest a while before boiling the noodles. If the pain went away after he took the pill, he'd know it was real. If it didn't, he'd blame all his agonies on Libby. She was already making him weak. Making him yearn after something that could only create a bigger hunger, a stronger craving.

He opened the pill bottle using the butt of his rifle, and picked the pills up out of the dirt, pocketing them. They were tiny things. He couldn't imagine they'd pack much of a wallop, or ease his misery. He swallowed one dry, then nabbed a beer out of the cooler and carried it to his place at the foot of the tall spruce. It was a comfortable spot to sit with his shoulders braced against the rough bark of the tree, the lake spreading out before him and the mountains walling off the far horizon. He clamped the bottle between his knees and used his left hand to unscrew the cap. Took a long swallow of cold, bitter brew. Leaned his head back and closed his eyes. He'd rest for a while before boiling the noodles and going back out on the lake. There were five hours of daylight left and he'd make the most of them. All he needed was a short rest....

"HE'S NOT COMING," Libby announced in response to Karen's questioning look when she entered the kitchen to help with supper preparations.

"That might be what he told you, but he could change his mind," Karen said as she spread chocolate butter frosting on a devil's food cake. "Tell you what. If he's not here by six-thirty, you take supper to him, before he can sneak back out onto the lake. I'll fix you a two-person gourmet meal, complete with a bottle of nice wine. You can still do the fireside thing, the talking, the getting to know each other."

"Wasted efforts, Karen, but I appreciate your intent. All we seem to do is rub each other the wrong way and we really don't have anything in common except searching for a wrecked airplane."

"Since when did that ever stand in the way of true romance? I've seen the way he looks at you. The sizzle is there, all it's going to take is a little spark from you to ignite his fires."

Libby laughed as she scrubbed her hands in the sink, relishing the feel of the hot water. "I think living in the bush is getting to you. You're missing those afternoon soaps." She dried her hand on a towel and hung it on the rack. "Now, what can I do to help?"

"Get one of the bigger baskets out of the pantry and pick out a nice bottle of wine you think might go well with chicken cordon bleu. And Libby? Before you go over there, change into something sexy."

THE AGONY WASN'T ALL Libby's fault, Carson realized as the little pill started to take effect. He felt his body melting into the earth as the pain eased and ebbed. He felt vaguely disoriented, as if he were becoming weightless even as gravity pulled him down. It was a strange sensation, but not unpleasant. He took the first swallow of his second beer and contemplated the lake. The wind had died and the chop was smoothing out. The loon was not far from shore, watching him. The sunset, when it came, would be perfect. Another beautiful sunset over Evening Lake. He tried drawing a deep breath and stopped halfway there. Not quite ready for that yet. But hell, another pill or two, and he could enter a triathalon and win. Goddam!

He wondered what they were serving for supper over at the

lodge, and if the penniless Libby Wilson was waiting on the fishermen, listening to their long-winded stories as she set their entrées before them, refilled their glasses, cleared their empty plates away. He was sure those men all realized they were in the presence of an extraordinarily beautiful woman, but he wondered if they realized they were being served by an heiress who could buy and sell them a thousand times over...when and if he found her plane.

Who would she be then? Who would she become when her father's bones sat up and talked to the world? Libby Libby? Must remember to ask her about that.

He should really be thinking about getting back to work, but the beer had robbed him of his motivation. The beer had also eliminated the immediate need to cook up a packet or two of noodles. He could do that when he got back in at dark. He wondered if any of the fishermen staying at the lodge were in love with Libby yet. He bet they were all married men, that they were all flirting with her and more than half were already contemplating divorce.

He heard the roll of gravel underfoot as someone walked along the lakeshore, but the sound was coming from above his camp. Huh. Who'd be walking from that direction? He turned his head, feeling the rough bark of the spruce and smelling the sun-warmed resiny tang of the earth and waiting with a feeling of benevolent calm and sleepy lassitude for the unexpected visitor to step into view. Would it be the old man who lived up on the Yaktektuk coming to tell him exactly where the plane went down? If so, that was a very fat old man. Those footsteps were heavy.

When the dark, massive bulk of a grizzly came into view, ambling slowly along the edge of the cove where his plane was beached, a mere fifty yards from where he sat, Carson felt a mild jolt of surprise. The great beast paused and lifted its head when it caught scent of Carson's camp. The huge head turned directly toward him. Carson set the bottle of beer down very carefully. Didn't want to spill any of it. Damn, he hadn't been practicing very good bear-country camping. The dried noodles and canned beans and white bread were in his tent, which was about as stupid as it got. His rifle was in the tent, as well. Didn't do him much good there. Better get up and get it, and hope the bear wasn't in an ugly mood.

While the bear stood and stared, contemplating its next move, Carson levered himself off the tree behind him and worked himself into a standing position. So far, so good. His leg didn't even hurt. Still, he doubted he was up for a quick sprint. Fifty yards sounded like a good distance, but a grizzly could charge at thirty miles an hour. Fifty yards wouldn't even give him time to start climbing a tree. He'd barely have time for a decent swear word or two before becoming grizzly fodder. He backed slowly toward the tent as the bear continued to test the air for possibilities. He felt the canvas behind him and turned, reaching through the door to heft the Winchester Model 71 hunting rifle he carried for just such a contingency.

He emerged from the tent in time to see the grizzly's big head swing away from him in a powerful arc and the silvery ruff over its shoulders stand up. He heard it give a low, dog like woof and felt the hair on the back of his own neck prickle as he followed the direction of the bear's stare.

And cursed softly. Libby was walking up the shoreline toward the point, and she was carrying a basket of food. She was striding along in that swift, graceful walk of hers, bringing him a delicious-smelling basket of food, and the bear was about to get wind of it. It couldn't see her yet, it could only hear the sound of her approach. But all too soon she'd reach the point, and a few more steps would bring her face-to-face with the great beast. She was walking into a danger-ous situation all because he'd declined her invitation to share the meal with her at the lodge.

He had to position himself between Libby and the bear. She was rapidly closing the distance, and he was running out of time to make his move. He braced the rifle against his forearm and levered a round into the chamber with his left hand. The bear's head shifted toward him, hearing the sharp metallic noise. *Go on, bear,* he silently willed, holding the rifle and moving slowly forward. *Turn around and go away.*

If he cut through the brush at an angle, he'd intercept the shoreline trail between Libby and the bear just on the other side of the point. The bear's hackles were still raised. God, that was a big grizzly. Huge. Carson moved as quickly as he dared, crashing blindly through the last few yards of willow and alder to emerge on the gravel shoreline, bringing the barrel of the rifle up and snugging the butt into his hip as he faced up the lake. He stuck his numb and useless finger inside the trigger guard.

Libby spotted him as soon as he emerged onto the shore. He heard her footsteps falter, then heard her stop when she interpreted what he was doing and guessed why he was doing it. She couldn't see the bear from where she stood because it hadn't yet rounded the point. "Start back to the lodge," he called quietly, half turning his head so she could hear. "There's a bear walking along the shore toward us. It's just up around the corner."

He waited. The seconds seemed endless. Libby had either become the most silent walker on the face of the planet, or she was still standing forty feet behind him, holding that basket packed with savory-smelling food. He half turned his head again and caught a glimpse of her out of the corner of his eye. "Get back to the lodge," he repeated. *"Now!"* And then a movement up ahead caused his adrenaline level to soar to new heights.

The big grizzly was rounding the point.

CHAPTER TWELVE

LIBBY HEARD CARSON'S WARNING and saw the rifle he was holding and realized that she should make all due haste back to the safety of the buildings, but when the bear came into view, she froze. The grizzly was maybe thirty yards from where Carson stood, and it was moving toward them in a powerful rolling walk. Libby felt her muscles turn to water and was unable to flee, and then the great beast paused again, lifting its massive head and swinging it back and forth, searching for the source of the smells. Human, mingled with warm dinner rolls, scalloped potatoes, corn soufflé, chicken cordon bleu and chocolate cake.

Libby could hear her heart pounding over the sounds of the waves against the shore.

"Back up, slowly," she heard Carson say to her. "Slowly." And then, to the bear, he said, in a low, persuasive voice, "Ho, bear. Ho, bear. Look at me. I'm bigger than you are. Stronger. Faster. You don't want to mess with Old King Cole. You're on my turf now. Turn around, bear, and run away while you still can."

She made her feet move. Back one step, then another, and another after that while her heartbeat shook her entire body. Carson stayed where he was, rifle ready, as she moved away. The bear remained still except for the movement of its head as it listened to Carson tell it how big and bad he was. She kept moving back, ever so slowly, pausing only when the bear lowered its head, turned and ambled out of sight around the point. Carson remained where he was for what seemed like a long time, standing in that same position, rifle leveled and ready. When he finally glanced back and saw her standing there his expression changed from wariness to anger.

"What are you waiting for? Get the hell back to the lodge. *Go on!*"

His urgency motivated her. She turned and began to walk a swift retreat, carrying the basket of food. The trembling didn't begin until she reached the dock, where she sat abruptly and watched up the shoreline, waiting for Carson to effect his own retreat once she was safe.

But he didn't. Incredibly, he walked back toward his campsite. Libby couldn't believe that he would be so foolish as to return there while the bear was so near. He disappeared out of sight and was gone for what seemed like an eternity before he reappeared, day pack slung over his shoulder and rifle dangling from his left hand. He walked slowly down the shoreline, his limp appearing to be less pronounced as he closed the distance between them. When he reached the dock he dropped the pack off his shoulder and lowered himself to sit beside her. He gave her a long, appraising look.

"You okay?" he said, in such a casual and laid-back manner that her blood pressure instantly soared.

"Why did you go back to the campsite?" Libby burst out, clenching her hands together in her lap to stop them from shaking. "That was stupid. It would have served you right if the bear had eaten you!"

"I couldn't leave my noodles and beans behind."

"*That's* why you went?" she said, incredulous.

"Partly. I got the rest of the beer, too. Ever seen what a grizzly can do to a camp when it's on a rampage?"

Libby stood on wobbly legs. "I guess your recent brush with death didn't teach you a thing about being careful!"

"That diving accident wasn't my fault," Carson said. "Look at you, you're shaking like a leaf. Better sit down before you collapse or faint or something."

"I don't faint." Libby felt the sting of tears and blinked, damning herself for being so unnerved, but she sat back down.

"What's in the basket?"

"I was bringing you some supper because you were too stubborn to eat here."

"Sorry." He glanced up at the lodge. "I didn't feel like making idle conversation with a bunch of strangers."

"They're only strangers until you meet them," Libby said.

"Yeah, but the thing is, I don't want to meet them, and I don't want to eat supper with them and have to answer all their questions about what I do, and so on and so forth. Right now that's just too much like work and I'm too tired to make the effort. You want me to walk you to your door in case that bear's still around? Do you even have a door? Or do you sleep in some common scullery room with the rest of the maids?"

"I have my own cabin and my own door. It's not that far behind the main lodge, and I'm perfectly capable of making it there on my own. I don't require a chaperone."

"Don't say I didn't offer." He pushed himself to his feet and took up the rifle. "I'll leave my pack on the dock for now, if it's all right with you, and pick it up when I quit for the night."

"Quit what?"

"Looking for the plane." He gave her a wry glance. "Or have you forgotten about searching until dark and all that stuff?"

Libby stood. Her knees were still feeling a little weak. "I've changed my mind."

"About looking for the plane?"

"About requiring a chaperone. I'll take you up on that offer, if you don't mind walking me to my cabin."

It was evident from his expression that he thought her sudden change of heart was suspicious, but he nodded obligingly. Good. The very least she could do was make sure he ate something, and that would give the bear a little more time to put some distance between itself and Carson's camp. She led the way down the narrow path that ended at the door of the cook's cabin, which was situated in its own private clearing.

"Nice," he said as she opened the door. "How many others share it with you?"

"Right now I have it all to myself because Karen's a little short on help." She held up the basket. "Come in and have some supper. You can't take it with you to your camp. That bear's probably ransacking your tent even as we speak."

He braced one arm in the doorway, glanced around the interior, then regarded her with just a hint of arrogance. "You sure? People might talk."

Libby set the basket down on the table. "Let them. They need something new to talk about besides lake trout and lunkers."

LIBBY'S CABIN WAS BUILT of peeled spruce logs and had four bunks, two over two against the far wall, a box stove for warmth, a table and four chairs arranged by the picture window, and a tiny bathroom and kitchenette. An empty jam jar on the table held a small bouquet of wildflowers, and the place was spotless. Carson heard warning bells ringing as he looked around and felt the homey aura of domesticity. Apron strings and all that. But the painkiller was working fine in combination with the beer, so he ignored all the warning signals and instead watched while Libby unpacked the delectable bounty of the picnic basket onto the table. The bottle of red wine startled the hell out of him.

"That's some kind of fancy supper," he commented, leaning his rifle in the corner behind the door and picking up the bottle of wine to study the label. "French wine to boot."

"But unfortunately no corkscrew or wineglasses." Libby frowned. "I'll run up to the lodge and get them, and give Karen a heads-up about the bear."

In a flash Libby was out the door, and Carson placed the bottle back on the table. He sat down on the edge of the lower bunk and let the last of the adrenaline from the bear encounter ooze out of him. As it did, the pain pill and beer seemed to take a much greater effect. It was a comfortable bunk with a real mattress on it. For the past few nights he'd been sleeping on a foam pad, a mere one inch thick. At eighteen he wouldn't have felt a thing sleeping on the ground like that, but at thirty-nine, he felt every pebble, stick and tree root after about fifteen minutes. For the past few nights he'd slept poorly, if at all.

Damn, that bear had been big. If it had charged, could he have stopped it in time? Could he have protected Libby?

He sat back a little deeper on the bunk and lifted his bad leg onto the mattress, careful to keep his boot clear of the bedding. God, that felt good. He leaned back against the logs. The food smelled good, too. Couldn't blame the bear for paying a visit. Every hamper that had been brought to his camp had no doubt infused the clearing with those same savory smells.

From a distance he could hear the sound of boat motors starting up. The fishermen and guides were going out for the evening hatch. They fished dawn to dusk and never seemed to tire of it. Strange behavior. Carson fished when he had a craving to eat a fish. When he caught what he was after, he killed it quickly and ate it. The concept of catching and releasing fish all day long was pretty peculiar, but it kept a lot of these sporting camps going. Kept Karen and Mike alive. He supposed that was a good thing. He heard the approach of footsteps and barely had time to push off the bunk before Libby came back into the cabin, carrying two wineglasses and a corkscrew.

"I found what I needed," she said, holding her prizes aloft. "Pull up a seat."

She sure liked giving orders. He sat and watched her dish up the plates of food and open the bottle of wine. She poured him a glass that was more than generous, allotted half that amount for herself, and then raised her glass to him. "To finding the plane."

He raised his glass in his left hand. "Amen."

The wineglasses were of good enough quality to make a fine chiming sound when touched together. "And to that goddam big grizzly bear, for not charging us," he added.

"Amen," she echoed, and their glasses chimed together again. Her hand, he noticed, was now as steady as a rock. "Would you have shot it?" she asked.

"Reluctantly."

"You deliberately placed yourself between me and that bear."

"Heroically."

She set her wineglass down and leaned toward him. "Well, I'm very grateful. When I was seven years old, I saw a grizzly kill my best friend. We were picking berries along the Koyukyuk and the bear came out of the willows. Ever since, I've always been afraid of them, and I've always wondered why that bear killed her and not me. I was so much closer."

No wonder she froze when she saw the bear, and had been so shaky after the encounter. Not that anyone wouldn't have been. Grizzlies tended to have that effect on people. Carson took a swallow of wine. He was feeling better by the moment. Hardly any aches or pains. "I'm sorry your friend was killed, but I'm glad the bear didn't kill you," he said. "Try the wine. It's pretty good."

She raised her glass and took a tiny sip. "Today's Wednesday. How much of the lake do you figure you've searched so far?"

"Hardly any," he replied. No point in lying. "But that doesn't mean I won't find the plane after supper."

She regarded him steadily. "What's the longest amount of time you've ever spent searching for something?"

He contemplated the question for a few moments. "Twenty-two years, and I still haven't found it."

Those blue eyes widened. "What on earth are you looking for?"

"When I was sixteen I lost my virginity to a woman twice my age who seduced me, stole my father's watch off my wrist, then told her boyfriend, who came in on the tail end of that episode, that I'd raped her. Her boyfriend beat the shit out of me, would've killed me if I hadn't jumped out the window and gone down the fire escape, but that didn't hurt nearly as much as losing the watch. It was all I had to remember my father by."

Her gaze held steady. "So for twenty-two years you've been searching for your father's watch?"

"Hell, no. For twenty-two years I've been searching for an honest woman."

Her eyes dropped. She picked up her fork and poked at her food. "Have you ever been married?"

"Once. It didn't last long. She wasn't as honest as I'd hoped. You?"

She shook her head and poked some more, took another tiny sip of wine and glanced briefly at him, a half shy, half curious look. "I've never been very good at relationships," she said. "I was too busy getting my education, then too busy practicing what I'd studied for."

"Why forensic pathology?"

She smiled faintly. "Because it fascinates me. What about you? How did you get into diving?"

"I joined the service because my dad was killed in Vietnam and for some reason I thought I could avenge his death if I followed in his footsteps. I wasn't all that bright when I was young, but I learned to dive in the Navy and stuck it out for eight years. Got a lot of good experience. Worked for a salvage operator in New York City when I got out and taught dive school on the side. When that Boeing 747 went down over the Long Island coast my old navy commander called me back to temporary duty to help recover the bodies. The silver lining in that gruesome job was making connections with another dive crew and getting hired by a big-time salvage outfit based out of Seattle. Two years later I started my own company in Spenard and here I am, mortgaged to the hilt, looking for your father's plane and fending off a grizzly. Ain't life strange?"

She gave him another half smile. "It's certainly never boring. Why did you call yourself Old King Cole when you were talking to that bear?"

Had he? Oh, God. "Long story," he replied. "Briefly, it's my mother's pet name for me, and I really don't like it much. .Just promise you'll never call me Cole...or old."

"But you're okay with King?" This time her smile was full and warm, with a hint of laughter. "Don't worry, I promise I'll never call you Old Cole."

Carson took another swallow of wine. He was feeling better and better and Libby was looking more and more beautiful but instead of feeling threatened by the power of that beauty, he was beginning to warm to it. In fact, it was becoming more and more difficult not to push out of his chair, pull her out of hers, and kiss her. He hadn't felt like this since before the accident. Hadn't felt like hopping in the sack with a woman and rocking the boat until the tide went out. Carson narrowed his eyes as the warning bell rang. Wait a minute. He'd never felt quite like this before, ever. He'd never felt like this because he'd never really thought beyond the rocking of the boat. That's why Gracie had been such a blessing. She understood what he was offering and never asked for more. There were no demands and no commitments, which had suited him right down to the ground.

But Libby was different. She was definitely no boat-rocking one-night stand.

He drained his glass of wine. The warning bells were clanging away, but the sound was becoming more and more muted, like a bell buoy receding in a thick fog. He refilled his glass and added more to hers, though she'd hardly touched the wine or the food. "So, Doctor Libby," he said. "What's the first thing you're planning to do with your inheritance?"

The smile faded and she gave her head a small shake. "I'm not planning anything until you find the plane. Time's running out, and it's a big lake. I realize I've asked a lot of you, and the odds are getting worse by the moment."

He felt that sharp kick to his ego in spite of the pain pill, the beer and the wine. She was right. Time was running out and here he was, sitting like a love-struck fool, wasting it in small talk and wishful thinking. He pushed his plate aside and stood. "Come hell or high water, I'll find that plane. I told you I would, and I will." Carson was already moving as he spoke, reaching for his rifle. He opened the cabin door and felt her hand close on his arm. Strong grip attached to a strong arm.

"Carson, please don't go. I'm sorry I said that."

She was so close. One step closer and she'd have him. He'd never be able to escape the intoxicating lure of her sexuality. Did she feel it, too? Was her hand charged with the same voltage that was passing into his arm, or was it a one-way circuit?

One step closer, and he'd know.

He might have taken that step himself except for the sudden earthquake. The floor beneath him trembled, the cabin shifted, and his sense of balance tipped right off the scale along with everything else. He thought it was odd that Libby seemed oblivious to the disturbance. He felt the door frame hit his shoulder and leaned against it to steady himself. Why wasn't this cataclysm affecting her? He stared hard at Libby, who was studying him the way a doctor might study an unusual and somewhat alarming case history.

"Are you all right?" she said, frowning, her hand still gripping his arm. She took the step. The step that brought her closer. Damn. If he wasn't holding the rifle, he'd… "Carson?"

"Don't you feel that?" he said, amazed that she didn't. "The cabin's moving."

"The cabin isn't moving," she said. "You're having some kind of dizzy spell. Come back to the table and sit down."

She was so close he could smell the sweet fragrance of her hair and skin. So close…

He shook his head. Small movement, big mistake. For some reason the room began to revolve around him. "I'm fine, just a little tired. Maybe some coffee, strong coffee, before I go back out…." He couldn't quite focus on her face. It was as if she was slipping into the fog the same way the bell buoy had.

What bell buoy?

The grip on his arm tightened. "I don't think you'll be going anywhere tonight. Come sit down."

He blinked hard. The cabin had stopped moving. He waited a moment to be sure, then straightened in the doorway. "I'm fine," he repeated. "All I need is some coffee."

She leaned toward him and stared him right in the eye. Lord almighty, she had beautiful eyes. He wanted to kiss her, but the entire cabin was starting to behave strangely again. Logs weren't supposed to act that way. Logs were supposed to be solid.

"You're not fine," she said, solemn as an undertaker. "What's wrong with you?"

"I took one of those prescription pills the doctor at the hospital gave me," he admitted. "It's the first one I've taken and it worked pretty good. I'm feeling fine, but the rest of the world's a little off-kilter."

"You took a prescription pain pill and drank two glasses of wine on top of it? All on an empty stomach? No wonder you can't even stand up." Her expression changed from pure concern to intense disapproval and he decided she was even more beautiful when she was mad, which was a good thing because she was mad a lot of the time. Most of the time, truth be told. Libby Wilson had been nursing a big mad since the day she was born.

He certainly wasn't about to tell her about the two beers.

"All I need is a pot of strong coffee," he said, speaking deliberately because quite suddenly everything seemed to be moving in slow motion, including his voice. "Just some coffee, and I'll get back out there and find that plane."

"Don't be an idiot. You're not going out on the lake again tonight. The only place you're going is to bed," she said in that firm, patronizing doctor's voice.

"Okay," Carson readily agreed. Only an idiot would pass up an invitation like that.

"Can you can make it over to the bunk, or am I going to have to drag you by your heels?"

Was she really inviting him to spend the night in her cabin? Carson could hardly believe his luck. Firm mattress and a beautiful woman… Things were looking up. He set the rifle against the wall and when he straightened another tremble shook the cabin and caused him to stagger off balance. She took that one dangerous step and suddenly she was right next to him, her arm slipping around his waist to steady him. She smelled so good. He leaned into her just enough to feel her hip press against him and then he brought his arms around her and pulled her against him in full frontal contact.

She was startled but didn't pull away. Carson took this as a good sign and would have kissed her because he sensed she was ripe and ready for kissing, but the act of moving caused that earthquake to intensify and he had to hold her close just to keep from falling over.

"Damn…!" he said, struggling for balance.

"Easy…" she responded, steadying him.

Not exactly the performance he'd intended to make. He'd intended to ignite her inner fires with his kisses. He'd intended to leave her breathless and wanting more. He'd intended to pick her up in his arms and carry her to the bunk where they would create their own earthquake, but in the end he wasn't even sure how he made it there himself.

CHAPTER THIRTEEN

LIBBY MANEUVERED Carson to the bottom bunk where she half rolled, half pushed him onto the mattress. The twin-size bunk was too small for him. His shoulders spanned the mattress and his feet hung over the end by a good six inches. She pulled off his boots while he muttered something about making earthquakes. She laid a blanket over him while he mumbled that the logs were crooked and caving in around them.

"The logs are fine," she told him. "The cabin is fine. There is no earthquake. Just lie here for a while. The effect of that pill should wear off in four to six hours."

She gathered up the supper dishes and cast frequent glances toward him, concerned about the potent combination of pain-killer and alcohol. Within a matter of minutes he was out like a light. Libby picked up his plate and stared down at the food he hadn't touched. She shook her head. Not good. No, the morning would not be good at all, and she was to blame. She was a doctor, but she was behaving like a slave driver. The reason Carson was lying there passed out on the bunk was because she'd demanded too much too soon from a man who should be in rehab.

He moved a little, moaned, and his arm flopped over the side of the bunk. She set the plates back down on the table and crossed to the bed, where she gently folded his arm across his chest. He never stirred. She tentatively lifted his bandaged hand and laid it back down. No response. Moments later Libby was changing the dressing, and he slept right through her ministrations. Maybe taking that pill would work to his benefit. He'd get a good solid night of sleep, which he wouldn't have gotten otherwise. He'd have gone out on the lake again and searched until midnight.

She packed up her medical kit and then paused before rising from the edge of the bunk. She wondered at the conflicting feelings that churned within her. She liked him, there was no denying that. There was also no denying that her feelings ran much deeper than mere liking. But he was dangerous. He was sexy and masculine and tough, the kind of guy who had a woman in every port. The kind of guy any self-respecting woman should avoid like the plague, yet moments ago, when he'd pulled her into his arms, she'd found herself hoping that he'd kiss her.

She was still sitting there when a tap on the door frame startled her. Karen poked her head through the open doorway. She raised an eyebrow when she saw Carson lying on the bunk and Libby sitting beside him. Libby quickly rose, crossed the small room and stepped outside. "He's asleep," she explained. "Passed out cold. You were right. He's exhausted."

Karen's expression had changed from surprised to concerned. "Did he eat anything?"

"He was too tired, but I'm sure when he wakes up he'll tuck into the food."

"He has a phone call. Someone named Trig who works for him. He said it was very important that he speak with him, and that he'd hold. He's calling from an off-shore ship."

Libby nodded, glancing back over her shoulder into the cabin. There was no way Carson could make it up to the lodge, and whatever the message was, good or bad, he was better off sleeping. "I'll take the phone call and relay the message to him when he wakes up," she said. "Thanks, Karen."

She ran up to the main lodge and picked up the phone. "This is Libby Wilson," she said, slightly out of breath. "Carson can't come to the phone right now but I can take a message for him. He's…out searching for a plane that sank in Evening Lake."

"Yeah," the man responded. "He told me about that job and he left the number of the lodge in case we needed to get in touch with him. Something's come up. A problem with the diesel engine on the *Pacific Explorer*. That's his salvage ship. The fuel pump's shit the bed. Can you tell him to call Trig as soon as he can? Carson's the only one who can bail us out of this mess, and it's a pretty serious one. We're dead in the water."

"Of course I'll tell him," Libby said, her heart sinking.

She walked back to the cabin wondering just how serious the problem was, and realizing that it could take Carson away before the week was up. If that happened, she'd be out of luck, just when she thought she was closer than she'd ever been to proving her identity and solving the mystery of her father's death. Libby paused on the path. She glanced down the shoreline toward Carson's camp, pondering her options. She knew how to run Carson's boat, but more importantly, she'd become somewhat familiar with reading the sonar screen. Maybe she wasn't an expert, but at least she had an idea of what she was looking for. The tail section of the plane rising above the lake bottom should be easy to spot and identify. Shouldn't it?

Karen was huffing and puffing up the path toward her on

her way back to the lodge. "You look pretty discouraged. Was it bad news?"

"Something's gone wrong with Carson's salvage ship. Karen, is Graham guiding tonight?"

"I'm not sure, but he's down on the dock if you want to ask him. Is there anything I can do?"

"Keep your fingers crossed," Libby said. "If Graham's free, maybe he could help me search for the plane tonight. I have a feeling I'm running out of time even faster than I thought."

Graham wasn't guiding that evening, and when Libby briefly explained her predicament he willingly volunteered to run the boat. "But I don't know anything about the sonar," he warned.

"I don't know that much myself," Libby admitted, "but I know how to turn it on and how to read the screen, and I don't think Carson will mind if we search until dark. It's a nice calm evening, and by now that grizzly must have moved on."

She could only hope that was the case as they walked back down the shoreline. Graham carried a rifle, just in case. Whenever a bear came near the lodge, all the guides carried rifles as a precaution, but the bear was gone. All that remained were its huge paw prints along the shore, and the incredible mess that the bear had wreaked on Carson's camp. The canvas wall tent was torn down, the metal-sided cooler was punctured with big tooth marks, and Carson's gear was scattered asunder. Libby felt a chill as she scanned the brush and woods behind the camp, and was more than glad to wade out to the rubber boat to get away from the shore.

Carson had already topped up the gas tank, so all she had to do was untie the boat from the pontoon while Graham started the motor, and then pull herself over the side. Soon they were motoring out onto the lake. When they had reached the approximate location, and it was very approximate, Libby lowered the sonar into the water and played out the line, but she was unsure just how much line to let out. She activated the screen and sat where Carson had, hunched over to shield the screen from the low angle of the sunlight so as to be able to read it on the easterly legs of the grid.

After five minutes it became evident how little talent she had for working any sort of search pattern and watching the screen at the same time. Also, the depth of the sonar was critical, and she couldn't quite get the resolution right. Furthermore, she didn't have a GPS, and even if she had one, she wouldn't have known how to use it. Still, at least she was doing something. The odds of doing it right and finding the plane were long, but if she'd had to spend the rest of the daylight hours on shore, frittering away the last chance she might have to find the wreckage, she'd have gone crazy. She thought about Carson peacefully sleeping off that pain pill while his salvage ship and crew were trouble and she hunched over the sonar screen for three more hours and squelched a rueful laugh.

The tough guy sure knew when to call a time-out.

CARSON CAME AWAKE with a start. For a few unsettling moments he had no idea where he was, but then the foggy memories rolled back in. He blinked and squinted across the empty room. His mouth was dry, but when he sat up and swung his legs over the edge of the bunk, the cabin remained stationary. He still felt muzzy-headed, but the pain levels were way down and he took that as a fair trade-off. He rubbed his hand over his face, stared at the fresh dressing on his other hand, somewhat alarmed that he had no recollection of Libby rebandaging it, and then studied the ends of his fingers that showed beyond the white gauze. He was sure he'd felt them move. He raised his arm and tried to curl his hand into a fist inside the bulky bandaging. Yes, the fingers definitely moved. He gave the order for them to wiggle, and they wiggled. Granted, the movement was weak, but what the hell. Relief flooded through him. What a beautiful, beautiful sight!

He stood, looked down at his feet, then cast around for his missing boots. There, over behind the woodstove. He retrieved them and sat on the edge of the bunk to pull them on. It was still light out. He could get out on the lake for an hour, maybe. Maybe less. But he'd do what he could before it became too dusky. He owed Libby that much for letting him crash at her cabin. Not that she'd had a whole lot of choice in the matter. He wondered if she were working up at the lodge, cleaning up after serving the fishermen their supper. Should he leave her a note?

There was a notebook on the table, pen clipped to the spiral binder. He opened it to pull out a blank page and saw that it was a journal of sorts. Dates and entries. He flipped until he reached the final entry. It was very brief, just gave the date and stated, "Time is running out. Only two days remain. I can only hope the weather holds, and Evening Lake gives up its secrets before Frey hides them forever."

Carson removed a fresh page from the notebook, closed the cover and penned a brief note to Libby.

Thanks for the use of your bunk. Carson.

He picked up his rifle on the way out the door and paused to wiggle his fingers one more time.

Beautiful.

When he rounded the point by his campsite and first saw
the sheltered cove where he'd beached the plane, he noticed
that the rubber boat was no longer tied off to the float plane's
pontoon. He stopped abruptly, wondering if he'd forgotten to
make it fast to the pontoon and the wind had carried it off,
and thinking with a sick feeling in the pit of his stomach
about how damned expensive that side-scanning sonar was.
Then he continued on, this time paying closer attention and
noticing the tracks along the shore. Not just the tracks of the
giant grizzly, but fresh tracks of two people, one being
Libby's, the other track considerably larger. The foot prints
continued right to the campsite, where Carson stared with
dismay at the havoc the bear had wreaked. He knew this was
his own fault for keeping a sloppy camp, but still, it was a dis-
couraging sight. Good thing he'd removed the last of his food.
It was doubtful the bear would return, having gotten nothing
for its bad-tempered efforts.

But where the hell was his boat?

He walked back to the shore and looked up the west arm
and cursed beneath his breath. He felt the slow burn of anger
coarse through him as he beheld one of the guides from the
lodge sitting in the stern, driving the boat about half a mile
off shore while Libby apparently watched the monitor. He
couldn't believe she'd taken his boat without asking him.
That she was using his extremely expensive equipment
without asking. What if she snagged it on something and
busted it? She hadn't a clue how to operate such sophisticated
equipment. And who the hell was with her?

He lashed out at a rock with his booted foot. Hollering
would be pointless. The distance between them was too great

and the wind was working against him. He watched for a while as his anger built, then wheeled around and returned to his wrecked campsite. Might as well vent that energy putting the tent back up and sorting out his ransacked gear. Damn bear. If it showed up again he'd bust its chops. He'd skin it alive. He'd... Oh hell, he wasn't really mad at the bear, but that doctor woman sure boiled his blood. She had no right to take his boat without asking.

LIBBY EASED A CRAMP in the small of her back and glanced up at the western sky. The last shreds of color snagged the snowy mountain range and faded even as she watched, and the air was getting chilly. She sighed. "I guess it's quitting time," she told Graham, who nodded and headed the boat back toward Carson's camp on the sheltered side of the point.

Graham had been silent for most of the past three hours, but as they drew near the plane he said, "I'll ask my father about the crash again. I'll tell him why it's so important you find the plane. Maybe he'll remember something."

"Maybe," Libby said, but she doubted it. Discouragement weighed her down. She felt exhausted and close to tears as the twilight thickened. She'd been so sure Carson would find the plane, but now it looked more and more hopeless. "Thanks for helping, anyway," she told Graham, who nodded. He brought the boat in next to the plane and killed the motor. Libby slid over the side and into the icy water, reaching for the painter on the stern to lash it to the pontoon, then doing the same to the bow. Graham was helping her secure the sonar when she heard movement on the beach and whirled around, heart in her throat, expecting to see the looming bulk of that giant grizzly.

But it was Carson. The pill he'd taken should have kept him under for at least six hours, but somehow he'd thrown off the effects a good two hours early. He stood and watched, and the very manner of his silence was ominous, as was the way he was standing. It was a Clint Eastwood stance, something right out of *The Good, the Bad and the Ugly*.

"Thanks again, Graham," Libby said as they waded ashore. Graham nodded to Carson, who made no response, and then he wisely continued on toward the lodge. "Hello, Carson," Libby said when she reached shore. "How are you feeling?"

"What do you think you were doing out there in my boat?"

Libby considered her response. "I didn't think you'd mind if I borrowed it and searched until dark."

"Well, you thought wrong."

"Yes, I can see I did, and I'm sorry, but you were out like a light and—"

"That equipment you were playing with cost me a small fortune."

His words cut deep. Libby glanced to where Graham walked along, then looked back at Carson. "Look, I apologize. I didn't mean to make you angry. I didn't think you'd—"

"It's getting darker by the moment," he interrupted. "You'd better get back to the lodge while it's still light enough to see."

Libby felt her face flush. She clenched her fists inside her parka pockets. "What about you? You can't stay out here. The bear might come back."

"I'll take my chances."

"One of your employees tried to get hold of you earlier. I told him you'd call as soon as you could. He said it was important. His name was Trig and the problem has something to do with the engine of your ship. The fuel pump wasn't working and he said that they're dead in the water. That's all I know. Karen said to feel free to use the satellite phone in the lodge."

"I'll call him from the plane." His words were delivered with a curtness that stung.

Libby nodded. "All right. Then I guess I'll see you in the morning."

"Maybe."

"Look, I'm sorry about borrowing the boat without asking you."

But he made no response, and she felt his eyes boring into her back as she walked down the shore toward the lodge. When she reached the point she turned. He was still watching her. She wondered if he'd be there in the morning, or if he would have flown away, taking the last of her hopes with him and leaving the secrets of Evening Lake buried forever.

LIBBY'S NIGHT WAS a sleepless one. She tossed and turned and got up several times to open the cabin door and listen, feeling the cold night air pour over the threshold and chill her bare feet while she wondered and worried about the grizzly returning to Carson's camp. Another listening session at the open door had her wondering and worrying about him flying away while she slept. Well before dawn she was dressed and in the kitchen of the lodge, where Karen was already beginning breakfast preparations. She accepted a mug of hot black coffee, aware of Karen's questioning expression.

"He was pretty mad that I borrowed his boat last night without asking," Libby explained.

"And even madder that you were out in it with another man, no doubt," Karen added.

Libby glanced up. "I doubt jealousy ever entered his mind. He was far more worried about me wrecking his equipment."

"You underestimate yourself. I think he's far more worried about you breaking his heart. Did he get in touch with his ship?"

"He said he was going to call from his plane."

"Hmm. So you don't know how serious the problem was?"

"No. But I'm afraid he might be leaving today. The guy on the phone sounded pretty serious, and the term 'dead in the water' didn't sound good."

"He promised you a full week, didn't he?"

Libby nodded. "But if there's some kind of emergency…"

"If he leaves today, he'll just have to come back, that's all. A deal is a deal."

Karen was making yeast pastries. She rolled out the dough, spread it with butter, brown sugar, cinnamon and chopped walnuts, then rolled it up and sliced it into one-inch-thick rounds. Libby watched her arrange the rounds on a greased cookie sheet and cover them with a clean linen dish towel. She set the pan on a warming rack above the woodstove, refilled her coffee cup and sat down across from Libby. "Daniel Frey was out on the lake last night," she said. "I've never seen him take that big boat of his out after supper before."

"Where did he go?"

"Just up to the point. I'm surprised you didn't see him."

Libby made a face. "The only thing I was looking at was the sonar screen. The *Titanic* could have crossed our bow, I wouldn't have seen it. Still, I'm surprised Graham didn't spot him."

"He wasn't out for long. He just motored up the point, then turned around and went back to his dock. I only mention it because I thought it was strange."

"Like he was spying on us?"

"Yes. Keeping tabs. Before, you were right out in front of his lodge. Now you're out of sight. Apparently that makes him curious."

"He wonders what we're up to, does he?" Libby took another swallow of coffee. "Well, he doesn't have much to worry about. The odds of finding the plane are beginning to look pretty bleak."

"If you did find the plane, what would that mean?" Karen said.

Libby sighed. "Oh, Karen. I'm not sure. At first I thought finding the plane would solve all my problems. Finding the plane would allow me to prove that Connor Libby was my father. But now I wonder."

Karen frowned. "You wonder *what?*"

"I wonder if finding the plane won't cause more problems than it solves." Libby closed her hands around the heat of the mug. "Don't get me wrong. I want to find it very much. I know it won't answer all my questions, but it'll bring me one step closer to finding some of the answers."

"Then I guess I don't understand. What problems do you think it will create?"

"All my life I've been Libby Wilson, the illegitimate daughter of Marie Wilson, an Athapaskan from the village of Umiak on the Koyukyuk. Don't you see? If I can prove that Connor Libby is my father, my whole identity will change. My life will change. Radically."

"Your public identity will change, there's no doubt about that, but who you are is who you are. Inside, you'll still be the same person. You'll just be a whole lot richer and you certainly won't need to be making beds and scrubbing bathrooms around this joint."

Libby stood and paced to the window, silently cursing the point of land that blocked his plane from view. Was Carson still there? Had he sneaked away in the night? Or was he even now loading up his plane and preparing to depart? Libby whirled, plunked her mug onto the table, and was almost out the door before Karen called out for her to wait, and with a wry smile handed her a basket she'd already prepared. "I figured you'd be leaving early," she said. "Good luck."

Libby ran as swiftly as she dared along the shoreline, leaping over big pieces of driftwood and dodging jumbled rocks. She rounded the point and suddenly there he was, sitting in the boat, working on the painter in the stern. No doubt he was having trouble with the knot she'd made the night before. Good. That would stall him. She came to a halt on the shore near the rope that tethered the plane to the beach, heart pounding in her ears. He had managed to untie the knot and he tossed the painter into the boat, shifting his position to untie the bow line. He barely gave her a glance. Libby plunged into the water and waded out to the boat, setting the lunch basket on the floor. She shimmied over the side and slid into the stern, taking her position on the seat and staring defiantly.

"I can only give you one more day," he muttered, eyes on his work as he struggled with the knot she'd tied.

Libby nodded. "I figured as much when that phone call came last night."

"The fuel pump failed in my salvage ship. Things're okay for now, the weather's supposed to hold for another twenty-four hours in the sound, but she's ten miles offshore. I have a spare fuel pump at the shop. I'll have to fly down, pick it up, then fly out to the ship and replace the broken one." He was still fiddling with the knot.

"I understand," Libby said. Her lips were so numb she was barely able to form the words. She was suddenly cold all over and she clenched up against a convulsive shiver. "We'd better get started."

He finally got the knot untied and looked at her steadily for the first time that morning. "I'm sorry I was so short with you last night."

"That's okay. I probably deserved it." She clenched up even tighter, fighting the emotions that cramped her throat. She started the motor. "Let's just get going."

He tossed the bow line into the boat but instead of pushing away from the plane, Carson took hold of the wing strut and pulled himself onto the pontoon. He stood, opened the door and pulled out a bulky orange pair of coveralls liberally striped with reflective tape. He tossed it into the rubber boat just in front of her. "Put that on," he said.

"What is it?"

"It's called a mustang suit. It's a flotation device designed for long-term survival in cold, rough waters. Put it on. We're supposed to get some wet weather today."

Libby pulled it toward her, lifted it up then hesitated. "But it's so big and awkward."

"Put it on or go ashore," he ordered bluntly. "Your choice."

She glanced up at him and his expression effectively quelled any further protests she might have made. She pulled the suit on, dwarfed within the bulk of it. It was quite obviously Carson's. He cast off from the plane, climbed back into the boat and took his place at the sonar screen. As Libby struggled to zip the front of the suit up and cinch the belt tight

around her waist, she noticed that the clouds were already
gathering over the mountains. At the rapid rate they were
piling up there would be no pretty sunrise this morning.

She was right. By 10:00 a.m. the sky was dark, and by
11:00 a.m. it had begun to rain. Carson protected his equipment
by pulling up a clear collapsible canopy he called a dodger,
which shielded two-thirds of the boat, but Libby, in the stern,
was at the mercy of the elements. The wind picked up and the
waves built up rapidly. The search pattern Carson had her steer
gave them one long upwind and downwind leg, which was
okay, but the short crosswind legs were rough. The images on
the monitor became rough, as well, and Carson let out more
cable to dampen the effect of the surface waves on the submerged towfish. They refueled at noon and when Libby started
to wade back to the boat after taking a bathroom break, no easy
feat in the mustang suit, Carson detained her by grasping her
arm.

"Go back to the lodge," he said. "It's getting too miserable for you to be out there."

She stared at him, watching the rain drip from the brim of
his cap. "Is it getting too miserable for you?"

"Libby..."

"No way am I staying ashore. If this is the last day you can
give me, let's make it a good one." She pulled out of his grasp
and waded back out to the boat. When they returned to the west
arm of the lake she passed him food from the lunch basket.
Thick ham sandwiches spicy with mustard. Tea in a cup laced
with raindrops and diluted instantly to lukewarm but still delicious. Carson had the advantage, sitting under the dodger. As
soggy as her sandwich quickly became, the food was restora-
tive. Libby felt the strength flowing back into her as she ate.

When the basket had been emptied of the last gingersnap cookie and every drop of tea had been shared between them, she packed everything back into the hamper and stowed it away.

Time dragged out as the miserable minutes passed.

Talk to me, Dad, she willed her father as the rubber boat wallowed through the chop. Back and forth, up and down. She watched Carson studying the screen; she watched her position by lining up with trees on the shore; she wiped rain from her cheeks and sometimes, tears. It no longer mattered if she wept the frustration she felt. Nobody would know.

Talk to me, Dad....

But the lake remained dark and cold and mysterious, keeping her ghosts and her secrets hidden, and Libby felt no closer to finding her father than she had for the past twenty-eight years.

CHAPTER FOURTEEN

At 5:00 p.m. Carson ordered Libby to head for the lodge's dock.

"You've been out for thirteen straight hours," he said, raising his voice to be heard above the wind.

"So have you," she shot back in that maddeningly defiant way of hers. "Let's just refuel and keep going until dark."

"Head back," he repeated. "We need to take a short break."

"How short?"

Clearly, she didn't trust him. She thought he'd get her ashore and then leave her behind, or stop the last hours of the search, but she had to be exhausted. Nobody could sit in the stern of a rubber boat in the pouring rain all day long and not be exhausted. She looked pale and wrung out, as well as soaking wet in spite of the hood on the mustang suit. Her dark hair was plastered to the sides of her face, her eyelashes were beaded with raindrops, her nose and chin were dripping with water. She looked whipped, and he was sure he didn't look much better.

"We'll stop just long enough for a mug of hot tea and a quick bite to eat, then we'll get right back out. We should be able to work four more hours before quitting."

The idea of hot tea and food had to appeal to her. She was

human, after all, and the effects of the lunch they'd eaten had worn off long ago. Once she got inside the warm lodge, her enthusiasm for the search would wane and he was sure she wouldn't want to go back out in the cold, driving rain.

"We don't have time to stop," she said.

"Look," Carson said, trying to reason calmly with her. "After I fix my ship, I'll come back and search the lake until I find the plane. I told you I'd find it and I will. I promise you, I will."

She shook her head in a fierce gesture. "*No!* If you don't find the plane today, that's it. The search is over! Don't you see? Frey will make sure that plane will never be found. He'll bring his own people in to make sure no evidence remains. He knows what's going on out here. He never thought it would happen, he never thought anyone would care about finding it, but now he knows differently, and as soon as you leave, he'll make sure that plane is never found. It'll go beyond trying to prevent us from purchasing the salvage rights. He knows where that plane is. He'll find a way to destroy everything!"

Carson leaned toward her, willing her to believe in him because suddenly nothing mattered more. "Libby, listen to me. I said I'd come back. I didn't mean next year, I meant as soon as the ship was fixed. I can't leave the *Pacific Explorer* dead in the water ten miles from landfall with my crew stranded aboard her. Do you understand?"

She leaned toward him, her eyes as dark and turbulent as the lake. "My father's been dead in the water for the past twenty-eight years. Do *you* understand?"

Carson felt his blood pressure climb. Was any creature on earth more irrational than a woman? "Dammit all," he burst out, "are you listening to anything I'm telling you?"

They glared at each other for a few moments, and then

suddenly Libby crumpled over herself, letting go of the tiller and dropping her head into her hands. Carson watched her and waited for the weeping storm that must surely follow, but she remained ominously rigid and still. He shifted toward the stern, hoping the rubber boat didn't swamp as he gently but firmly moved her out of the seat and into the middle of the boat, under the sheltering canopy of the dodger. She hardly seemed aware of him as he took the tiller and headed back to the lodge. She just sat on the bottom of the boat with her knees drawn up to her chest, looking vulnerable and exhausted and more beautiful than anyone in a bulky orange mustang suit had any right to look.

By the time he was tying the boat off at the lodge's dock, she had come up with her latest strategy. "I'll wait for you right here," she said when he extended his hand to help her out of the boat. "It's nice and sheltered. Maybe you could bring me back something hot."

"Now listen," he said, striving for calm. "You're getting out of the boat right now or I'm climbing in there and throwing you out. You're coming up to the lodge with me and you're going to drink a hot cup of tea and you're going to eat whatever Karen gives you to eat. You got that?"

A sudden gust of wind-driven rain lashed into her face and she blinked up at him, and it wrenched his heart to see her sitting there like that, all played out in the bottom of the boat. "Get up," he ordered, holding out his hand.

She reached for him and he pulled her out of the boat as it lurched up and down against the dock in the rough chop. She leaned against him for a few moments when she was standing on solid ground. "I'm sorry," she said. "My legs must have fallen asleep."

"I'd pick you up and carry you to the lodge, but I'd need a few more of those magic pills to pull that off."

"No more painkillers for you," she murmured.

"Then you're going to have to walk."

She gripped his arm as the blood started to circulate through her limbs. "Oh, it hurts…. My legs are all pins and needles…."

"I know it hurts. C'mon. Walk with me." He put his arm around her, silently cursing his bad leg and his bad lung and his bum hand because he so desperately wanted to help her more than he was. He so desperately wanted to be the man he used to be, the man she needed him to be right now. "That's it, Libby. One step at a time."

KAREN WAS IN THE KITCHEN, putting the finishing touches on the evening meal. She took one look at Libby as Carson half carried her through the door and whisked out a seat at the kitchen table. "Sit her down," she said to Carson. "My God. Have you been out on the lake all day in this miserable weather? Never mind, I already know the answer to that one. Poor girl. She needs to get out of that suit and get a cup of hot tea in her."

Libby felt only great weariness as she tried to shrug out of the bulky confines of the mustang suit. As much as she'd protested wearing the thing, she was glad she had. The suit had kept her reasonably dry and quite warm. She was aware of Karen helping her, and then pressing a hot mug into her hands. "Drink that slowly. There's a big slug of apricot brandy in it."

She took a sip and her eyes watered. "Carson?" She blinked and gazed foggily around the room, certain that he was going to sneak out and leave her sitting there but he was standing right beside the table. "Don't you dare go back out on that lake without me."

"Wouldn't dream of it," he said.

"Libby, you can't be thinking of going back out," Karen protested, handing Carson a mug of what Libby assumed was the same potent stuff she was drinking. "The forecast is for rain straight through the weekend, and it's a cold rain, too. I think I saw some sleet mixed in a little earlier. All the fishermen came in as soon as it started, and they've spent the day playing cards and napping. It's been kind of quiet and peaceful here at the lodge."

The warmth of the kitchen felt wonderful after the raw cold rain of the lake. Libby took another swallow of tea and felt the slow burn clear to the soles of her feet. She glanced up. "Carson?"

"Right here, behind you. Just taking off my wet jacket."

"Don't you even think of leaving this room without me."

"It'll never happen."

"I'll help you get supper ready, Karen. Just give me a few more minutes."

"Right," Karen said with a strong hint of sarcasm. "Then maybe afterward you can help me clean up and get the prep work done for breakfast and then go socialize with the guests for a few hours, maybe play some cribbage or a few hands of poker. Oh, and how could I forget? Listen to fish stories."

"Right," Libby echoed.

"I thought fly fishermen were obsessed, but people searching for planes are even worse." Libby felt Karen give her shoulder a squeeze to take the sting out of the words. "I'm just glad you're okay. I hate not being able to keep an eye on you, now that you're searching up beyond the point. I worried all day long, especially when the wind came up. You must be starving. Sit down, Carson, and I'll feed the two of you."

Carson dropped into the seat beside her, and Libby glanced at him. He'd shrugged out of his parka and removed his hat but he was still dripping wet. "You should've worn one of those orange suits, too," she said.

He shrugged. "There's only the one. The rest of them are with my crew."

Karen placed a plate of food before each of them. Libby smelled roast chicken and her mouth watered. She hadn't realized how hungry she was. She picked up her fork and dug in. With each bite she felt her strength and resolve return. When her plate was clean she was aware that Carson was staring. She stared back, cheeks warming. "I was hungry."

"You'll have to give me a few more minutes," he said. "I'm not as speedy as you."

Karen heard the phone ring and left the kitchen, only to return immediately. "Libby? Your mother's on the line."

Libby hurried into the living room and picked up the phone. "Mom? Are you all right?"

"I'm fine, but I was worried. You didn't call Susan today."

"Not yet, I was just getting ready to." Truth was, Libby had forgotten all about calling.

"When are you coming home?"

"Soon. I'm going to help Karen with the rooms this weekend then fly back on Sunday afternoon when the air service brings a new batch of guests in."

"I wish you'd come home now. I don't like you being there. You haven't found the plane, have you?"

"We still have a few more hours of search time, Mom. It could still happen."

"It doesn't matter, Libby. Nothing matters except that you are safe."

"It *does* matter, Mom," Libby said. She lowered her voice. "I want you to have the kind of life you should have been living all along. I want you to have a nice house in a nice place."

"I love my little house and I don't want to leave here. This is my village and these people are my people."

"But things could be so much better…."

"Better for you, maybe, but I am happy. I have everything I need, except my daughter. Come home, Libby. Come away from that dangerous place."

"I love you, Mom, and I'll be home very soon. Why don't you let Susan win just one cribbage game before I get back?"

Libby returned to the kitchen, picked up her mug of tea and sipped it standing next to the woodstove. She watched while Carson finished his plate, and then set her mug on the table. "You ready to go?"

He pushed to his feet. "You don't have to come. I can do it alone. And I told you I'd come back. This isn't the end of the search."

"And I told you that might be too late. You promised me a week and we have four more hours of good light."

"And very bad weather," Karen interjected. "Don't go back out there, Libby. The rain…"

"I'm not made of sugar." Libby picked up the bulky orange flotation suit and held it toward Carson. "You wear it this time. My parka's pretty waterproof."

"Libby, don't be foolish," Karen said. "Let me see if Graham's here. He can go out with Carson. He's perfectly capable of driving the boat."

"Graham's done enough as it is," Libby said, but Karen had already left the room. She looked at Carson. "It's just a few hours more," she said. "Please. Let me go. I *have* to go. This is the last chance I'll ever have of finding my father's plane, and your last chance of getting that big salvage fee."

Carson hesitated for a long moment then gave her a reluctant nod. "All right. Suit up. It's going to be a long, cold four hours and you're not going back out onto that lake unless you're properly attired."

DANIEL FREY WAS IN a foul mood and had been all day. Luanne thought it was because of the weather, but she realized after hearing him muttering out on the porch after supper that the dreary rain was only partly to blame. She was stepping out the screen door to bring him his brandy and box of cigars when she heard him say, as he peered through his binoculars, "No, no, no…they won't go back out tonight. Lake's too rough. Too rainy… Pointless for them to be out in it. They'll stay at the lodge…."

And then, even as she set the tray on the little table, Frey lurched forward in his seat.

"By God!" he muttered. "They're going back out. Both of them. What does it mean? What does it mean? They'd only go back out in this if they thought they found something…."

"Here's your after-dinner brandy, Mr. Frey," Luanne said.

Frey never responded, just stared through the binoculars and continued muttering beneath his breath. He was clearly agitated. Luanne could barely make out the opposite shore through the gray veil of rain, but she saw the people getting into the rubber boat and guessed that it was Carson Dodge and Libby Wilson.

"There's only one reason they'd go back out on a night like tonight…only one reason," he said. "I should've taken care of this a long time ago. A long time ago…." His face looked ashen, almost blue in color.

"Are you all right, Mr. Frey? Do you need me to bring you your heart pills?"

He jerked his head around, eyes blazing with anger. "I need you to leave me the hell alone!" he barked.

Luanne backed swiftly away. Before she reentered the lodge she cast a brief glance over her shoulder. Frey was staring through the binoculars again, muttering. She felt chilled. What a strange and evil soul he was. Graham was right. She shouldn't be working here. Tomorrow she would give her two-week notice, and if he gave her any grief she would leave at once, without working it out. Karen Whitten had already said she'd hire her. It would be nice to work for a pleasant employer even if she had to take a pay cut, and it would be wonderful to be nearer to Graham. She'd find another way to finish her thesis. Working for Frey wasn't worth it.

She watched the rubber boat motor up the west arm and after it had disappeared around the point she stepped back inside the lodge and started for the kitchen, glad to put some distance between herself and Daniel Frey.

He scared her.

BY 9:00 P.M. LIBBY WAS beginning to regret her decision to return to the lake. The mustang suit protected her from the brunt of the weather, but the wind had worsened and the waves sometimes broke over the sides on their crosswind legs of the search pattern. Twice now Carson had asked her to quit, and twice she'd stubbornly refused.

He looked up again from the sonar screen after a big wave rocked the boat up on its side. "We have to go back in," he said, voice raised to carry over the sound of the wind and waves. "The weather's getting worse and the resolution is so bad it's getting difficult to make out anything on the monitor. I've let out all the cable I can, and it isn't helping." The wind was picking the water off the surface of the lake and making visibility poor. Libby knew he was right. It was becoming more and more difficult to control the boat, and she was having to bail as well as steer the proper pattern. But the desperation inside of her burned brighter by the moment. She hated to give up the search. She knew there would be no second chance.

"Just one more hour!" she shouted back, blinking the rain out of her eyes.

Carson raised his arm and gestured emphatically. "Now!" he bellowed. "There's no point in continuing. We could drive right over the wreckage and I wouldn't be able to see it. I'll come back, Libby, I swear I will. As soon as I fix my ship I'll be back and I'll find the damned plane. Frey can't stop me from looking, and he won't be able to do anything in a few days time. Now head for shore and keep the bow into the wind. We'll make the nearest landfall and wait until the wind dies down."

Libby bit back her protests. She wasn't just risking her own life, she was risking his, and that was just plain wrong. They were about half a mile from shore, but keeping the bow into the wind would mean angling across the west arm and making landfall at least a mile above Carson's point. It was the longest way back, but the safest.

She hunched down inside the warm protection of the mustang suit as rain pelted her face, and kept the bow into the wind.

LUANNE HAD JUST FINISHED tidying up the kitchen when she heard Frey bellow her name. She started for the porch but then realized his shouting was coming from the back hall. She found him in a state of great agitation, trying to pull on an oilcloth raincoat. He'd caught one arm in a tangle of musty-smelling green cloth and was struggling to free it.

"Help me with this damn rain gear," he snarled.

"Are you going out in this, Mr. Frey?" Luanne said as she freed his arm and then held the raincoat so he could don it more easily.

"I should have done this long ago," he said. "Long ago...."

"Mr. Frey, maybe you should sit down. You don't look well. Have you had your pills?" He brushed past her so roughly that she staggered into the wall. "Mr. Frey?"

He went down the back hall to the servants' entrance, down the narrow stairs to the rain soaked ground, along the path that led down to the dock. Luanne stood just inside the door and watched him. The chill she'd felt earlier returned in force as he walked out into the storm, descended to the dock and began untying the lines that secured the Chris-Craft. What was he doing? Where was he going in this awful weather?

He started the motor and immediately advanced the throttle. The engine was powerful and the sleek boat took the rough water in stride as he accelerated, not toward the other lodge, but toward the point of land that hid the west arm from his view. Luanne felt the cold creeping into her as she watched the boat rapidly dwindle into the distance, pass the point where the plane was tethered and disappear from sight.

Without realizing that she'd made any conscious decision, Luanne burst out of the servants' entry and into the storm, heading for the boathouse where the old canoe was stashed. It would take her a good half hour of hard paddling to reach the other lodge, but Frey had the only motorboat and she had to warn Graham and Karen Whitten of her suspicions. The cold she felt was born of the fear of knowing just how deep the evil ran in the old billionaire's bones, and that fear gave her the uncommon strength to drag the canoe to the water, weight the bow with rocks from the shore and leap into the stern, paddle in hand, ready to do battle with the stormy weather.

CHAPTER FIFTEEN

CARSON REELED IN THE towfish, protected his gear as well as he could, then shifted his weight forward to keep the nose of the inflatable down in the face of the stiff wind. He bailed while Libby drove. The boat had a ten horsepower motor but it was slow going, and the waves were building by the moment. He didn't have to holler any piloting instructions to Libby. She was a natural. She read the surging lake waters as well as he could have, and her instinctive skills were the only thing that kept the boat from breaching when several rogue waves lifted it and the wind spun it around. Her feet were braced, her head was canted sideways against the rain, and she had both hands wrapped tightly around the tiller. There was no quit in her. Her spirit matched that of the lake itself, and the wildness of the storm. She was magnificent.

He threw back his head and shouted into the wind,

"The time and my intents are savage-wild,
More fierce and more inexorable far
Than empty tigers or the roaring sea!"

She flung the rain from her eyes with a dash of her head and shouted back, "What's that?"

"Shakespeare. Didn't you have to memorize any of his damn plays?"

"Not where I went to school."

"Lucky girl. I had the lead in *Romeo and Juliet.* I still remember most of the lines, but unfortunately I died in the end."

"Carson, the waves are getting worse!"

"You're doing fine. Steady as she goes."

"We don't seem to be moving."

"We're moving. Mark your progress by the trees along the shore. We're making headway. Slow but steady."

"I'm sorry I made you come back out here."

"I had nothing better to do," he said, bailing. He straightened to slat the water over the side and his eyes fixed on a dark object looming out of the wave-tossed murk behind them. He cursed aloud when he recognized the shape of the Chris-Craft.

Libby shot a quick glance over her shoulder, then faced forward again to do battle with the oncoming waves. "It's Frey, isn't it!"

"Looks like it, and I doubt he's out here looking to catch a fish. Can you make any better speed?"

She shook her head. "No, we'll take too much water. Do you think he sees us?"

"I think he's aiming straight for us," Carson said, fear tightening like a fist in the pit of his stomach. They were still a long way from shore. On a calm day that distance would be nothing, but tonight the lake was anything but calm. He reached for the edge of the dodger's framework and jerked it back, collapsing it onto the bow. "Listen to me, Libby," he said, moving toward her, reaching down and cinching up the leg belts on her mustang suit, tightening her waist belt as the big wooden cruiser bore down on them. "If you go overboard, that mustang suit will keep you afloat and protect you against hypothermia. You'll be okay, just keep swimming for shore." He glanced up. The Chris-Craft was gaining on them rapidly.

He reached behind her. "There's a zippered pocket below your hood that contains an uninflated air bladder," he told her as his fingers worked the zipper, dug inside and pulled out a length of black tubing with a mouth valve on the end. He took the tiller from her and handed her the end of the tube. "Blow into the tube!" he shouted over the wind. "It will inflate the flotation device inside that pouch. *Hurry,* goddamit, we don't have much time!"

Carson opened the throttle but he knew it was a futile gesture. The small motor on the rubber boat was no match for the Chris-Craft, which was quickly closing the distance between them. Over his shoulder and through the dark veil of rain Carson could see Frey standing at the helm. The crazy bastard! There was no way out of this situation. No way to outrun Frey's boat, and no way to outmaneuver it.

"He's going to ram us!" Carson shouted. "We're going to have to jump before he hits our boat. Understand?"

Her eyes were round with fright, but she nodded.

"It'll be hard for him to see us once we're in the water. It's getting darker and the waves are big but we'll stick together and swim to shore."

"Carson…!"

He glanced back again. They were out of time. He stood and seized the belt around Libby's waist, wrenching her to her feet with him. With the same movement he shifted his grip, hooked his arm around her, and hurled her overboard just before the heavy wooden Chris-Craft struck the rubber boat. Carson felt the boat heave out of the water as he flung himself over the side and into the dark and shockingly cold depths. He came up in time to see the stern of the cruiser pass within inches of his head, throttle wide-open. Waves battered him and he spat a mouthful of water. He looked for the rubber boat, but it was gone.

So was Libby.

Panic gripped him as he looked for her. She had to be close. Really close, but those mustang suits sometimes slowed a surface ascent. Maybe she'd gone under too far when he'd thrown her from the boat. Maybe she couldn't get to the surface in time....

He shouted her name. Saw the dark ominous approach of Frey's boat making a return run over the impact sight. Carson dived beneath the surface and kept himself submerged until the sound of the motor faded. He checked the murky depths before he rose to the surface but couldn't see anything. Couldn't find Libby. He surfaced, lungs burning, and scanned the choppy water. Saw a flash of orange farther away than he would have thought. He swam toward it, casting a backward glance to locate Frey, but the Chris Craft had already vanished into the twilight. He saw Libby floating on the surface, her head bent to one side, arms flung out and oddly motionless, and his panic level deepened. When he reached her he saw that she was unconscious, a fresh dark welling of blood streaking her temple every time a wave washed it clean.

If she was bleeding, she was still alive.

Carson gripped her with his good hand, shifted her to get a better hold around her torso with his arm, then began swimming toward the shore. The wind was lifting water off the crests of the waves and blowing it in a solid gray sheet across the surface of the lake. He had to swim at an angle to the wind in order to reach shore, which made the distance longer, and conditions were rough and getting rougher. He knew the odds were against him making it, but somehow he had to save Libby.

She had to survive.

LUANNE MADE GOOD TIME in the old canoe, in spite of the driving rain and gusting winds. She tied it to the dock, raced up the steps and onto the porch, and burst into the lodge's living room. Lamps had been lit against the early gloaming and men were seated in various groupings around a big field-stone fireplace. Some were playing cards, some were smoking pipes and reading. The scene was so tranquil it seemed otherworldly in contrast to the wild weather outside and the clutch of fear that constricted her chest. They all looked up, startled, when she entered.

"I need to speak with Karen and Mike Whitten!" she blurted out, breathless from her run and dripping wet. "I need to find Graham Johnson."

"Graham's down at the guides' camp," one of the men said, rising to his feet. "Mike and Karen are in the kitchen. I'll get them."

But having heard the commotion, they were just coming into the room. "Luanne? What is it?" Karen said. "Has something happened to Mr. Frey?"

"No. But Mr. Dodge and Libby Wilson might be in trouble out on the lake."

"I'll go get Graham," Mike said, leaving the room.

"What makes you think that?" Karen asked. "Did you see something?"

"Mr. Frey saw them go around the point in that rubber boat

after supper. He became very upset and not long after that he went out in his own boat. He's been acting strangely. I think he might try to do something to them."

Karen's face paled. "How long ago did he leave?"

"About half an hour. I came as quickly as I could."

"You did well. We'll get a couple boats out right away to look for them." Karen moved to the lodge window. "I can't see Frey's boat at his dock, but the visibility is poor."

They heard running footsteps and Mike came back into the lodge trailed closely by Graham. Luanne caught his eye across the room and didn't have to say a word.

"I'll get the boats ready," he said, and dodged back out into the rain.

IT WOULD HAVE BEEN EASY if it weren't for the frigid water, the strong winds, the lashing rain and the waves. It would've been effortless if it weren't for his bad leg and useless lung and crippled-up hand. But as the long minutes passed Carson felt his strength slipping away, and the dark line of the shore seemed no closer. He took a fresh grip on Libby and kept up with the side stroke, kept spitting out water as the waves crashed over his head and the wind-driven rain blinded him, kept taking his bearings on the shore and kept trying because that's all he could do. Keep swimming. Keep moving. Keep trying. Had to save her, had to get her to shore.

He began to sing because the wind had somehow picked up the strains of the old song and carried it over the water, and he recognized it as a hymn he'd learned in the navy. He sang choppily, ducking to avoid mouthfuls of water. He sang in spurts around painful, gasping breaths, and half the time he wasn't sure he was even singing aloud, but he sang to keep

Libby's spirits up because he thought she might be afraid and he thought she might hear him and he thought the words might give her courage and hope and keep her alive because above all, she had to live.

"Eternal Father…strong to save…whose arm…doth bind…the restless wave…"

His own arm was failing by the moment. Libby kept slipping out of his grasp, and his responses were becoming more and more sluggish.

"Who bidd'st…the mighty ocean deep…its own…appointed limits keep…"

What the hell did that mean, anyway?

"O, hear us…when we cry to Thee…for those in peril on the sea…"

Most of his life had been spent on the sea. He'd had his share of rough moments and close calls. He'd always thought he'd die there, some day, in some kind of peril or other, but was it this lake that would claim him in the end? Would his bones lie on the bottom along with the bones of Libby's father? Would more secrets haunt these deep, mysterious waters?

He remembered the friends he'd lost. There were many, but one in particular. Best friend. Navy diver who worked in combat demolition, same team as his, same outfit, same mission, but somehow Brad was killed and Carson survived to sit through all those hymns they sang at the endless Catholic mass. Glad he wasn't Catholic. Didn't want a funeral. Didn't want all that droning Latin fuss....

Still had Brad's diving helmet...how odd that a helmet could outlast a man....

Cold. Damn, it was cold. One fight more, the best and the last.

The last, hell. He'd live to fight many more fights, and so would Libby. She'd live to find her father. She'd live because he wasn't going to give up. He was going to fight hard enough for the both of them.

He blinked the water out of his eyes, coughed and felt the agonizing burn intensify deep in his chest. The shore was closer. He could make out individual trees snagging at the dark sky with darker teeth. He could see the wind-whipped breakers crashing up against the gravel. He stroked with renewed energy. Closer. It was closer.

So close, but he was so cold. So tired. It would be so easy to just slide under the waves.... The night is upon us...dark are the waters...asleep in the arms... Fragmented thoughts and words streamed through his mind as he dragged Libby through the water. Hours passed. Days, months and years passed. He looked again, sure they must be nearly there, but it had been an illusion. He was no closer. The shore was always going to be just out of reach, and just a heartbeat away....

THEY TOOK TWO BOATS OUT, with two guides in each boat and bright lights to search the stormy waters. Luanne waited in the lodge with Karen and watched the boats disappear around the point. She wrapped her arms around herself and shivered, and felt Karen's arm slip around her shoulders. "They'll be all right," she soothed. "Come into the kitchen. I'll get you some dry clothes, and we could both use a cup of tea."

Luanne changed into the borrowed clothing then sat at the table and shared a pot of tea with Karen while the minutes dragged. "I'm not going back to work for Mr. Frey," she said. "If you would hire me, I'd work hard."

"Graham's been hoping you'd quit that job. He doesn't like you being over there. I probably won't be able to pay you as much money...."

Luanne shook her head. "That doesn't matter anymore. I'll get through school, one way or the other. I don't need Mr. Frey's money. And Mr. Frey will still have a cook and a housekeeper and groundskeeper living with him. He won't be all alone."

By the time they finished the pot of tea, it was nearly eleven-thirty. Luanne heard the sound of an approaching motor and grabbed her jacket. Karen was right behind her as she raced down to the dock. Graham and Joe Boone were climbing out as the two women arrived. Luanne's heart dropped at Graham's solemn expression.

He shook his head in answer to their mute question. "The only things we found were some pieces of the rubber boat that were still afloat, a life jacket and one wooden oar. Mike's gone over to talk to Frey. His boat is back at the dock. We searched the shoreline for a while, too, but didn't find anything. The water's pretty rough. It's wild out there, but that guy, Dodge, I don't think he'd drown too easy."

"Libby was wearing an orange flotation suit," Karen said.

"We're going back out again as soon as we've refueled," Graham told her. "We'll keep looking until we find them."

Karen nodded grimly. "I'll put the coffee on, and call the wardens."

THE SOUND OF THE WAVES broke into Libby's consciousness, drew her up out of the dark place and into an even darker one. She became aware of a terrible crushing pain in her head as she opened her eyes on a hostile world of shadows, high winds and hard rain. She was lying on her side and her feet were still in the water, stinging with cold. She drew them up and curled into a ball. The movement made her nauseous and she lay still for another long moment until she could roll onto her hands and knees. This time the nausea overwhelmed her, and she retched painfully onto the gravel shore as the rain pelted down.

She remembered the boat, the big wooden boat bearing down on them, and Carson lifting her up as though she weighed no more than a child. She remembered being thrown into the water, but that was all. Everything else was a blank. She had no idea how she got to shore, but she knew she hadn't managed it on her own. Not from so far out on the lake, and not with this terrible pain. She raised her fingers to the side of her head and felt the thick sticky warmth of blood. Must've hit her head on something. God, it hurt....

Carson! Where was he?

She sat back and looked up the shoreline, then turned and looked behind her. Her relief at seeing him lying almost within arm's reach was immediately replaced by a surge of dread. He was sprawled facedown, lying half in the water, and he wasn't moving. She crawled to him on her hands and knees and grabbed his shoulder. "Carson!" She bent closer with a whimper of pure terror. Was he even breathing? She shook him again, harder. *"Carson!"*

Was that a moan? Yes. Yes! Libby collapsed beside him, overcome. "Oh thank God, thank God!" She wept, not caring about anything at the moment except that he was alive. She sobbed while the storm raged around them, and then a dull awareness came over her and she pushed herself back onto her knees. This wouldn't do at all. She had to get him out of the water. "Come on," she said, latching onto his arm with both hands and tugging. "Carson? You have to move. You have to get out of the water."

His eyes opened. She bent closer. "Carson, please, you have to help me."

He moved then, but oh, so slowly. He moved until he had crawled up out of the water, and then he knelt, braced his hands on his thighs, and remained like that, head ducked against the rain, long enough for Libby to pull on his arm again. "Carson?"

He spoke without raising his head. "I'm okay. Just give me a minute."

He didn't look okay but she wasn't going to argue the point. She was sure she looked pretty awful, too. She knelt beside him while the waves crashed behind them and the wind blew and the rain came down. She squinted painfully through the wet twilight, looking up and down the shoreline, and saw what she thought was a familiar landmark. She'd been here before, with Graham. She was sure of it. Hope gave her strength and she tugged again at Carson's arm. "Come on," she said. "If you don't keep moving you'll die of hypothermia. Get up. I'll help you as much as I can, but you have to get up and get moving."

Somehow he made it to his feet. They swayed a little in each other's arms from the exertion, then Carson steadied and looked down at her, dull-eyed with exhaustion. "You okay?"

"Yes, and I think I know where we are," she said. "Remember that river I pointed out to you a while ago, the river that Graham's father lives on? Well, somehow we came ashore right beside it. There should be a path running along the riverbank. It's not far from here to Solly's cabin. We can take shelter there. We have to get someplace warm."

She hoped she was right about their location. She had no idea how many rivers fed into this lake. For all she knew there were fifty, and the one she was looking at was the wrong one. Carson started out very shakily and before he'd taken five steps he went down onto his knees in a paroxysm of coughing that left him curled over in agony. She waited for it to pass, then helped him to his feet again. "Come on," she urged. "Keep moving."

She led him one step at a time to the place where the river fed into the lake, and there was the footpath, just as she remembered. Relief flooded through her. "This is it, Carson. We follow this trail a bit farther and we'll come to a warm little cabin."

What had taken just over ten minutes on that hike with Graham took almost an hour with Carson struggling behind her, fighting for every breath he drew, but he kept moving. Every step was a painful limp, every coughing spasm dropped him to his knees, but he kept moving. Up and up, following the river, until they finally reached the plateau where Solly's cabin stood. The clearing was murky in the arctic twilight and the strong rush of the river became a sigh that faded quickly away. No lights shone from the cabin windows, but the sled dogs tethered out back roused and began to bark. "We're here, Carson," Libby said, her eyes stinging. "Just a few steps more."

Awakened by the dogs, Graham's father opened the cabin door when they were halfway across the clearing. "Solly? It's

Libby Wilson, from the lodge," she called out. "We need your help. My friend's been hurt."

Solly lit the lamps while Libby helped Carson over to the bunk and set him down. The cabin was warm compared to the raw night air, but Solly took one look at them and was already building up the fire in the woodstove. Libby began stripping off Carson's parka. She flung it aside and started on his flannel shirt.

"Stop," he said, trying to parry her hands. "I'm okay."

"Of course you are." She glanced over her shoulder. "Solly, do you have any hot tea? Anything at all that's hot, and has some sugar?" She peeled the wet flannel off one arm, then the other, and tossed the shirt to the floor. She worked the thermal top over his head and added it to the pile of wet clothing. A shiver of pain ran through her as she saw for the first time the raw scars that laced his torso from that terrible diving accident. How in God's name had he ever survived such terrible body trauma? She reached for his belt and unbuckled it. "Forgive my familiarity, but this is no time to be modest. Lie down, tough guy, and let me have my way."

"I'm all yours," he muttered as his shoulders hit the mattress, and she was oh, so glad to hear those brash words, however faintly spoken.

Five minutes later his clammy wet clothing was off, he was covered with several warm wool blankets, and Libby was stirring heaping spoonfuls of sugar into a cup of strong-smelling herbal tea.

"Good stuff," Solly had said when he handed it to her, and Libby had to refrain from making a face. If odor were any indication of the strength of the herbs, this was powerful stuff, as well. She got some of it into Carson, but he wasn't all that enthusiastic about swallowing it down and she couldn't blame him. She suspected that's why he fell asleep so abruptly in the middle of her ministrations.

It wasn't until she left his bedside and put the cup down on the table that her hands began to shake, and then her entire body. She used the last of her own strength to peel out of the orange survival suit before collapsing into a chair at the table, where she closed her eyes, leaned her elbows on the tabletop and pressed her hands to the sides of her aching head to keep it from breaking apart. She sat very still, counting her own painful heartbeats, until she heard a faint noise beside her. She raised her head out of her hands and glanced up.

Solly was holding a wadded-up clump of dried plant material in one hand. He lifted the gnarled fingers of the other to tap the side of his head, then pointed to her injured temple and extended the poultice. Libby sat up and took it from him. She tried not to wince as she pressed it against the wound, and managed a wan smile at the old man. "Thank you."

"What happened?" he said.

"Daniel Frey didn't want us to find the plane that sank in the lake, so he ran us over with his big wooden boat. I'm sure he thinks we both drowned, and I would have, except for Carson."

The old man stared. Libby waited for him to say something, anything, but she was waiting in vain. "That was my father's plane we were looking for, Solly. My father had the yellow three-legged dog, the same dog you told Graham about when he was a boy. The dog that haunted the shores of the lake. I think Frey did something to make my father's plane crash, and that's why I'm looking for it. To prove his guilt, and to prove that the man flying that plane was really my father."

Solly listened, but his wizened expression never changed.

He fed a few more sticks of firewood into the stove and pointed to the top bunk. "You sleep there," he said.

Libby tried to shake her head and winced. "No. You take that bed, Solly. I better stay close to Carson. He isn't out of the woods yet."

For a moment she wondered if Solly could even climb into the top bunk, but the old man had not only made a remarkable recovery from the pneumonia that had nearly claimed his life, but he was far more nimble than most men his age. Within minutes of settling onto the mattress, he was fast asleep. Libby lowered her hand, laid the poultice on the table and sighed. If Solly knew anything about that plane, he was never going to tell his secrets. Like the lake, he would keep them for all of time.

She pushed wearily out of the chair, blew out the oil lamp, and checked on Carson when her eyes had adapted to the cabin's dim interior. She slid her hand beneath the blankets that covered him to check his body temperature. The skin of his chest was warm to the touch. His breathing was shallow but steady. After seeing the extent of his injuries, the fact that he was breathing at all seemed miraculous, to say nothing of what he'd just been through. She tucked the blankets back around him and sank to the floor beside the bunk. The trembling was easing now as her own exhaustion and the warmth of the cabin pressed against her limbs and weighed her down. She let her head rest against the bunk's mattress and drew a shaky breath.

When the rubber boat had sunk, it had taken the side-scanning sonar with it, and her last chance to find her father's plane. She didn't have the money to extend the search. She didn't even have the money to pay Carson what she already owed him. She couldn't ask him to return because the odds of finding the plane were nil. Carson would leave Evening Lake and return to run his salvage company in Spenard and she'd go back to her mother's village for a while, maybe go to fish camp with Marie and spend the rest of the summer in Alaska before thinking about applying for another residency at another hospital.

Life would go on. There were worse things than remaining an illegitimate daughter. She'd lived with that label for the past twenty-eight years and she could live with it forever if she had to. She knew she was lucky in many ways, but most of all, right now Libby knew both she and Carson were lucky just to be alive.

CHAPTER SIXTEEN

SOMETIME BEFORE DAWN the rain stopped, the wind died, and the silence became as large as the wilderness itself, broken only by the sound of the songbirds awakening to the new day. Carson woke in that same early hour, though he didn't come close to bursting into song like the hermit thrush that filled the surrounding woods with clear, flutelike notes of ethereal beauty. Instead he groaned as the awareness of every part of his agonized being became more and more acute. He shifted slightly, and was startled to see that Libby slept on the floor beside the bunk. She slept sitting up, leaning against his mattress, head turned to one side.

Her black hair had dried in a loose glossy tangle over her shoulders and her lashes were dark against her cheek. Not even the ugly gash over her temple or the purpling bruise gathering around it could mar her beauty.

It had been a miracle, the two of them making it to shore. A combination of the wind dying, a back eddy from the river's current drawing them in the right direction and just plain luck. By the time his feet hit the gravelly bottom he felt as if he'd swallowed half the lake. There wasn't an ounce of strength left in him, and he'd dragged Libby out of the water by sheer willpower, falling on top of her as he heaved her onto shore and rolling off just before the blackness came.

Pure miracle.

He was watching her sleep when Solly crawled down from the top bunk, pulled on his boots and went outside. He was still watching her when she wakened. He saw her lashes flutter against cheek, the gentle movement of her head, the sudden opening of her eyes. For a moment she gazed vacantly at the far wall, then she sat up and turned to look at him. He saw those blue eyes widen when she realized he was awake. She pulled herself up to sit on the edge of his bunk and studied him intently for a few moments more before gracing him with a tentative smile. "You look pretty good for a half-drowned salvage diver," she said.

"You look pretty good yourself," he replied. "And you don't have to whisper. Solly's already up. He went outside just before you woke."

"What happened? I remember you throwing me out of the boat just before Frey hit us, but that's all, until I woke up on the shore."

"That mustang suit saved your life."

"Oh, I think I had a little more help than that," she said. "I'd still be out there if you hadn't brought me in. Did Frey look for us after he sank our boat?"

"He made one pass trying to run us over, hit you, then headed back. I think he figured we'd both drown."

"That bastard." She whispered the words, but he could feel the scorching heat of them just the same.

"He'll get what's coming to him," Carson said. "How's your head feeling? That's a nasty-looking gash."

"A handful of aspirin would be nice, but I'll live. What about you? You were in pretty rough shape last night."

"That was last night. Look at this." He held up his hand,

stripped off the wet bandage and wiggled his fingers. "I can move 'em, and I can feel 'em."

She took his hand in hers very gently and closed her own around it. "I'm glad. How does the rest of you feel?"

"Fighting fit."

"Right." She raised his hand and surprised the hell out of him when she held it to her cheek in a gesture so sweet and tender he was sure he was hallucinating. "Thank you," she said.

"For what?"

"For saving my life." She lowered his hand and then, while he stared in absolute shock, she kissed his palm, ugly scars and all.

"I had to," he finally managed over his wildly beating heart. "If you'd drowned, I never would've collected my hundred and fifty grand."

His try for humor fell flat when her eyes flooded with tears. "Oh, Carson, forgive me. Until I saw you last night, I had no idea how badly you'd been hurt in that diving accident. All this time I've been pushing you to find the plane, and..." Her voice choked off.

"Don't make a fuss," he said, more gruffly than he intended, but dammit, there was nothing worse than an emotional woman. "Do you suppose there's any coffee in this cabin, or is it all nasty medicinal teas?"

She shook her head and sniffed, laying his hand down to wipe her cheeks with the palms of her hands. "I don't know. I'll have a look. Graham's been staying here and he likes coffee. Maybe he stashed some."

He watched as she stirred up the coals in the woodstove, added some dry kindling and put a pot of water on to heat. She moved around the rustic cabin with the same practiced ease that she moved around the kitchen at Karen's lodge, and no doubt around the bustling high-tech halls of a big city hospital. She was the kind of woman who would be at ease in any situation, in any environment. He heard her make a small sound of triumph as she held up a can of coffee. Within minutes the water was boiling and coffee was brewing. Did anything smell any better than hot fresh coffee?

He sat up and had to swing his bad leg over the edge of the bunk using both hands. It was pretty damn stiff after last night, but he was sure once he started moving it'd loosen up. He sat for a moment, wearing nothing but his boxer shorts, and was disturbed that he couldn't remember getting undressed. Scanning the room, he located his clothing hanging on wall pegs behind the stove, alongside the bulky mustang suit, but he had no recollection of hanging them there. "I don't suppose you could bring me my clothes?"

Libby took them down and brought them to the bunk. "You shouldn't be getting up. You need rest."

"No time for that, and I have a thing or two I'd like to say to Daniel Frey before I head for Anchorage." He forced the clumsy fingers of his lacerated hand to close on his blue jeans and do their part in getting him dressed.

"You can't still be planning to fly out of here today?"

"Have to. My ship's dead in the water. Remember?"

"Can't you have someone else fly the part out there?"

"Sure," Carson said, abandoning the blue jeans for the red thermal top. "But they wouldn't know how to replace it. I designed and built that fuel pump myself. It'd be a mysterious gadget to anyone else." He pulled the shirt over his head, stuffed his arms into the sleeves and dragged the waist down to hide the latticework of scars from Libby's further scrutiny.

He picked up the jeans again and tried for the second time to get his feet into the pant legs. Wished she wasn't watching him. Using his hand to crank his bad leg up, he shimmied the jeans on, zipped them up, buttoned the waist. He looked around. "Are my socks here somewhere?"

Libby brought them over. "I really think you need to rest."

"Don't be put off by the scars," Carson said, pulling on his socks. "I'm not nearly as bad off as I look." He reached for his flannel shirt. Moving around was gradually loosening up all those tight, painful muscles. The first moments were always the worst. "That coffee smells good."

He joined her at the table and they shared it hot, strong and black, and just as Libby was refilling their cups, Solly reentered the cabin, made himself a cup of that foul-smelling herbal tea and drank it standing by the stove.

"Thanks for letting us stay here last night," Carson said, but got no response. The old man just gazed across the room and drank his tea, wearing that same thoughtful expression, as if he were about to impart some weighty words of wisdom, but he never spoke.

At length Libby rose and gathered their cups together. She took them to the little sink, washed them out, then set them on the sideboard. "Solly," she said, drying the first cup with the dish towel, "may we borrow your canoe to return to the lodge? They'll be worried about us by now. We'll bring it right back."

Solly finished his tea, put his cup in the sink, then walked to a shelf and took down a small pot. He upended it into his palm and put the pot back up on the shelf. Closing his fingers around whatever the pot had held, he walked to where Libby was drying the second mug and held out his hand. Libby hesitated, then put the cup down and held her own hand out, palm up.

While Carson watched, the old man made the exchange, and Libby stared down at her palm with a frozen expression for several long moments. Then with the fingers of her other hand she lifted what looked like a long loop of thin leather. Dangling from the end of the loop was a ring of gold. She reached for the ring and held it at an angle, turning it to catch the light from the small window above the sink. She gasped aloud and he saw her expression change all at once, as though something had just caused her excruciating pain. She looked at the old man with eyes that were suddenly brimming with tears.

"Solly, where did you find this?" she said.

LIBBY COULD SCARCELY BREATHE when she realized what it was the old man had put in her hand. Inside the plain gold wedding band was an inscription that read "Marie W. to Connor Libby," and was followed by the date of the plane crash.

It was her mother's wedding band, the band of gold Marie Wilson had never gotten to wear. Libby felt hot and cold all at once as conflicting emotions battled within. She'd given up on the search for the plane, she'd come to terms with letting go of her father, and now she held in her hands the proof of her parents love for each other. She looked at Solly through a shimmering blur of tears and the old man gazed steadily back at her. "You know what happened to my father's plane, don't you?" she said. "Please, Solly, tell me what you know!"

Oh, he was so slow to answer! He stood in that stoic silence for so long that Libby was filled with a sudden sharp rage and the urge to shake the words from him. But then, finally, he began to speak.

"I don't remember the day. When you start to get old, the

days and seasons run into each other. And, anyway, the day is just the day. But it was good fishing then, just getting good, and I got my first good fish that day. A big one, but not too big. I could get some steaks out of it, and smoke the rest for later. It was good fish and it would be good eating." He paused as if waiting for his memories to play catch-up.

Libby had to restrain herself from telling Solly that she didn't give a damn about him catching a good fish twenty-eight years ago that would be good eating. Instead she forced herself to be patient and wait in silence.

"I remember I was cleaning that fish on the edge of the lake when I heard the plane," the old man continued at last. "There was only one lodge on the lake back then, the one on the warm shore where Daniel Frey lives. The plane was taking off from that lodge. It was a bright yellow plane. The young one flew it. It was his plane.

"Back then, I seen it take off a lot. Every time, he would come down the lake the same way. So I knew he would come down the lake like that, like a duck flying just above the water, and then the yellow plane would fly up steep and disappear to the west. He always flew out the same way. He always headed west."

Libby's fingers tightened around the ring. "He was going to Umiak, to visit my mother." Her knees suddenly felt so weak that she lowered herself into the nearest chair.

"This day, I thought it would be the same," the old man said. "But it wasn't. The plane went straight up in the air and all the noise stopped, and then it fell forward into the lake and sank. It sank fast. I thought it would float a while, like a canoe, but it just disappeared."

Her heart was beating so hard she was sure the old man could hear it. "How did you get this ring?" she repeated.

"After the plane disappeared, something came to the surface and swam to shore. It was the yellow dog with three legs. It was on the shore when Frey came down the lake in the boat."

"Frey went to the site of the plane crash?" Libby fought for breath.

"He came very fast from the lodge. The legs broke off the plane when it hit the water and floated there on the surface. Frey tied them together and towed them back down the lake. He didn't see me, and he didn't see the yellow dog."

Libby felt as though she might faint. She raised her hand to the side of her head and her fingertips touched the scab of blood at her throbbing temple. The jolt of pain helped to clear her head. "Solly, how did you get the ring?" she repeated for the third time.

"The yellow dog stayed on the shore," the old man continued. "He never left that spot. When I went down to where he was, he wouldn't let me near. I could see he had a strip of leather around his neck, and I could see the gold ring hanging from it. But the dog wouldn't let me near him.

"He stayed there all that day and all the next. I brought food for him but he wouldn't eat it. He just watched the lake, like he was waiting for something to come out of it. I guess he was waiting for the young one who flew the plane. Sometimes, he would howl. In the evening when it was quiet, the sound carried a long ways. I thought Frey might hear the howling, but if he did he never came for the dog. Maybe he thought it was a wolf.

"A week went by. I kept putting food out, but the yellow dog never touched it. He just lay on the shore with his head on his paws and stared out at the lake.

"One day I came down and I walked toward him and he

was lying that same way but he didn't move when I got close. He never moved again. So I took the strip of leather with the gold ring from around his neck and I buried him up above the waterline. I piled rocks over his grave so nothing would dig him up. The rock pile is still there." The old man nodded that he was finished.

There was a long silence that stretched into eternity.

That was it. There was no more. Libby stood so abruptly that the chair clattered to the floor behind her. She rushed to the door, opened it and fled into the early morning, drawing deep breaths and fighting to stay in control. She walked to the river's edge and knelt there, rocking back and forth in a silent agony of grief as she gripped the ring in her hand. She thought about the loyalty of the three-legged dog her father had brought back from Vietnam and the young woman who had waited for a young man who never came on her wedding day and the girl who had grown up without a father and Daniel Frey, who had lived here all these years without paying penance for all the pain and suffering he'd caused. Wave after wave of emotion overwhelmed her. She heard a slow, limping approach from behind and felt a hand close firmly on her shoulder.

"You okay?" Carson said.

She nodded jerkily, unable to speak, but when she regained her feet and his arm went around her, she turned and plastered herself against him with a harsh, wrenching sob. She couldn't help herself. She broke down completely in his arms. He didn't say anything to try and make it better. He didn't soothe or placate with meaningless words. He just held her. He held her while the river ran past and the hermit thrush sang and the sun came up and life went on around them. For a few brief moments in time they became an island of two, insulated from the random chaos of a cruel and uncaring universe, and in those moments Libby felt the beginning stirrings of something she had never felt before.

Peace.

It was an extraordinary feeling, profound in its simplicity, flowing into her the way the river flowed into the ocean. She felt the agony within her gradually ebb, and she lifted her head and looked up at Carson.

"Thank you," she said, marveling at the beauty she saw inside of him.

THE OLD MAN WALKED down the path with them, following the river as it rushed toward the lake. It was a slow walk, though Carson did his best to make good time. He was as anxious as Libby was to have Solly point out the place where the plane had gone down. He was wondering how deep the wreckage was, and if the ice had moved it. He was thinking about the side-scanning sonar that was now at the bottom of the lake, and wondering if Trig could be persuaded to make a trip back with him, once he got the *Pacific Explorer* up and running. He wanted to speak his thoughts aloud to Libby as they descended the steep trail, but it was all he could do to keep to his feet. She cast frequent quiet glances back at him, and once she waited when he dropped too far behind. He wanted to tell her to go on ahead but was too winded to speak. He could only struggle painfully along while his chest burned with every breath he drew.

By the time he reached the lake, the old man and Libby were waiting for him and he pushed himself to pick up his pace. Solly walked down the shoreline about a hundred yards, not far at all from where Carson had dragged Libby ashore hours earlier. He poked around a bit in the alders that grew along the high-water mark, then gestured down at his feet and held the alders aside, revealing a jumbled pile of weathered stones.

Libby stood over the grave for a moment, then knelt and pressed her hand to a stone in a tender gesture that Carson thought the yellow three-legged dog would have understood. She rose to her feet and the old man turned and looked out at the lake. He raised his arm and pointed, and Carson followed with his eyes.

"The plane went down there."

Carson squinted into the morning sun. *There* was a relative term that could cover a lot of territory. He couldn't tell how far out the old man was pointing. "How deep is the water in that spot?"

"Not so deep," the old man said. "But the runoff from the river flows over it."

Carson rubbed the rough stubble on his chin. "That's why the search planes couldn't find it," he mused. "Not only were they looking in the wrong spot, but even if they flew right over it the glacial silt from that river must've covered it almost immediately, especially if the plane dug in and kicked up a cloud when it hit bottom."

"If it's buried in silt, how will you find it without your sonar?" Libby asked, echoing Carson's own thoughts.

"We'd have to bring in another piece of sonar equipment," Carson said. "I'll have to do that anyway, to find the sonar we lost when Frey rammed us. In the meantime I have my dive gear in the plane. If someone were to stand on shore and signal me to the right spot, I could go down and have a look." Carson knew it would be a crapshoot trying to find the wreckage that way, and even if he did, it would no doubt be buried beneath twenty-eight years of glacial silt. All he'd be able to locate was the tail section. Still, he was itching to see what shape it was in and what it was going to take to raise the Beaver to the surface. Only then would Libby know if her father's remains were still in the plane.

Only then would she be able to prove her paternity.

Libby had slipped the leather thong holding the ring around her neck, and her hand was closed tightly around the gold wedding band. "That's not a good plan," she said with a shake of her head. "It's too risky, and the odds of you being able to spot the plane if it's covered in silt aren't very good."

"I'll take one shallow dive for a quick look-see," Carson said, "but by noon I'll have to be out of here. I have to pick up the engine part at my shop and fly it out to the ship. I'll come back just as soon as I fix the *Explorer*'s engine and I'll bring another side scan sonar." Carson turned to Solly. "Do you think you could signal me from shore to the spot where the plane went down?"

The old man nodded. "I think so."

They heard the approaching drone of an outboard motor and looked down the lake. One of the boats from the lodge was approaching at a good clip. As it drew closer Carson recognized the man who'd gone out with Libby to search the lake and he felt a dark twinge of jealousy mingle with all the other twinges of pain he was experiencing that fine morning.

"It's Graham." He heard Libby speak at his shoulder. "Solly's son." She lifted her arm in a wave. Graham cut the motor and let the skiff drift to shore. When it beached he jumped out and waded toward them, his relief at finding them alive brightening his expression.

"Everybody okay?" he asked, his gaze drawn to Libby's bruised and bloodied temple. "What happened?"

"We're fine," Libby replied. "Frey chased us down in his boat last night and he ran right over us. Carson got me to shore, and from there we made it to your father's cabin. Solly took good care of us. Your father fixed me a poultice, and made us some very nasty-tasting tea."

"That was good medicine." The old man nodded with a satisfied gleam in his eye. "Powerful."

"The wardens should be here soon," Graham said. "Karen called them as soon as we came back from the first search, around midnight, I guess it was. They were going to wait until sunrise to fly in. We've been searching all night, ever since Luanne came to the lodge saying that Frey had gone out after you. She suspected he was up to no good."

"Bless Luanne," Carson heard Libby murmur. "Graham? Don't let her go back there. Keep her away from Frey. She can move into the cabin I'm in. There's plenty of room, and I'm sure Karen would be happy to hire her."

"She already has. Luane'll be working for Karen for the rest of the summer. I'll let her know about sharing the cabin. The two of you want a ride back to the lodge, or were you planning to walk?"

Libby turned to Solly. "Come with us. Karen will fix us breakfast, and then we'll look for the plane."

The old man shook his head. "I have to go back and feed my dogs. I'll come down to the lake when it's time."

Libby hugged him, and Carson didn't have to wonder at Solly's startled expression. "Thank you, Solly," she said in a voice choked with emotion. "Thank you for telling me about my father."

THEY WERE HALFWAY BACK to the lodge when the warden's plane flew over. It made a long banking turn when they waved a paddle, and flew back over them again. Then the plane landed across their bow and as they drew alongside the prop feathered to a stop. The pilot popped open his door and leaned out. "Everyone okay?" he said, echoing Graham's words.

"We're okay," Libby said, "but Daniel Frey sank our boat and tried to kill us."

The warden piloting the plane was young and zealous-looking, which Libby took as a good sign. The warden riding shotgun, on the other hand, looked old and mellow. He probably didn't have the spit and vinegar to chase down real criminals anymore. The young warden gave her a curt nod. "The woman at the lodge explained the situation. We'll talk to Mr. Frey."

"You need to do more than just talk to him. You need to arrest him!" Libby said. "He should be in jail. He tried to kill us last night. He's a dangerous man!"

The warden nodded again. "We'll be sure to look into it, ma'am. We're just glad you're both okay."

He slammed the plane's door shut and taxied off toward the lodge's dock. Libby blew out an angry whoosh of air. "You wait and see," she fumed. "Frey'll somehow talk his way out of this."

"His money will do the talking," Carson said. "Billionaires rarely go to jail. They don't have to play by the system's rules. But don't worry. One way or another he'll get what's coming to him."

"That's easy for you to say," Libby responded, staring across the lake toward the big fancy lodge. "He's lived pretty high off the hog for a long time."

Karen met them down on the dock and gave Libby a heartfelt hug. "You scared us all to death!" she exclaimed, holding Libby at arm's length. "What happened? How did you cut your head?"

Libby explained as they walked up toward the lodge, where Karen sat her down in the kitchen, poured her a cup of coffee, and then very tenderly administered to the gash on her temple. "The wardens have gone to speak with Daniel Frey," she said, applying antibiotic ointment to the gash and then taping a clean bandage over it. "They'll probably haul him straight to Fairbanks and throw him in a jail cell after what he did last night. Would you like a couple of aspirin?"

"Love some, thanks," Libby said. "Where's Carson?" She stood with a surge of anxiety and moved to the window, staring up the shore toward the point, but there were no signs of activity.

"Relax. Mike took the wardens over to Mr. Frey's lodge in the big boat. Graham and Carson went along with them. I guess you didn't find your father's plane last night?"

"Not exactly," Libby replied, refocusing her attention on Frey's dock, where she could see another boat tied off next to the Chris-Craft. "But we came a whole lot closer. Solly showed us where it went down. He saw the whole thing. He also saw Daniel Frey drive his boat out to the spot right after the plane crashed to tow the two pontoons away with him."

"Dear God!" Karen said, handing her the aspirin and a glass of water. "Then he knew all about that crash, even where the plane went down, and never told anyone about it."

"Carson wants to find the spot this morning, but Karen, as much as I want to locate the plane, he's in no shape to do anything right now, let alone dive on the wreckage."

"He's very experienced. Surely if he thought he couldn't do it, he wouldn't take the risk."

"Of course he would," Libby said. "Would his stubborn, prideful ego let him do anything else?" Libby swallowed the aspirin and set the water glass on the table. "Karen, if you don't mind, I think I'm going to go lie down for a while. I have a world-class headache and last night wasn't very restful."

"You go ahead. And don't worry, I'll wake you when Carson comes back. The wardens will want to get a statement from you."

Libby retreated to her little cabin, where she lay on the bunk and tried to sleep, but as exhausted as she was, all she could think about was her father's plane lying just offshore in water that Solly said wasn't too deep.

How deep was not too deep?

Maybe it was only ten feet down. Could *she* dive down to it? If she had one of those face masks all she'd have to do was hold her breath and... Ridiculous to even think about doing something like that.

Or was it?

She closed her eyes and pictured how she'd go about it. She'd need a raft, something to swim off of and climb back onto easily. She'd need a face mask and a snorkel. She could snorkel along above the surface until she saw the tail section, and then hold her breath and dive down into the cold, dark, deep water....

CHAPTER SEVENTEEN

SUNLIGHT SPARKLED ON THE surface of the lake and not a breath of air marred its glassy expanse. She could see the outline of the Beaver so clearly. How could the search planes ever have missed it? The yellow color glowed like the sun itself on the lake bottom. She could even read the numbers on the tail of the plane. The water over the crash site wasn't that deep at all. She'd easily be able to swim down to it. She held her breath and began the descent. It wasn't nearly as difficult as she'd feared, nor was the water very cold. As she swam closer she could see the front of the plane and how it had gouged into the silt when it bottomed out. The prop was bent but the windshield was intact and clean. She could see inside the cockpit and as she drew near she could hear her heart clubbing in her ears and the pressure in her lungs intensified.

There was a skeleton strapped in the seat, and she knew the anatomical name of every bone in that skeleton, just as she knew the name of the man whose bones they were. One of the skeletal arms floated in an unseen current. It lifted up and beckoned to her, and she jerked back, gasping with fright, and drew icy water into her lungs. Suddenly she was drowning in the cold dark depths, sinking toward the plane and the pale gleam of the bones in the cockpit. The bones were talking to her. Calling her name. She tried to scream but couldn't make a sound. She tried to swim to the surface but her limbs were leaden and unresponsive.

"Libby. Libby?"

She cried out in terror as she felt something grab hold of her arm.

"*Libby*. Wake up!"

She sat bolt upright, gasping for breath, and stared at Karen for a few panic-stricken moments. "I was dreaming," she said.

"That had to have been more like a nightmare."

Libby brushed her hair back with one hand. "Are the wardens waiting?"

"Yes. They've gotten statements from everyone. I had them save you for last, so you could get some sleep. You've been napping for about two hours."

Libby followed Karen back up to the lodge. Her head ached worse than ever. The wardens were drinking coffee in the kitchen and eating sandwiches Karen had prepared. They glanced up when she stepped into the room and the younger one gestured to a chair. "We'll need to get your account of what happened," he said around a mouthful.

"Did you arrest Daniel Frey?"

The younger warden fidgeted while the older one said, "If he's found guilty of reckless operation and leaving the scene of an accident, he'll be fined accordingly."

"Reckless operation? Fined? That man is guilty of murder and attempted murder and he belongs in jail!"

"Now look," the older warden began.

Anger made a bitter taste in Libby's mouth. "Where's Carson Dodge? He'll tell you what happened."

"We have Mr. Dodge's statement. He was in a hurry to get

back to Anchorage so we took his first. Now we need to get yours. If you'll have a seat…"

Libby whirled to look out the window and felt her heart skip a beat. He was packing up, preparing to sneak off while she was being detained and questioned by two wardens who had no intentions whatsoever of seeing that justice was served! Heedless of the startled protests made by the wardens, she raced for the door, flew down the steps, and ran along the shoreline path.

"Carson!" she shouted as she rounded the point and drew near enough for him to hear. He was standing on the pontoon and tossing a duffel into the rear of the plane. He glanced over his shoulder and then jumped off the pontoon and came ashore. She skidded to a stop in front of him, out of breath but full of fire. "Were you planning on leaving without saying goodbye?"

"I was just packing up some gear," he said. "The paperwork took a long time, and I have to fly that engine part out to the ship and fix what's busted before dark."

"Frey's going to get away with it, isn't he?"

"He told the wardens he was out fishing when the weather turned dirty. He said he was making for home as quickly as he could and didn't see us. He felt the collision and went back to look but didn't see anything, so he returned to his dock. He would have summoned the wardens himself to report the incident, but when he got back he suffered some sort of heart malfunction and his medications didn't work and he's been bedridden ever since."

Carson's expression remained carefully neutral while he related this to her. Libby clenched her hands into fists.

"You mean, they're just going to let him stay here?" she said in disbelief.

"No. As a matter of fact, he's getting a free trip with the wardens to the Fairbanks hospital to get his heart checked out and his medications adjusted."

Libby turned her back to him and stood in rigid silence, staring toward Frey's lodge. Words couldn't begin to describe what she was feeling. When Carson touched her shoulder she had to fight to compose herself before turning to face him. He looked exhausted, and not even his typically stoic tough guy expression could hide the pain that shadowed his eyes. "You shouldn't be flying anywhere," she said. "You shouldn't be doing anything but sleeping right now. I wish you wouldn't go."

"I'm not leaving yet. Not for a little while, anyway. I told you I'd check out the crash site before I left, and I plan to."

For the first time Libby noticed the pile of dive gear on the shore behind him. It was unbelievable to her that he would even consider such a risky endeavor in the shape he was in. "No way. Not in your condition. It's way too dangerous."

"It's no more dangerous than commuting to work in busy rush-hour traffic. Graham's picking me up in a few minutes. Go talk to the wardens."

She shook her head. "I mean it, Carson. The plane has waited twenty-eight years. It can wait a few more days. If you insist on doing something, go fix your ship."

"I plan on it. I also plan on making one short dive and locating the plane. Solly's probably waiting to point out the spot."

"Graham can tell him we've postponed things."

"He's an old man, Libby. He could die in his sleep tonight."

"And you could die while diving on the crash site. You could have one of your coughing spells and drown. That's possible, isn't it? We know the general area. Isn't that enough?"

His eyes narrowed. "You really want me to leave here without checking out the crash site?"

"Yes." Libby forced herself to nod coolly when what she really wanted to do was to beg him not to leave, ever, and ask him to hold her again, the way he'd held her by the river up at Solly's cabin. Hold her until she felt safe because she was so sure she'd never feel that way again unless she was in his arms, and she was so afraid that if he left now, he'd never return. "I really do. It's too risky. You could bring back your other divers when you come and let them be the ones who look."

"No way." He took one step closer so Libby had to look up at him, and she recognized the move for the power play it was. "I've put a lot of hours in on this search and I'm going to be the one who finds the plane."

"That's foolish macho talk and you know it," Libby said, trying unsuccessfully to make herself taller. "You can supervise the recovery. Let someone else take the risks for a while, at least until you're back on your feet."

"Get this straight," he said in a voice as hard as granite. "I *am* on my feet and I'm diving on the site. I said I would, and I'm a man of my word, remember? Now go talk to the wardens and let me finish packing. I'll be flying out of here by midafternoon."

LIBBY FUMED HER WAY BACK to the lodge. Stubborn, egotistical tough guy. The kind that always died young. Or almost always. A few survived. Carson had made it this long, maybe he was smarter than most, or luckier. But one thing was certain; he was compromised right now, and as much as she wanted to find her father's plane, it wasn't worth risking lives for.

Especially Carson's life.

But how could she stop him?

She burst back into the kitchen, where she surprised the wardens, who were just finishing off two pieces of Karen's apple pie. "Okay, listen up. My name is Libby Wilson and this is my statement," she said, bracing her hands on the table and leaning intently toward the wardens, who sat back in their seats with full mouths and startled expressions. "Daniel Frey knows I'm looking for a plane that crashed in this lake twenty-eight years ago, and he doesn't want it found. He'd do anything to prevent me from dredging up the past, because that would prove that he caused the plane crash that killed the pilot, Connor Libby, who happened to be his godson. A godson, may I point out, that he didn't particularly care for all that much, especially since he was planning to marry an Athapaskan girl and bring her back to the lodge to live. Ask Daniel Frey how he feels about the indigenous help he has to hire and you'll understand why he refused to attend his godson's wedding and why he refused to acknowledge the existence of his godson's child.

"He tried to kill us last night because the conditions were perfect for a boating accident. There was a storm. Visibility was poor. He could run us down with his boat and if anyone suspected anything he could feed them the pack of lies he's already fed you. There's just one problem. He failed. I'm still here, and so is Carson Dodge. And not only that, we've located my father's plane. So do me a favor. When you ferry the oh-so-rich-and-powerful Daniel Frey back to Fairbanks to meet with his heart specialist, be sure to tell him that by the time he gets back, he'll probably be seeing that long-lost yellow de Havilland Beaver floating on the surface of Evening Lake, giving up all its secrets. Tell him there's a witness that places him at the crash site right after it happened. A witness who saw Frey take the pontoons and tow them two miles to the outlet of the lake just to throw your fellow wardens off the search. And tell him that he'll definitely be seeing me, Connor Libby's daughter, in court, fighting to get back what's legally mine and what should have been my mother's for the past twenty-eight years. Did you get all of that?"

She straightened from the table and was about to leave the kitchen with the two wardens staring after her, slack jawed, when Karen met her in the doorway.

"Libby? That guy Trig's on the phone again. He's looking for Carson and he says there's a storm brewing in the Pacific."

"I'll take that call," Libby said.

CARSON WAS WAITING ON THE shore when Graham arrived with the big aluminum boat. He was glad the boat could beach right on the gravel shore because the dive gear was awkward to handle. Graham carried most of it to the boat then gave him a long speculative look. "This stuff's pretty heavy, man. You sure you want to do this?"

He gave a curt nod, irritated by the unspoken implication that he might not be up to it. "It shouldn't take too long."

As they motored around the point and into the west arm, Carson wondered if he'd ever get it back again. He wondered if he'd ever lift another heavy object or take another step without feeling weak and inferior, without feeling his own mortality. He wondered if he'd ever feel like a real man ever again. Not for the first time he found himself wishing that Trig had just left him to die down there, in the cold, dark deep. How could he learn to settle for less than he'd been?

How could he learn to live with the limp, with the hand that wouldn't function properly, with the lung that burned as if it was full of hot coals? How could he ever come to grips with a woman the likes of Libby Wilson looking at him, not with strong stirrings of sexual attraction, but with concern and pity?

He was going to dive on the crash site and the way he felt right now, he didn't give a shit if he died while doing it. Dying in action, doing something you liked to do, sure beat dying an old man in a nursing home with years of uselessness piled up behind him, years of self-pity and reminiscing about his younger years.

Besides, he might find the plane and end up with a nice chunk of change in his severely depleted bank account, which would feel almost as good as proving those damn doctors wrong.

"TRIG?" LIBBY SPOKE INTO the satellite phone. "It's Libby Wilson. I have some questions for you about Carson. Do you think he's capable of diving on the crash site of the plane he's been searching for?"

There was a pause. "Capable? Are you kidding me?"

"What I mean is, did his doctors okay him for that?"

This time there was an abrupt laugh. "Doctors? Lady, Carson hates doctors. He signed himself out of the hospital a week before they wanted to release him. He'd still be in there if they'd had their way, but he hates 'em. Hates hospitals and hates doctors. They told him, all those specialists did, that he'd never dive again. Too much damage, they said. They told him he'd need months of physical therapy and he was lucky to be alive."

Libby slumped against the wall and closed her eyes. "I thought as much," she said. "I need some advice. How do I stop him from diving?"

Another laugh. "Gotta gun? 'Cause that's what it'll take."

"That's not helpful."

"You could try to subdue him, but even now Carson could probably whip all of us with one arm tied behind his back. He's tougher than hell. I'm sure he can handle whatever dive job you throw at him. I wouldn't worry." A brief pause followed. "Look, put the king on the phone and let me talk to him. We have a situation here."

"I can't. He's out on the lake preparing to dive on the crash site."

There was another pause, then she heard a frustrated swear. "Okay then, tell him we're still dead in the water. Tell him there's a storm brewing, and without her engines the *Pacific Explorer* could be lost. Maybe that'll get him down here quicker. The Coast Guard is prepared to fly the fuel pump out to us by chopper, but Carson cobbled the engine together and he's the only one who understands how it ticks. We're just cooling our heels out here on the deep blue sea, waiting for him to rescue us. And lady? That's no lie. We're going to be in real trouble if he doesn't make his appearance soon. They're predicting twenty-foot seas and seventy-knot winds when this storm kicks into high gear."

Karen was waiting with a questioning expression when Libby hung up the sat phone. "Can I borrow a boat?" Libby asked.

"Mike's is down at the dock. Is there anything I can do?"

"Pray," Libby said on her way out the door. She ran down to the dock, aware that Carson and Graham were already out on the lake and hoping she wouldn't be too late. It would take time for Carson to get into the diving gear. A lot of time, considering how crippled up he was. She jumped into the boat, threw off the lines and started the motor.

THE OLD MAN WAS WAITING down near the mouth of the Yaktektuk, squatting on his heels and smoking a cigarette. Carson thought he had to be at least ninety years old and was glad he'd lived a few hours more. He stood as Graham maneuvered the boat close to the shore.

"Dad, we're going to take the boat out really slowly. You stand there and give me hand signals to the right or left. Wave your arm over your head if you want me to go farther out. When you think we're in the right place, wave both arms over your head. Okay?"

The old man nodded.

Graham backed the boat away from shore and while Carson continued the slow and painstaking process of donning the wet suit. Graham politely avoided watching him by keeping his eye on his father.

"I guess you've been diving a long time, huh?" he said.

"Yeah," Carson replied. "A long time." He struggled awkwardly with the zipper and felt the boat alter course in response to the old man's gesturing.

"How deep can you go in that gear?"

"Deep enough. Your father said the water was fairly shallow where the plane went down."

"That was years ago," Graham said. "Things change. The plane could be farther out than he thought, and this is a pretty deep lake."

Carson heard the sound of an approaching boat and glanced up, swearing under his breath when he saw who it was. The last person he wanted to see right now was Libby. The wardens had questioned him for nearly an hour. She shouldn't be out here this soon. He should have been done with the dive before she got out on the lake.

She charged toward them at full throttle, cutting the engine back at the last moment and swerving sharply to bleed off speed. Her boat came up neatly beside theirs, its wake rocking up against them. Libby's face was set in determined lines. "You just had a phone call from Trig. He was calling from your ship. You have to leave right away. They're in trouble. There's a storm coming up and if you don't fix the engine as soon as possible, the ship could be lost."

Carson listened to her terse delivery and narrowed his eyes. "Nice try."

She leaned toward him, face flushed and eyes flashing. "It's the truth. Call him yourself if you don't believe me. He said they're predicting twenty-foot seas and winds to seventy knots when the storm hits."

"They can wait another hour," Carson said.

Graham suddenly cut the motor. "That's it," he said, gazing toward shore to where the old man stood, waving both arms over his head. "We're over the crash site."

"Drop the diver's buoy over to mark the spot," Carson said, reaching for his air tank.

Libby reached out and grasped the side of their boat. "Carson, I'm asking you not to dive. Don't make me beg."

"Don't even bother trying," Carson said. "I've never cared much for beggars." He hefted the air tank, swung it up and shrugged into the shoulder harness. Damn, the thing felt heavier than lead. He waited out a cramping burn that might have turned into a coughing fit. "This won't take long. I'm going down to check out the site, that's all." He was buckling the waist belt when he felt the boat rock and glanced up to see that Libby had jumped aboard.

"Trade boats," she said to Graham, who wasted no time claiming her craft and heading immediately for friendlier waters, abandoning them without a backward glance. Libby dropped into the seat in the stern, started the motor and throttled away from the dive site. She stared directly over his shoulder as she steered the boat down the lake, refusing to meet his eyes.

"Where the hell are you going?" he shouted over the sound of the motor, anger warming his blood. "Dammit, Libby, the plane was right there. We could have been right on top of it!"

"The plane isn't going anywhere, and your ship is in danger." She kept her eyes fixed dead ahead and her expression was determined. "Your crew needs you."

"And all of a sudden you don't? A few days ago you were frantic for me to find that plane!"

"A few days ago, I believed that was the most important thing in my life," she said.

"And now it isn't?"

They were approaching the point, and she throttled down. "It's still important," she said, speaking in a more normal tone and looking at him for the first time. "But other things are more important."

"What the hell could be more important than proving you're the rightful heir to the Libby fortune? What could be more important than proving that Daniel Frey killed your father?"

She cut the motor as they came alongside the plane and she steadied the boat against the pontoon. "I'll help you load your diving gear," she said.

"That dive wouldn't have taken long. Half an hour, max."

"Your air tank, please." She stepped toward him, balancing lightly on her feet, and waited for him to unbuckle and shrug out of the harness.

"You think you don't need me to find the plane because Graham's father knows where it is? Is that it? You think you can save yourself a hundred and fifty grand by sending me away? Well, let me tell you something about lake ice. That plane could be miles away from where Solly Johnson saw it go down. The ice shifts everything all around, and the ice floes coming out of that river at breakup could've pushed it way out into the deep."

Libby wrenched the air tank out of his hands, balanced her way carefully to the side of the boat, and slid it onto the plane's pontoon. She scrambled up beside it and lifted the tank into the plane, then returned to the boat. "Get out of your wet suit," she said in that bossy doctor's tone of voice that only fueled his anger and frustration.

"Did the wardens tell you they'd send their own divers out to find the plane? Is that it?" he said as he stripped out of the wet suit, glad he was wearing a set of warm long johns underneath. The last thing he needed was for her to scrutinize his scars again with those pitying blue eyes. She took the wet suit from him piece by piece as he peeled out of it and then stowed that in the plane, as well. "Is that why you're booting me out of here so quick?"

"The wardens couldn't have been less helpful, and you're wasting time," she said. "It's going to be dark in another six hours." She untied the painter from the pontoon and grabbed onto the plane's wing strut to steady the boat while he climbed out.

He moved toward the stern and took hold of the strut just

above her hand, leaning over her as the aluminum boat rocked beneath them. "I'm not flying out of here until you tell me what the hell is suddenly more important to you than finding that plane."

"You imbecile!" she said, staring up at him with an expression he could only interpret as seriously pissed off. "How do you think I'd feel if anything else happened to you because of me? Don't you understand? I can't let you dive on the crash site. Not in your condition."

His eyes narrowed on hers as he processed what she'd said. Could he have heard her correctly? Had she become just another patronizing doctor insinuating he'd never be able to dive again? "I don't need your pity," he said, his voice rough with anger. "I don't need you to tell me what I can and can't do. If I want to dive, I'm going to dive, but if you really and truly want me out of here, I'm out of here. And you can keep your goddamn money, every last cent. You'll need it if the wardens can't find the plane." He turned to pull himself onto the pontoon but her hand shifted and closed tightly around his forearm.

"Wait!" she said, yanking him back into the boat. "I'm not implying you aren't a competent diver, but be sensible! You don't have to prove anything to anyone, but Carson, you have to be realistic about your physical limitations."

"My physical limitations didn't keep me from hauling you to shore yesterday, did they?" he shot back. "My physical limitations are all in your head, Doctor. You need me, call me. I'm in the phone book."

He spun around in a tight half turn and reached for the wing strut to pull himself out of the boat. It would have been a perfect exit with him having the last word if the unsecured boat hadn't drifted away from the plane while they'd been shouting at each other, but as it turned out he lost his balance and plunged headfirst over the gunnel and into the lake with an undignified shout. The icy immersion cooled his temper instantly, which was probably a good thing, and he had to give Libby credit for not laughing at him when he pulled himself out of the water and onto the plane's pontoon. He stood glaring at her in a pair of dripping-wet long johns, looking about as ridiculous as a man could look, and she never even cracked a smile.

CHAPTER EIGHTEEN

LIBBY WATCHED CARSON'S PLANE lift off the surface of the lake, bank gently to the west, and then bank again as it gained altitude and headed south toward Anchorage. She watched until it was out of sight, until the deep throaty roar of the engine was swallowed up in the vast silence of the wilderness, until the realization that he was gone and would probably never come back became so painful that she could scarcely draw breath. She motored back to the lodge's dock and was relieved to see the wardens preparing to depart Frey's dock in their own plane, presumably with Frey aboard. She secured the boat and walked up to the lodge's kitchen. As expected, Karen was working on the next meal.

"Well?" she said, when Libby came into the room. "Did you stop him from diving?"

"Yes. He's gone to fix his ship."

"Good. That should keep him occupied and out of harm's way for a while."

"Maybe," Libby said, collapsing into a chair and dropping her head into her hands. She was desperately tired and her head was killing her. "What day is it?"

"Saturday."

"Karen, do you have the number that Trig was calling from?"

"It should be logged in the satellite phone's memory."

Libby raised her head. "Can I make a call?"

"Help yourself."

Minutes later she was talking to Trig again. "Carson just left here to pick up the part," she told him. "Is he going to be able to land his plane with that storm moving in?"

"Yeah, he shouldn't have any problem. Conditions are getting a little choppy but the storm isn't supposed to hit until tomorrow, and he's a good pilot."

Libby hesitated. "Look, I may have overstepped my bounds, but I told him I didn't want him diving on the plane's crash site because I was concerned about his physical condition. He didn't take it very well."

"No, I can imagine he didn't. Carson's one of the best divers in the business. They don't call him the king for nothing."

"But if he signed himself out of the hospital and the doctors told him he shouldn't dive…"

"Look, lady, those doctors don't know him, okay?" Trig interrupted. "They talk in terms of ordinary men. They don't have a clue what someone like Carson's made of."

Libby drew a deep breath and blew it out silently. "In that case, could you please give him a message for me when he arrives? Tell him I need him. Tell him I'll take him any way I can get him. Tell him he has a job to finish at Evening Lake."

LIBBY WAS JUST FINISHING up her last guest room early Sunday afternoon when she heard the sound of a plane. She carried her tote of cleaning supplies into the kitchen. "I'm just in time," she told Karen. "I think your next batch of guests is about to arrive."

Karen was up to her elbows in a bowl of bread dough and

gave Libby a puzzled look. "They're early. They don't usually fly in until five o'clock." She leaned over the counter to peer out the window toward the lake. "That's not the flying service's plane. Looks to me like your salvage operator's back. He must have made mighty quick work of fixing that engine."

A quick glance outside and Libby felt her heart skip a beat. She was out the door and waiting at the dock as the plane taxied up. She tried to act nonchalant as the prop came to a stop and the pilot's door opened. Carson leaned out, his expression dead pan.

"I heard you needed a diver," he said.

Libby shoved her hands into her jeans pockets. "I was told you were the best in the business."

"I don't come cheap."

"If I'm hiring the best, I expect to pay for it," Libby said.

"Good. I'll go set up camp and get my gear organized."

"All right."

His deadpan expression never changed. "Aren't you going to offer to help?"

"Why? So you can tell me you don't need it?"

He jerked his head to the passenger door. "Thanks for offering. Climb aboard."

Libby stepped onto the pontoon, ducked into the plane and settled herself in the copilot's seat as he started the plane's engine back up and taxied to the point. He tethered the Otter in the same spot as before and Libby jumped down into the cold water without even feeling it. She helped carry his gear ashore, acutely aware of each time they passed, each time he handed her something and their fingers touched, each time they exchanged brief glances. She could hardly stand the tension. Her

heart was hammering a painful cadence as she drove tent pegs
and strung guy ropes and set up the canvas wall tent.

When everything was done and no busywork remained,
they stood facing each other and Libby wondered if he felt
even half of the electrical turbulence that was flowing between
them. She could barely breathe. "Thanks for coming back,"
she said. "How long can you stay?"

"As long as it takes."

"That shouldn't be too long if the plane is anywhere near
where Graham's father saw it go down."

"Finding it's one thing. We still have to raise it and get it
ashore. That could take some time, especially if Frey throws
up any roadblocks."

The wind was blowing up the lake, raising a light chop.
"I'm sorry about how I acted before," Libby said. "I should
never have questioned your abilities."

Carson shook his head and ran his fingers through his hair,
leaving it more tousled than before. "All my life I've been
searching for an honest woman, and when I finally find one
I behave like a jerk. I'm sorry for treating you that way. That
said, let's go find your father's plane."

THE DIVE MARKER WAS still in place, and they worked the first
search pattern with new side-scanning sonar around the
marker. Thirty minutes into the search Carson spotted what
he was looking for and gestured for Libby to cut the engine.
"Mark this spot with the other dive buoy," he told her over his
shoulder. "We're right on top of it."

"You can see it?" Her expression was a curious combination of excitement and dread.

He leaned back so she could see the sonar screen and with

his finger traced the vague outline of what looked like a sunken cowboy hat. "See that? That's the tail section. You can barely make out the outline of the wings, there and there. I'm surprised to even see that. The plane is approximately fifty-four feet beneath us."

Libby glanced at him. "It'll be dark down there, won't it?"

"I'll have a powerful light with me." Carson was already in his wet suit. All he had to do was strap on the tank, pull on his face mask, adjust his headlamp and go over the side. He sat on the edge of the boat and gave Libby a thumbs-up.

"Good luck," she said. She looked pale and grim, but then again, who wouldn't if their father's bones were about to be dredged out of the deep.

Or not. He knew he'd be lucky to find anything down there today. Finding the pilot's remains would probably have to wait until the plane was raised.

He hit the water, tested his regulator, switched on his headlamp and began the dive. The water was murky with silt from the glacial river. Visibility was less than fifteen feet by the time he reached bottom, and the river's current pulled at him constantly, making it difficult to maintain position. But he was diving. He was doing what the doctors told him he'd probably never do again, and it felt good. Hell, it felt great. He had to breathe shallow and fast, but he was getting enough air, and after being around Libby for a week he'd gotten used to living without much air. Damn, just being near her left him breathless. Good training for this stuff.

When he came upon the tail section he was surprised that it was so yellow in the beam of the underwater light. The tail numbers were as crisp and black as the day they'd been painted on. He scanned ahead of the tail and could see the rounded crown of the plane's fuselage, the faint demarcation of the wings. He swam just above the wreckage, grasping the leading edge of the port wing and hanging on to it while he reached over with his other hand to dig down through the silt that covered the plane's windshield.

Only, there was no windshield. His hand went beyond where the barrier should have been. He reached deeper, scooping out handfuls of silt that clouded the area and created zero visibility, but that was okay. He could work by feel. He pulled himself a little closer and dug deeper, trying to envision the plane's cockpit, trying to anticipate what his hand might encounter, but he was unprepared for what he felt. There… something protruded out beyond the framework of the windshield. Something that shouldn't have been there.

For a moment he stopped and lay suspended in the murky darkness. He then put his hand into the silt again. He was feeling the top of the seat but it wasn't where it was supposed to be. Carson stopped for the second time, trying to understand how the seat could have become wedged within the windshield's framework. He felt along the seat toward where the yoke would be. There was something between it and the seat.

Something smooth and hard and fairly long.

He closed his hand around it and tugged, surprised when it came loose. The thick swirl of silt kept him from immediately identifying what it was he held, but the current gradually swept the worst of the silt away and he became aware of a pale gleam in his headlamp. He felt his heart rate accelerate and his lungs struggled to keep up. He was fairly certain he was looking at an arm bone. Somehow it had become stuck and had remained there for the past twenty-eight years, which was nothing less than a miracle, considering the current here.

He knew it was time to go up. Libby, for all her forced non-chalance, would be worried out of her mind if he stayed down any longer. He'd seen what shape the plane was in, seen how much work it would take to raise it, and he held in his hand the bone she needed to prove her paternity. It was time to go up, but he knew when he did, everything would change.

So he stayed down just a little while longer, wondering if maybe he shouldn't put the bone back where it was to buy himself some more time. She'd still get her proof, but he'd get another week or so of the Libby Wilson he'd come to care about way too much. The Libby Wilson he couldn't get out of his head…or heart.

He stared at the bone in the murky light of his lamp, reluctant to let go of a woman he'd never even had in the first place but couldn't imagine living without.

LIBBY SAT IN THE BOAT and watched the sonar screen intently, her hands intertwined so tightly in her lap that she became aware she was causing herself pain and had to force herself to relax. What was taking him so long?

If he got into trouble, could she possibly swim down fifty feet in that dark and ice-cold water and rescue him? No way. Which is why she'd thought the idea of him diving was a bad one in the beginning and an even worse one now. She should have stuck to her guns and never let him go down there. By giving in to his stubborn and prideful arrogance she may have just signed his death certificate.

Three agonizing minutes later she stood up, kicked off her sneakers, shrugged out of her parka and took off her jeans. He was in trouble. He was down there somewhere and he was in trouble and she was going to have to try to save him. Heart pounding and adrenaline surging, she dived over the side. She surfaced, treading water while she drew a few deep breaths before diving back under, then cried out as a hand closed around her ankle. Air bubbles, invisible in the rough chop, shivered up her bare legs as Carson rose out of the darkness and surfaced beside her. He pushed up his face mask, removed his regulator and said, "Libby, what the hell are you doing?"

She wanted to rage at him, but already her limbs were growing numb and she realized that in moments she would be in trouble. With his urging she pulled herself back into the boat, then leaned over the gunnel and took his dive bag from him, tossing it into the bow before helping him aboard. When he was safe she collapsed into the forward seat, pulling her parka on, her entire body shaking with cold. Carson stripped off his mask, peeled back his diving hood and sat for a few minutes bent over with his elbows on his knees, catching his breath.

"What…took you…so *long!*" Libby finally asked around chattering teeth. "I…thought you…were in trouble down there!"

He straightened up and said, "I wasn't in trouble."

"You were…gone for a long time, and you…promised you wouldn't be any longer than…ten minutes!" Libby huddled inside her parka and glared.

"So you jumped into the water to rescue me?"

"Yes!"

He stared at her for a moment and Libby swore to herself that if he made fun of her, she was going to push him overboard. But he didn't. "I found the plane, in case you're interested," he said. "And I found something else." He nodded toward the bow of the boat. "Can you hear it talking?"

Libby followed his glance, saw the dive bag she'd tossed

so carelessly into the bow and felt a wave of dizziness wash over her as his words sank in. Through the dark mesh she saw a pale gleam and felt her heartbeat race. "You mean… Did you…?" With trembling hands she reached for the bag, opened the top and removed the bone. She huddled over it, convulsed with shivers, feeling the smooth cold wet of it beneath her fingers. Over the years the bone had become porous and yellow, but it had been a part of her father when he was young and handsome and alive. Her vision suddenly blurred, knowing that this was as close as she'd ever get to her father.

Carson remained silent. He sat with his shoulders rounded over and waited in silence until she raised her eyes to his. She cleared her throat and blinked hard. "Where did…you find this?"

"I'll tell you everything just as soon as you get warmed up. Let's go ashore."

"N-No. I'm fine. Tell me now. Was it…outside the plane?"

He shook his head. "The plane's windshield was missing and I was able to reach inside the cockpit." He hesitated, then added, "Want me to tell you what I think happened?" When she nodded, he continued. "When the plane hit the lake, I think the windshield was blown out and that's how the dog was able to escape, but your father was trapped." He paused. "Are you sure you're okay with me talking about this?"

Libby nodded again. The convulsive shivers were easing as she warmed up, though Carson's words struck a different kind of chill in her heart.

"I found that bone between the yoke and the seat. Now, those Beavers are built like rocks. The seat isn't going to come unbolted when the plane hits the water, and no way in hell is it going to come loose when a pilot pulls the nose up to gain altitude, but that's what I think happened. I think he started his climb and the seat slid right out from under him and left him hanging on to the yoke. The pull on the yoke caused the plane to go straight up until it stalled. When it nosed over and fell into the lake, the seat slammed forward through the windshield and wedged there. He was trapped, water came in, and the plane sank."

Libby stared, horror washing the numbness away. "So Frey really did tamper with the plane."

"It looks that way to me, yes."

Libby stared down at the surface of the lake. "Can we prove that after you bring it up?"

"Raising the wreckage is going to be a tough job because the fuselage is loaded with silt. My ship's probably in port by now. I'll file for salvage rights first thing tomorrow morning and start ferrying the equipment we'll need out here. No telling how long the paperwork will take, sometimes only a few days. If Frey puts up a stink we could have a fight on our hands, but it's one fight Frey won't win. No state or federal court in this country would deny your claim to that plane once the DNA testing proves you're Connor Libby's daughter, and once Frey knows we've located the pilot's remains he may just give up. At any rate, we'll pay the state the fee they demand for the plane, and after we raise it we'll have it air-lifted to Anchorage. The FAA will send investigators but even if they verify everything I just told you, that doesn't mean Frey's going to be convicted of tampering with the plane. There's no way to prove he did it."

"But, he's the only one who lived here at the time, and the only one with motive, and Solly saw him drag the pontoons to the outlet!" Libby said.

"You and I know Frey's guilty and Solly can testify about what he saw the day it crashed, but convincing the rest of the world might not be so easy. Frey didn't exactly strike me as the kind of man who would confess any of his past transgressions."

Libby raised one hand to her aching temple while the other closed around her mother's wedding band, which hung from the leather thong around her neck. "For twenty-eight years I've been moving toward this moment, and now that I've reached it I don't even know how I feel. I guess I'm just overwhelmed."

Carson reached across the boat to give her shoulder a squeeze. "I think we could both use a good stiff drink. I have a bottle of sipping whiskey in my gear. Talisker, made on the Isle of Skye. Good stuff. What do you say we head back to camp, warm you up by the campfire, and break into it?"

Libby regarded him for a long, steady moment, then nodded. "I'd like that very much."

CARSON HAD LONG SINCE discovered that the distance between a man and woman could be measured in light-years and had long since given up trying to bridge that mysterious gap. But right now, sitting in front of the tent and across the campfire from Libby, none of that stuff mattered. All that mattered was the moment, because he knew that these final hours were all he would ever have with her. She was wrapped in a wool Hudson Bay blanket he'd brought out of the tent, her hair was still wet, and she was still shivering a little with a combination of cold and shock, but to him she had never looked more beautiful.

He poured the whiskey into two clean but battered tin cups and held one out. Her hand trembled as she took it, and her eyes were wide and dark and slightly unfocused, dazed by everything that had happened, but she managed a small smile and a quiet, "Thank you."

He lifted his own cup. "To your father. May his bones talk loud and clear."

"To my father." She raised her cup to his, then took a sip, blinked her eyes and coughed. "Wow."

"Powerful stuff for a powerful moment."

The sun was setting and the air was cooling off as twilight stretched blue fingers into the forested campsite. A hamper of food had been waiting for them when they'd returned, compliments of Karen, but Libby shook her head when Carson offered the basket to her. "No, thanks. I'm not hungry." She stared into the flames of the fire, cradling the tin cup of whiskey on her updrawn knees for a long, contemplative moment before taking another tiny swallow. "Well, you did it. You found the plane, just like you said you would."

"With Solly's help."

"You'd have found it eventually." She raised her eyes and held his gaze. "Thank you."

"What'll you do now?" he asked after she'd dropped her eyes from his to stare back into the fire, making it easier for him to breathe.

"Call my mother and let her know we found the plane, send the bone you found off to the best forensics lab in the country and then stay on here and help Karen out at the lodge while you bring the wreckage up."

"You'll keep on cleaning rooms?"

She managed a half laugh. "And scrubbing toilets. It'll keep me occupied, and she needs the help. Besides, I like that little cabin and I love the food." Those blue eyes fixed on his yet again. "How long do you think it will take to get the plane up?"

Carson shrugged. "Depends. I'm thinking it's in good shape, and it's worth taking some time to bring it up in the best condition we can, especially if you're gunning for Frey, and from what I've already seen, your instincts were right about him. I'm guessing a month at the outside. Maybe less, if I can get a full crew in here. And if I can't, maybe I could sign you up. You seemed pretty anxious to do some diving today."

"Don't make fun of me."

"I'm not. I think you're gutsy as hell."

She set her cup down, rose abruptly and walked to the edge of the lake. She stood there for so long in stillness and absolute silence, wrapped in the blanket and watching the sun set, that Carson tossed off the remainder of his whiskey, pushed to his feet and joined her. He was dumbstruck to see tears streaming down her cheeks. He put his arm around her shoulders and pulled her near. He couldn't think of anything to say to ease what she was going through, but he became aware, when she looked up at him, that all those light-years between a man and a woman could be spanned with just a touch.

"Just hold me for a little while, Carson," she said in a shaky voice, and it felt like the most natural thing in the world to oblige her. "I'm sorry," she murmured, laying her head against his chest and wrapping her own arms around his waist. "I don't know why I'm so emotional."

Ah, the pain. This time it wasn't his leg, it wasn't his lung and it wasn't his beat-up body. It was his heart. He held her in his arms and breathed the sweet vulnerability of her and felt the agony of a body that fought for control but was rapidly losing the battle. She was just too damn close and too damn desirable. He knew he should put some distance between them before he embarrassed the both of them, but he didn't know how. "You have a right to be emotional," he managed. "You finally have what you need to prove that you're Connor Libby's daughter. This is the turning point of your life."

Her arms tightened around him, pulling their bodies closer together, and he practically groaned aloud. "That's just it," she said. "I thought I'd feel different. I thought it would make everything right, but now I realize it's not enough. Not nearly enough."

In spite of his increasing agonies he was baffled by her words. She was about to become the rightful heiress to the Libby fortune, and that wasn't enough? Good God, what more could she possibly want? Once again Carson didn't know what to say. He seemed to excel in long silences. He thought she'd pull away when she realized what she was doing to him, he thought she'd open up those light-years of distance between them, but she didn't. Instead, she lifted her head and gazed up at him, and then, to his absolute amazement, she stood on tiptoe and kissed him on the mouth. Her kiss was tender, sweet and sensual, and there was absolutely no mistaking her intent. The electrical jolt that passed through him as her lips first touched his only intensified as he did the only thing he could do. He kissed her back. He wanted to ask her what it was she really wanted, but he couldn't, because after that first kiss he was breathless. They both were.

And, as it turned out, no further words were necessary.

THE SUN, WHEN IT ROSE over the Brooks Range, sent long streamers of light into the clearing. Libby woke only when the heat inside the canvas wall tent became too intense. She opened her eyes and lay for a moment before reaching over to Carson but her hand encountered nothing but empty space.

He was gone. Startled, she sat up and saw that the sleeping bag and blanket they'd shared were now hers alone, and there was a note pinned to the door flap. She unpinned it and read the masculine scrawl.

I've gone to pick up the crew, file the salvage papers and get some necessary gear. Check out the bear tracks on the shore. Back by supper. Carson.

Libby dressed in haste, unable to believe he'd taken off in the Otter and she hadn't heard a thing, but when she padded barefoot to the cove she saw that the plane was indeed gone. His note had been so impersonal after such an intimate night that at first her feelings were hurt. But then, as she pulled on her socks and sneakers, she realized he was just being Carson. She would never have guessed that the search for her father's plane would have led to her falling in love with a man like Carson Dodge, but she knew her life would never be the same.

When he guided her into the dimness of his tent she was barely aware of the masculine world surrounding her, the smell of canvas and leather, gun steel and wood smoke. She was focused only on the man whose kisses were so passionate and whose expert touch made her cry his name aloud.

And finally, just before the dawn, as their mutual exhaustion lulled them into deep sleep, Libby came to understand that without Carson, and without the love that he alone could give her, nothing would ever be enough. Not the Libby fortune, and not the Libby name.

Nothing would ever be enough without Carson.

CHAPTER NINETEEN

"WE FOUND THE PLANE, MOM."

The words sounded strange, even to Libby. She could only wonder how her mother must feel, hearing them spoken aloud. She huddled in the chair beside the phone and was glad that it was so early nobody else was up in the lodge, except for Karen.

"Libby!" Marie's voice was choked with emotion. "Are you all right? When you didn't come home yesterday, and didn't call…"

"I'm sorry. I really am. Are you okay?"

"You found the plane?"

"Yes, and everything I needed to prove that Connor Libby was my father."

"And so," Marie said. "Now, will you come home?"

"Soon," Libby promised. "Very soon." She paused, hand tightening on the phone. "Mom? I have your wedding ring. It's beautiful."

The silence lasted so long that Libby wondered if her mother had heard, but then Marie said quietly, "I know how beautiful it is. I've worn that ring in my heart all these years."

KAREN WAS A ROCK IN the chaotic days that followed, as Carson ferried his crew and gear into Evening Lake. Libby leaned on her quiet strength, and tried to repay all her kindnesses by helping out as much as she could, but her heart was in such pain she wondered if anything she did at the lodge was even remotely helpful. All she could think about was Carson, all she wanted was to be near him, but he was now completely focused on the salvage project, surrounded by his crew, unreachable, untouchable, and what hurt the most was that he didn't seem to notice the agony she was in.

Finding the plane had been a tremendous victory. She was on the verge of proving her paternity, something she'd dreamed of doing all of her life, and yet she was miserable. She wanted Carson to touch her the way he'd touched her that night, to have him hold her in his arms, to have him kiss her and make her feel as if she were the sole reason he lived and breathed. She wanted him desperately, but he worked nonstop, rain or shine, eighteen-hour days, using every minute of daylight. His crew was always around him. Nice guys, wonderful guys, but their constant presence made a private conversation with Carson impossible.

Daniel Frey had not returned to the lodge after the wardens flew him to Fairbanks, nor had he tried to block the purchase of the salvage rights. The most Libby could find out was that he was staying in private accommodations in town, in order to be closer to the hospital while his heart medications were being adjusted. Libby believed he was just readying himself to flee the country when the wreckage was raised and then inspected by the FAA and the truth of his tampering was revealed.

Solly had given his statements to the proper officials and had recovered completely from his bout of pneumonia. Marie was feeling good and looking much improved. She'd come out to the lake the day Libby had called her to spend an af-

ternoon at the lodge, and ended up staying on with Luanne
and Libby in the cook's cabin.

And then, suddenly, after two and a half weeks, the salvage
operation was over. The remains of her father had been recovered and sent to the medical examiner in Anchorage. Half of
Carson's crew had already left on the huge chopper that had
airlifted the plane to Anchorage for FAA inspection and
ultimate restoration and the others were up at the lodge,
wowing Karen with stories of daring, high-risk salvage operations and eating yet another delicious meal while Carson
packed up gear and cleaned the campsite. Libby took advantage of the fact that he was finally alone and walked down the
shore in the light drizzle, wondering what she would say,
wondering what he would say, wondering if this was going
to be a final goodbye.

But how could it be, after that night she'd spent with him?
The heat from that encounter had sizzled between them
throughout the long process of bringing the Beaver to the
surface of the lake, and though no other shared intimacy had
been possible, just a glance or the touch of a hand had been
enough to keep the fires smoldering. Or maybe the fires had
only smoldered in her. Libby had to accept the fact that the
encounter had no doubt meant a great deal more to her than
it had to him. He was, after all, the kind of guy who had a girl
in every port. But still, how could they possibly say a forever
goodbye after all they'd shared?

He spotted her coming and stopped in the process of
cramming his sleeping bag into the stuff sack. "Well, I guess
this is it," he said.

"I guess so." Libby glanced around the campsite to avoid
looking at him. "I won't be able to pay you for a while. I don't

exactly have a hundred and fifty grand in my savings account. Not yet, anyway. It could take a while for the DNA testing to be completed, and even longer for the legal paperwork."

He tossed the sleeping bag into a pile of gear that was waiting to be loaded onto the plane. "I'm not worried. I know you're good for it."

"I have your retainer fee. Well, almost all of it. Some of it got used up flying myself out here and some other stuff and…" Libby pulled the crumpled envelope out of her pocket. "It's only four thousand, but I'll add the other thousand to the salvage fee. I'm sorry it took me so long to come up with it and I promise you'll get the rest. I'll let you know as soon as the lab contacts me with the DNA results."

He took the envelope from her and without even glancing at it he shoved it in his pocket. His eyes held hers. "Like I said, I'm not worried."

"What will you do now?"

He shrugged. "Get started on the next job. I guess that's something you don't have to worry about anymore, now that you're about to become an heiress."

She felt a flush of anger and shoved her hands into her coat pockets. "I have no intention of changing my lifestyle." Then, realizing how sharply she'd spoken, she added, in a softer tone, "This has been quite a journey."

"Yeah," he said, still holding her gaze. "For me, too."

"I just wanted to thank you for everything. I mean, I'm almost sorry the job's over, but I know you have other jobs to get to and…" Libby felt the heat in her face intensify. "I guess what I'm trying to say is that, after all that's happened, I…I've become very…fond of you." She stumbled over the words, wishing she had the courage to tell him how she really felt about him, but not daring to make a fool out of herself. She just couldn't face listening to him explain, in a careful and considerate way, that while he'd enjoyed their time together and liked her very much, he was a busy man with no time for long-term relationships. He would break her heart so badly she'd never be able to piece it together again.

"Fond." He regarded her thoughtfully, then his eye shifted over her shoulder, and she turned to see his crew walking around the point toward them. They were a great bunch of guys, especially Trig, but their timing was incredibly lousy.

"Fond," he muttered. "Tell me something, Dr. Libby. Does being very *fond* of someone merit a goodbye kiss?" Before she could respond he closed the distance between them, gripped her shoulders, ignored her shamelessly offered lips and kissed her on the cheek with no hint whatsoever of the intimacy they'd shared. He released her and stepped away as his crew arrived, leaving her breathless and humiliated and burning for him to kiss her the way he must know she was yearning to be kissed. "I hope things work out for you, Libby," he said just before he left. "I really do."

EPILOGUE

LIBBY'S FLIGHT from Boston was scheduled to arrive in Anchorage at 5:00 p.m. and had taken most of the day, with an endless layover at Chicago O'Hare. She was anxious to get back. It felt as if she'd been gone for months, though after the DNA results were finally proved out, the legal paperwork and endless meetings with the lawyers had taken less than three weeks. Being the exciting new toast of the Libby Foundation had whirled her into an exhausting social scene, and Libby was actually looking forward to Marie's suggestion to spend some time in Umiak, to stay until the arctic winter swept down from the pole and froze the river in its tracks.

But first she had to settle things with Carson, with whom she hadn't spoken since that gray dreary August morning on Evening Lake, when the salvage of her father's de Havilland Beaver was finished. He'd gone back to his other women, no doubt, and Libby had gone to Umiak and stayed with her mother for most of a month before flying East when official confirmation of her paternity came from the country's top forensics lab in Washington, D.C. She'd hoped that Carson would call, but how would he know where she was, or how to get hold of her? Nor could she call him, because until she actually had the hundred and fifty thousand she'd promised him in her hand, what would she say? He'd given no indication that he wanted any sort of lasting relationship with her. On the contrary. He had just given her a chaste, impersonal goodbye and flown away.

Libby swore she would never use the word *fond* again, in any context.

When her flight touched down in Anchorage, she rented a car and drove out to Spenard, knowing it would be past 6:00 p.m. but hoping Carson would still be at Alaska Salvage. She parked in front of the Quonset hut and walked inside. His office was empty, but she heard a clattering from one of the bays and found Trig there, working on a piece of equipment. He glanced up when she walked in.

"Hey, Libby," he said as casually as if he'd just seen her that morning. She doubted anything ever phased Trig. He was, as Carson had said, as cool and steady as they came. He stood up and wiped his hands on a greasy rag. "You just missed Carson. We got back from a salvage job in Valdez this afternoon and as soon as our gear was unpacked he called it quits early and headed over to the marina. He's getting that old leaky house boat of his ready to be hauled for the winter. I'll tell you how to get there."

"He didn't know I was coming, Trig," Libby said. "If he's busy, I don't want to bother him. I can just stop by in the morning...."

Trig shook his head and held up his hand. "If I didn't send you over there now, as in *right* now, and Carson found out? I tell you what, the king'd murder me in cold blood. He's been moping around like a kicked dog ever since we left Evening Lake. C'mon into the office and I'll draw you a map of the marina. That place is big and there are lots of boats."

Ten minutes later she was breathing chilly October air at the marina and, with the help of Trig's map, she searched the lighted docks for the vintage wooden power boat Carson lived on called *Vertigo*. She found it easily and stood on the wharf, suddenly overcome with doubts. She knew Carson would be glad to get the money, but would he be glad to see her? In spite of what Trig had implied, Carson might have been moping because his company was reputedly in serious financial trouble, not because he was missing her.

She wondered how one knocked on a boat when the owner wasn't on deck. Wondered if perhaps he was entertaining one of his many love interests below deck. She didn't have to wonder very long. Even as she stood there pondering her next move there was a thumping sound from inside the hull and then footsteps climbing the stairs. The cabin door kicked open and quite suddenly he appeared, nearly two months on the mend since she'd last seen him, looking borderline salty, a day or so unshaven and very virile. He was carrying a cardboard box in his arms and when he caught site of her he tripped on the last step, fumbled and nearly lost his grip.

"Hello, Carson," she said. "It's good to see you."

He recovered his composure, leaned over the side of the boat, dropped the box onto the dock and braced his hands on the railing. He gave her a long stare. "I heard you went back East."

"Just temporarily." She held up the brown paper bag she carried. "I brought you a little something."

He straightened but his expression remained cryptic. "Come aboard."

He helped her onto the boat and then gestured for her to descend the steep stairs. Below deck Libby was surprised at how neat and cozy his living quarters were and grateful for the warmth thrown by the small cast iron stove, especially after Carson's less than warm welcome. An oil lamp burned in a brass gimbal, casting a soft glow on the polished woodwork inside the cabin. He helped her out of her overcoat and gave her another appraising up-and-down. She was still dressed in her traveling clothes, a conservative dark wool skirt suit, white linen blouse and low heels. "Nice outfit," he commented.

"Trig told me you were preparing to haul this boat for the winter. Where will you live?"

He shrugged. "Most of the cannery workers've gone back to the lower forty-eight. I'll find a cheap apartment somewhere. When did you get back in town?"

They stared at each other for a few awkward moments while the boat rocked gently at the dock. "My flight just arrived an hour ago," Libby said, struggling to match his cool tone of voice. It was patently obvious from his behavior that he hadn't missed her. Hadn't thought about her or lain awake at night, tossing and turning and wishing she were there beside him. Those torments had been hers alone. "I have your money. It's inside the bag in a plain envelope. I hope a certified bank check is acceptable."

Carson took the offered bag and set it on the table without so much as a glance inside, not the least bit curious about why the bag weighed so much. He regarded her for a few moments more, then turned away abruptly, heaved an exasperated sigh and turned back, instantly shedding his aloof demeanor. "Goddammit, Libby, it's been nearly two whole months. I thought you'd dropped off the edge of the earth!"

"I told you it would take some time for the DNA testing and the legal paperwork," Libby said, immediately on the defensive. "I brought the money as soon as I could."

"Money? Hell, that's not what I'm talking about," he said, his voice gaining strength. "You could have called and let me know you were all right, let me know how things were going, let me know you were going back East. I had to read about you in the newspapers. You could've called. You knew how to get hold of me!"

Libby was completely taken aback by this accusatory outburst. "I'm sorry, but I wanted to make sure I had good news before I contacted you, and I told you it would probably take two months."

"One phone call, Libby. I'd have traded that entire goddamn certified bank check for just one phone call from you!"

His words astonished her. His eyes burned into hers and she felt trapped by their intensity. Had she been wrong about him having a girl in every port? Did he really and truly care about her, above and beyond all others?

"The newspapers ran the stories about Daniel Frey, even back East," she said in a voice that trembled with emotion. "I read about how Frey accused your company of salvaging the plane for your own interests and violating Connor's resting place, and how he dragged your financial situation through the mud. He didn't dare mention me, so he took it all out on you. When I read those awful stories…" Libby felt the sting of tears and drew a sharp, painful breath. "As soon as I had the results from the DNA testing I called the reporters who wrote them and told them the truth, and then I pushed hard to move the legal paperwork along. I tried to get the money to pay you as soon as possible. I knew it would be a big help so I came back with it as soon as I could. I'm sorry for not calling you, Carson. I…I guess I didn't know how much you wanted me to. Back at the lake while you were salvaging the plane it was like you were trying to avoid me."

"Avoid you? How in hell could I have gotten anywhere near you after you brought your mother there to act as your bodyguard?"

"Bodyguard?" Libby could hardly believe he'd said that. She felt a hot surge of anger. "The reason I brought my mother there was because she's been ill and I wanted to keep an eye on her. It certainly wasn't to keep you at arm's length. And as long as we're talking about bodyguards, your salvage crew did a pretty good job of running interference on your behalf."

He turned away from her but could only pace two steps in the confines of the old cruiser's cabin before having to turn back. As he stood there, the anger and frustration visibly drained out of him and he gestured wearily with his arm. "It doesn't matter. I'm sorry I blew up at you like that. I guess I'm just tired. It's been a rough week." He moved to the stove and fiddled with the draft. "No doubt you heard about Frey dying while you were gone."

"Yes. My mother called me. She thinks the stress of being suspected or accused of the crime caused him to have that massive heart attack."

"No doubt. That evil old bastard got off easy."

"Too easy." Libby desperately wanted to touch him. Wanted him to touch her. Being so close to him was making it increasingly difficult for her to breathe. "You look well, in spite of the fact that you're still diving."

"You mean, because of it," he corrected.

"Salvage diving is dangerous work."

"You're damn straight it is. I've nearly starved to death three times since starting up Alaska Salvage, and the business isn't out of the red yet." His wry, tough guy demeanor was as brash and arrogant as she remembered. "So. What happens to you now that you're the official heiress of the Libby fortune? Do you plan on sticking around, or did you buy yourself a Hinkley yacht and an island off Hawaii to sail her to?"

"I told you I wasn't changing my lifestyle, and I'm not," Libby responded testily. "I'd give my mother the world but she doesn't want it. The Libby Foundation is a good organization. They've asked me to serve on the board, and I've agreed. My first recommendation was that they turn Frey's lodge into a summer camp for native children and set up some permanent medical clinics in the outlying villages. As for me, I've accepted a residency at the hospital here in Anchorage. I'm sticking around. There's no place else I really want to be."

A long silence stretched between them while Carson looked as if he was struggling to make sense of what she'd just said. Libby gestured to the bag on the table. "Are you hungry? I brought Chinese food, and a bottle of wine. I would have picked up some of your Talisker sipping whiskey, but…" She paused a moment, then took the plunge. "But I was in too much of a hurry to see you. The truth is, I've missed you."

"Is that so." His eyes narrowed and he rubbed the stubble on his chin. "How did you miss me? Was it in a fond way?"

Libby felt her cheeks flush. "You'll never let me live that down, will you?"

"Most people feel a lot more than fond about their pet dogs," he said.

Libby closed the distance between them. "I'm sorrier than you'll ever know for using that word. The words I should have used were *crazy about,* and *passionately in love with* but I was too much of a coward. I've gotten braver since then. I've had a long time to think about how I would change that one moment between us, but right now I'm just wishing you'd kiss me, because for the past two months that's all I've been thinking about. And I don't want a fond kiss, like that last one you gave me," Libby said, breathless and trembling before he even touched her. "I want passionate."

Passionate, as defined by the American College Dictionary, included such descriptive words as vehement, emotional, strong, enthusiastic, compelling, sexual and sometimes violent. As Carson brought the definition to life in the many ways he kissed her, Libby felt the fire between them rekindle, and just when she thought he couldn't fan her flames much higher without causing spontaneous combustion, he swept her off her feet, kicked open the door that led to his bedroom and paused before carrying her inside.

"For the past two months I've been thinking about doing a whole helluva lot more than just kissing you," he warned, "and fond behavior never figured into any of my thoughts."

"Good," Libby said as her universe shifted oh, so perfectly into its proper place. "Make sure it never does."

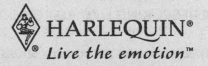

Silhouette® BOMBSHELL™

ATHENA FORCE

CHOSEN FOR THEIR TALENTS.
TRAINED TO BE THE BEST.
EXPECTED TO CHANGE THE WORLD.

The women of Athena Academy are back.
Don't miss their compelling new adventures
as they reveal the truth about their founder's
unsolved murder—and provoke the wrath of a
cunning new enemy....

FLASHBACK
by Justine DAVIS

Available April 2006 at your favorite retail outlet.

MORE ATHENA ADVENTURES
COMING SOON:

Look-Alike by Meredith Fletcher, May 2006
Exclusive by Katherine Garbera, June 2006
Pawn by Carla Cassidy, July 2006
Comeback by Doranna Durgin, August 2006

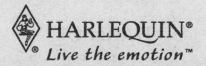

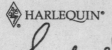

HARLEQUIN®

Super Romance

LEARNING CURVE

by *Terry McLaughlin*

(HSR #1348)

**A brand-new Superromance
author makes her debut in 2006!**

Disillusioned high school history teacher
Joe Wisniewski is in a rut so deep he's
considering retirement. The last thing he wants
is to mentor some starry-eyed newcomer, so
when he gets an unexpected assignment—
Emily Sullivan, a student teacher with a
steamroller smile and dynamite legs—
he digs in deeper and ducks for cover.

On sale May 2006
Available wherever Harlequin books are sold!

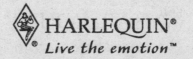

HARLEQUIN®
Live the emotion™